the celebration of hogmanay

by
Constance Weston

PublishAmerica
Baltimore

© 2006 by Constance Weston.
All rights reserved. No part of this book may be reproduced, stored in a retrieval system or transmitted in any form or by any means without the prior written permission of the publishers, except by a reviewer who may quote brief passages in a review to be printed in a newspaper, magazine or journal.

First printing

At the specific preference of the author, PublishAmerica allowed this work to remain exactly as the author intended, verbatim, without editorial input.

ISBN: 1-4241-0824-1
PUBLISHED BY PUBLISHAMERICA, LLLP
www.publishamerica.com
Baltimore

Printed in the United States of America

Dedication

I offer my deepest gratitude to my husband for his encouragement, and support. I would also like to thank Elizabeth Perry who convinced me to go to Scotland for the first time, and was crazy enough to want to go back there with me again! Thanks also go to my cousin, Rebecca Lucy, who waited patiently to read the next installment and whose optimistic attitude pushed me to write the best story I had within me. Lastly, I would also like to acknowledge FirstFoot.com for their extensive Scottish vernacular dictionary.

For Nana, my namesake.

Author's Note:

The Great Glen Way is a popular walking trail in Scotland, but the town of Inverwick and its inhabitants are purely the offspring of the writer's imagination. Actual historical occurrences are detailed, but the characters, whether they resemble someone living or deceased, are purely fictional.

Contents

Prologue 9
Chapter 1: News in the Highlands 11
Chapter 2: Again, why was this such a great idea? 16
Chapter 3: Family Ties 20
Chapter 4: Birds of a Feather 25
Chapter 5: Simple Life On The Farm 30
Chapter 6: Witches Brew? 40
Chapter 7: A Call to Dinner 46
    Recipe: A Simple Dill Sause for Salmon 50
Chapter 8: Is This A Place Ya'd Call Home? 51
    Recipe: Basil and Parsley Pesto Sause for Pasta 65
Chapter 9: No Seasons of Change 69
Chapter 10: A Pair of Kilts 75
Chapter 11: Good Food, Good Wine, Good Company, And Good God! 85
Chapter 12: So, Do Ya' Come Here Often? 104
Chapter 13: A Welcome Guest 114
    Recipe: B&B Buttermilk Salad Dressing 116
Chapter 14: A Reason to Give Thanks 120
Chapter 15: The Big Feed 136
    Recipe: Perfect Pumpkin Pecan Pie 137
Chapter 16: Taken For A Ride 157
Chapter 17: Asking for Directions 171
Chapter 18: A Night Like No Other 173
Chapter 19: The Morning After 181
Chapter 20: Another Chore 185
Chapter 21: Bolstered by Friends 189
    Recipe: Holiday Egg Nog 191
Chapter 22: Little Things Mean A Lot 194
Chapter 23: Going Somewhere? 201
Chapter 24: Presentation Of A Present 203
Chapter 25: An Unwelcome Christmas Delivery 209

Chapter 26: The Strange Gifts Christmas Can Bring 224
Chapter 27: The Emotions of the Season 232
Chapter 28: A Change Of Heart 241
      Recipe: Heather and Thyme Boursin Cheese Spread 246
Chapter 29: A New Year, A New Beginning 247
Epilogue 255
Appendix 257
Thistle 258
Savory 260
Basil 262

PROLOGUE

Clarinda had had it! She was struggling to control her emotions as she feverishly shoved her belongings into a travel suitcase. Her bottom lip was being bitten to death so it wouldn't quiver and by doing so it kept the tears from brimming over. Her arms were flailing so if anyone were near enough, they would feel as if they were about to be assaulted by an octopus. Clothes were strewn around the bed and the rejects lay where they landed; the accepted were balled up and stashed in the bag. She figured what she left would be thrown out or donated to the local homeless shelter. She didn't plan to come back.

This was it! This was going to be last time she would feel this way in her life—remorse. She had given him the best years of her life, or so she thought—and what did it get her? Misery. Deceit. Sorrow. She had stood for this mistreatment long enough and was not going to subject herself to any more emotional trauma.

Once she had selected what she felt she needed, she took the phone off the hook, collected her purse and locked the door to the spacious and bright apartment behind her. Her travel bag had wheels but even so, the stairs made the bag awkward and heavy and the struggle only fueled her anger. Muttering expletives under her breath, she reached the doors to the apartment building. She was slightly sweating from the exertion, and her hair started to fall out of its pony-tail in wisps around her face. She took the back of her hand and swiped both aside. Straightening up and reestablishing her attire, she hailed a cab and one pulled up immediately; the cabbie helped wrangle her bag into the trunk. She let out a sigh as she fell back into the glossy seat and the cab hurtled toward Newark airport. She had loved New York, her friends and her job, and now she was leaving them all behind — all because of him. As she watched the familiar buildings of her neighborhood whiz by, she wondered if she would ever return. Part of her hoped so, but the other part wondered why. Why would she ever return to a place so cold and heartless?

chapter 1
news in the highlands

Every day was the same for Alistair Campbell—rise, breakfast, chores, a quick shower, and off to work. He would come home and do it all again but in reverse—shower, a few more chores, and a small supper and off to bed only to repeat the routine again. At least he got to work with clients who didn't try to express their ideas over his, and also appreciated his dedication to his craft. Sometimes clients baulked at his ideas, but he always won them over with his soft voice and easy gift of persuasion. He had plenty of customers, thus the reason for the seven-day workweek especially in early spring when the year and budgets were young. Luckily, there was always another hoof to shoe. Yes, Alistair's profession is one of a farrier—and one of the best in Inverness-shire.

"Alistair, please come in and try some of my new tablets! I just took them out and they are simply delightful," cried a shrill and cheery voice. Alistair closed his eyes, sighed and resigned himself to the fact to keep the Mrs. Fitzrandolph happy (and as a well paying client), he would have to come to her doorstep and taste some of the awful concoction she had just invented. If Dr.

Frankenstein were still alive, he would have loved to have her as an assistant in his laboratory. She had an uncanny method of blending together ingredients that have no right to be near each other at all, in an effort to scare the tongue into taking up a diet and avoid any further punishment.

"Yes Mrs. Fitzrandolph, I will be there in a wee bit. Shamus still needs one more shoe before you can let him trot on the main road." This would bide him some time and maybe after a few moments she would forget and he would escape and bill her for his services later. Of course what Mrs. Fitzrandolph heard was: "I weel be there een a whee bit, Shamus steel needs woun more shu b'for yew caan lit heem trrot un the mean rud." This thrilled the old dearie to no end! Yes, she did she love to watch Alistair working on her old dappled-gray, Shamus, in the paddock—a key reason she moved to the highlands of Scotland was to hear the wonderful brogue. When she heard from the townsfolk about Alistair and saw him for the first time, she felt like she had won the Lotto—a highland accent and a wonderful specimen of man all in one prize. She would ring up Alistair the minute Shamus lost a shoe and count the days until he would arrive. Hopefully the day would be a warm or humid one, and Alistair would take off his shirt to cool himself from the hard work. He was very well toned—and somewhat tan since he was out in whatever sun there might be—and he would gleam in the sunlight with a thin layer of sweat once he got to Shamus's third shoe. Mrs. Fitzrandolph tried very hard to fit in, but she knew her curious American ways were always obvious and strange. However, Alistair felt she was harmless—except when she had been in the kitchen. Once Alistair was finished with Shamus, he let the old horse into the paddock and reluctantly made his way to Mrs. Fitzrandolph's doorstep.

Secretly he had been wishing for a bit of something to tide him over until supper, but he had forgotten to bring any energy bars with him this day. He could imagine what her tablets would taste like, and he braced himself for the worst, but back in the small corner of his mind, he hoped these would not be representative of her earlier experiments. He knocked on the screen door, "Mrs. Fitzrandolph, Shamus is finished. I need tae be aff. Did you want to speak with me?" Maybe she wouldn't hear him and he could slink into his wee panel lorry and be gone.

"Oh, just a sec Al, I will be right there!" Oh Lord, he hated being called 'Al'; this was clearly an American tendency to give everyone the endearment of a nickname. "Oh, please do come in. Here are some fresh tablets I have just made. I substituted the heavy cream for half and half and instead of sugar I have used NutraSweet and added some lime to the lemon juice. I think you will find them quite tasty and only one-third the calories—not that you need to worry about that, but I do. A girl has got to watch her figure!"

Yeah, watch it grow is what Alistair thought as he took a wee bite. Horrid as expected. These tablets were dreadful and would surely kill small animals. "Lovely," he muffled as he tried to swallow without using his tongue. Praise the good Lord, she sensed he needed some liquid to wash the concrete down, and thankfully gave him a nicely chilled glass of water.

"Well have you heard about the new American in town?" Mrs. Fitzrandolph inquired. "I understand she is quite a modern thing so I don't think she will need any horse maintenance of any sort. I know the kind—coming here to try 'to find themselves'. What she is probably doing is to find herself a new husband! Although I don't know why she would come to the Shire—this is a remote area so the pickings are slim, if you know what I mean."

He was using all the best manners his mother taught him to continue to choke down her tablets and quite honestly wasn't really paying attention to her diatribe. He was certain his mouth would soon be glued shut, and prevent him from attempting a reply.

"Yep," Mrs. Fitzrandolph continued, "I understand she was jilted by her husband and she decided to come to Scotland to try on a new lifestyle. She sure has chosen a tough way to try to start a new life. She went and purchased that big, old Cameron house off Telford Lane. That house needs so much work! And she thinks she will open it up for guests—clearly the girl does not understand highland life and what is involved to run a place like that. She is such a wisp of a thing and doesn't look strong enough to even pump the well. At any rate we will see."

"These are great, but I really must be going. Thank you Mrs. Fitzrandolph." Alistair raised himself out the chair to make his way to the door. She continued with her report of her new neighbor while washing dishes and gazing out of the window and really wasn't paying attention to the fact Alistair was making his leave.

"Oh yes, bye now. Do you want some tablets to take with you?" Alistair of course shook is head no. "Are you sure? OK, well then drive safe and I will see you in about three weeks?"

"Yes Mrs. Fitzrandolph—the paddock is no as clarty now, sae Shamus might nae need shoes for about four to five weeks, but I will ring ya' to see if he is gettin' along alright."

"Yes—good!" she replied, "and I will do the same. Good to see you again. Let me know if you ever need any thing—like a casserole or something. Bye-bye." She was now standing on her stoop waving vigorous and the bottom of her arm acting as the counter balance. Alistair could only imagine if her casseroles would still contain live animals even after baking, but he felt they were best to be avoided. He waved out the window of his lorry as he turned to go down her lane and to the next clients he has scheduled for the remainder of the afternoon.

The day was wonderful—some people would not think of 'Scotland' and 'good weather' in the same sentence, but this month had been wonderful. Yes, the summer had been rainy and the midges awful, but September was dry with puffy white clouds framed against a deep blue sky. He couldn't really believe what wonderful weather this season had provided. The air was clear; a touch of chill in the air, and no midges with the heather loamin' in the hills. Glorious!

He turned down the next road to make his way up to the Sheffield's to repair the shoe of their bay gelding. As he did, he passed the old Cameron house. There seemed to be new life there, but the house was still in such a state of disrepair. Generally it needed new paint, the garden was overrun with weeds, the adjoining out buildings were missing windows and overall the place had the appearance of sadness and uselessness. Alistair noticed some movement in the garden. He spied a tall woman tugging at the weeds and it appeared the weeds were winning. *This must be the new American* he thought. *Well, good luck with that,* and he continued to drive to the Sheffield's farm.

chapter 2
again, why was this such a great idea?

Clarinda was exhausted. She had spent the week in the garden digging up weeds, indeed backbreaking work. Arrangements had been made to have someone come and paint the old house, and he agreed to do so as long as the weather stayed clear. Clarinda crossed her fingers on that one—the weather had indeed been wonderful—not what she had heard or imagined when she thought of Scotland, but it had been fabulous so far. *Casting away the New York glare*, she thought as she realized she actually was getting a slight tan on her arms. As she sat at her large kitchen table and enjoyed her meager dinner-for-one, she had made a list of all the items that needed to be done and the list continued to grow:

~ *Get the place painted*
~ *Get the chicken house livable (and buy some chickens!)*
~ *Weed the garden for herbs (basil, dill, savory, rocket, rosemary and chives)*
~ *Paint the rooms*

~ Find a plumber to fix the toilets and add showers to each room (lots of $$$ there!)
~ Buy new bedding for the rooms
~ Find a chef to cook meals
~ Find a maid to keep up the rooms
~ Hire an Assistant Manager
~ Find a friend

The last one was a difficult task indeed. She realized when she came to Scotland her life would not be the same and she came here to 'heal'. But what she didn't expect was to have to try so hard to make a good friend. Oh sure enough, the local ladies were very nice and tried to make her welcome—but their average age was seventy-five plus, and they were not well versed in the skill of "girl talk". Granted, Clarinda never considered herself a very "girlie-girl", but it would be nice to giggle a little bit and fantasize about a new man

"Stop! What ARE you thinking?" she scolded herself aloud. "This is not the time to think about men. You have WAY too much work to do and they are only a denigrating distraction. Get those thoughts out of your head."

She was a bit overwhelmed with the amount of work the old house needed, but it was a bargain even considering her American dollar went only about half as far as the British pound sterling. Nevertheless, the house had charmed her and was in an ideal location. The "Old Cameron House" is what the townsfolk called it, but Clarinda was thinking of a new moniker more fitting and inviting. The house had once been built by one of the wealthier clan descendants as a "hunting" cottage. It had lots of rooms, hard wood floors, large fireplaces on either end, and a spacious dining room and kitchen. She would be able to have about eight rooms that she could let, and most of them were en suite. The others she hoped to convert soon. There was a separate area on the main floor that would be her "apartment"—it contained a small bedroom, bath and sitting area with a small fireplace where she could get some "quiet time." It also made the house economical since she would heat just her rooms and close off others if she didn't have full capacity. The house had also been used as a dorm of sorts. After the "Laird" ran out of money, a local school purchased it for students to use in the summer. The students roamed the woods and moors and collected several specimens over the course of their studies. It was rumored one of the out buildings contained dozens of jars of flora and fauna—the latter category were deceased, of course. Soon after the school ran out of money and a large family came to own the house and logically their name was Cameron. From what Clarinda had learned from the solicitor, they had eight children, and a mother-in-law, so the house was perfect for the large brood. However, as children do—they grew up and went to university. The elder Cameron's no longer wanted, nor could manage, the large house. Sadly, they let many maintenance necessities slide, so the value of the home depreciated. Although they were able to get the asking price, Clarinda still considered it a "steal"—she knew she could recoup the value of the home and more by returning it to an being inviting inn for guests. The old house would be one of the few in town and Inverwick was a busy settlement.

One of the large attractions of Inverwick was the large river which flowed through one end of town. A unique feature of the river was a series of several small dams created to trap native salmon as they swam upstream. A permit was required and the waiting list several years long, but anglers would come to Inverwick to fill their creels out of the bountiful waterway. Good salmon fishing is rare since the seas are depleted, and salmon farms are supplying most of the world's demand, so to catch a healthy wild salmon is a treat. There are 'smokers' in town who will smoke anyone's catch so it is easier to transport. Clarinda had not had the pleasure to have some of the salmon from the Inverwick River, but she understood it to be a delicacy.

The other draw to Inverwick is the walking path that comes

very close to the town. Hikers, as they are called in the States, who like to take long distance walks come to Scotland to enjoy the highland views. The Great Glen Way is a seventy-three mile walk beginning in Fort William on the west coast near the Atlantic Ocean, ending in Inverness near the North Sea. The Great Glen is primarily comprised of three lochs: Loch Lochy, Lock Oich and Loch Ness. These are connected by the Caledonian Canal essentially creating an island of north-east Scotland. The Great Glen can be traveled on foot, by bike, or in a boat, and in either direction. Inverwick is about two miles from the Great Glen Way pathway, so Clarinda hoped she would be able to attract weary walkers and bikers and eager anglers all coming to visit the wee town. Yes—the old Cameron House would be a busy place, if only Clarinda could get it in order. She decided to retire to bed, get some rest and tackle more of the restoration tomorrow. A decaf chai tea in hand, she trundled off to bed. She tried to write in her journal, but exhaustion got the better of her. As she drifted into a restful slumber her dreams were of riding a magnificent horse—starting from the woods of Vermont and carrying her over the moors of Scotland.

chapter 3
family ties

"Alistair Campbell! You clot-heid! Will ya' please mind your feet? Och, I just washed this floor! Do you nae see I have the mop still in my hand?" Alistair jumped back onto the doorway rug and looked up at his reprimander with a sheepish look. "OK, but dinnae do it again! Come in here and have some tea and biscuits, will ya'?"

Alistair's older sister, Janet, was a fine woman, but since she lived without a man in her life, she was quite set in her ways. One of those habits was to have a spotless house. The other was she had time to cook, as her pear-shaped figured revealed; her skills were some of the best in the Shire. Alistair was glad to have some tea and biscuits. Today was a bit cool, and the tea was warming and the shortbread right out of the oven.

"Perfect timin', aye?" he asked. His sister gave him a look to indicate he knew exactly what time she was baking each day, and he had perfectly timed this visit in according to the well kept schedule.

Janet's husband had died several decades ago, but nevertheless Alistair made a point to visit her about twice a week. Her home was her sanctuary and always tidy and cheery, but she was not the most able-bodied person when it came to maintaining her wee farm. She had a tiny chicken house with about a dozen hens, a cock, and three or four ducks. Alistair would come over to make sure the coups were cleaned and to re-stock the grain. Janet was capable of getting the eggs, but keeping the birds healthy was not her strong suit.

Janet was eight years Alistair's senior. In her early twenties and while attending University in Edinburgh, she met an American man named Richard Adams. They were immediately smitten with each other and soon planned to wed. Not long after the simple nuptials, he persuaded her to return with him to America, so they left Alba for Indiana. Richard studied to become a doctor and wanted to get into a top-rated medical school to obtain his degree. He discovered if he enlisted into the military, he would get a first-rate education and be able to repay this debt by serving in the National Guard. He presumed this arrangement was ideal—he would be receiving an education he wouldn't normally be able to afford, and on the weekends he would be forced to keep in shape. While Richard attended classes during the week, and completed reps of push-ups on the weekend, Janet got a job working in a small dress shop. It wasn't a great job, but it was something to earn wages and she was not afraid of hard work. Richard assured her if she would help to make ends meet now, in five years he would be able to create a life they both had envisioned—complete with laughing and playful children. Janet worked in the store every day and if she was not helping the customers with their frock choices, she performed alterations to match the customers shrinking or expanding waistlines. Given her pleasant disposition and charming Scottish lilt, she was quite popular with the store's patrons and the shop's sales improved. Luckily the storeowner, Mr. Shapiro, saw Janet was bringing in new customers and increased her wages. To reciprocate, Janet suggested new items to Mr. Shapiro, convincing him his customers would buy these new fashions as quickly as they could. As time went by Mr. Shapiro showed Janet the "math" behind a retail store—she learned how to calculate mark-up, understood the value of good margin, and how to run a high-revenue sale and still make a profit. Before long Mr. Shapiro and Janet were a solid team and as his store prospered, it was reflected in Janet's wages and bonuses.

Janet and Richard seemed happy but since they both spent so much time focused on their duties and occupations there was not much time to be together. But they relished their evenings, and would fall asleep embraced in each others' arms—tired, but happy. Regrettably, their harmony was soon to end.

Because Richard was part of the National Guard, and also a medical student, he was one of the first selected to go to Desert Storm. "You cannae go and leave me alone," Janet pleaded, but Richard saw this as an opportunity to learn trauma care firsthand in a triage unit. He believed his service would give him an advantage when applying for residency—military personnel were sometimes given some favoritism as repayment for wartime service. Despite her objections, Richard enlisted into one of the first battalions and his orders were to establish medical units near the battle lines.

One month passed and although Janet had received news he had safely arrived, Richard had not sent subsequent letters to relate the war's progress and to provide reassurances he remained safe. On the day of November 15, 1985, there was a knock at Janet's door. The uniformed officers were polite and to the point. It was obvious they had to convey the same sort of bad news to other families of men who had also lost their lives. Janet's knees could not support the weight of grief that came over her, and she crumpled to the floor. The sorrow was so overpowering she couldn't even breathe to gather a sob; she whined and moaned and attempted to catch her breath. The uniformed officers quietly left—they offered no comfort; they tried not to be rude but at the same time they could not allow themselves to become entangled in the mourning of those they were ordered to confront with dreadful news.

That was almost twenty years ago. Having no family, the widow decided to leave America. Mr. Shapiro begged her to stay and would have easily doubled her wages to entice her to do so, but there really was not much anyone could say or do to break though the cold barrier which Janet had surrounded herself. A necessity she needed to get up and carry on each day. She felt lost in a country where she wasn't comfortable and wanted to return to the security of home—Scotland. At the age of twenty-four, Janet Campbell Adams returned to her homeland to find some sort of solace and comfort in the land she so loved.

When she returned, she used her retail skills to get a job in Portree. Although her friends and family missed her and wanted her to come back to Inverwick, she felt the seclusion on the Isle of Skye was just what she needed. Once again, she was able to make good wages by charming tourists and helping the shop owner with her keen eye for fashion trends. She continued to make some good money performing alterations—not only for the store trade, but also for expecting brides and mothers. She saved most of her income and only spent what she needed for food, some alteration supplies, and her small one-room flat's rent.

The life on Skye is hard—the only way to leave is via the new bridge or by ferry, and the latter's schedule was followed only when the weather allowed. She was frugal and strived to save as much money as she could so she chose not to own her own car. That left the ferry as her only method of transportation to the main island. She would diligently make a trip back at least once a month. Not only to get provisions not available on Skye, but also to check in on her younger brother who had left university and was beginning a successful career in finance. Years passed, and her routine did not alter until Alistair's accident and she decided to move back to Inverwick. Their parents had both since died, so the family home was now hers. Her diligent saving afforded her the ability to leave her job and care for her only kin. When she looked at her strong and handsome brother, she found it hard to imagine him helpless and needing anyone's assistance.

"Sis, I'm gonna look at the coup. I am sure those birds are starving under your care," he jeered and Janet heard the door close behind him. *I dinnae ken where she would be if I dinnae come and look after her,* he mused to himself. He knew she was a very capable woman, but he also knew she liked him to help with her less-favorite chores, and likewise he liked trying to repay her for all her kindness and care in his time of need.

chapter 4
birds of a feather

George Wallace was a man of sixty with the strength of a forty-year-old and the compassion of a man in his twenties. He didn't live far from the old Cameron house and when he spied the young American lass who had bought the place, he felt his time could be better spent trying to help her than it would be sitting at home alone. Light chores kept him limber and strong, and who better to assist than the young lass making him feel useful again.

George was driving by 'the old Cameron house' one day when he spied her struggling with atrocious weeds in her overgrown garden. "Now is as good a time as any," he stated and pulled into the spacious drive. She stood up to look at who would be paying her this unexpected visit. As in her habitual way, she took the back of her hand to wipe away both sweat and hair from her brow. She then stood with one hand on her hip and the other holding a dull hoe as the wiry older man approached. She had the engagingly thin figure of a lovely woman, but looked as though she could easily defeat him if it came to blows.

"Ya' bought the old Cameron house, aye? Hullo, I am George. I wanted to stop by and introduce meself." He offered his hand understanding American women felt this custom was an appropriate greeting gesture.

"Nice to meet you, Mr ," she paused.

"Wallace, George Wallace. But please call me George. If you call me Mr. Wallace, people will think of my father." He winked.

OK, George—nice to meet you," she grinned as she shook his hand. She noticed his hands were callused from hard work, but his bright blue eyes had the devilish glint of youth.

"How are you findin' our wee town?" he asked as he bent with Clarinda to pull some weeds where she had been working before. "I hope Mrs. Fitzrandolph has nae brought you anythin' to eat. If she does, just take it and toss it immediately—it is pure rubbish and no sow in town will touch it. She means well but I think she has killed her taste buds with acid."

This remark brought a smile to ~~a smile to~~ Clarinda. She was happy for the company and this small, wry man was helping her to rid the garden of the most heinous and stubborn of weeds.

"So why are you working so hard on the garden?" George asked.

"Well, I plan to open this place as a small guest house and I want to supply my kitchen with fresh herbs. Granted, I don't even have a chef yet, and although I would like to, I can't really cook and run the place at the same time. However, that doesn't mean that when I do get a good chef, I don't want them to have the freshest of supplies. How will I get a good Scottish Tourist Board Rating if I don't have wonderfully appetizing meals?"

"Well ya' have got a plan there, lass," George countered, "but I think ya' have more worries than a few thistles in ye yard. First of all, ye need to get the place covered with a fresh coat of paint, and I ken the interior also needs some fixin' up too."

"You are quite correct, so I have a painter lined up, but he is still working on the last job and will only continue to paint this season if the weather continues to hold up. So in the meantime, I can work on other chores."

"Who is doin' the paintin' for ya'? Please tell me it is the MacKenzies—they are the best."

"Well no—I chose a man by the name of Thompson—he was the cheapest," she replied.

"Och no! That drunk Thompson—you will no see him until he needs another drink. Let me talk to Jamie MacKenzie and he will be over in no time. He may cost ya' a wee bit more, but the job will be good and last a long time. I will stop by his place t'morrow and have him give you a ring."

As the afternoon wore on, Clarinda wasn't sure if she was being taken for all she was worth by this new acquaintance; or if George could actually assist her with the local tradesmen, and was indeed going to improve her previous arrangements. He seemed to know everyone, their vices, and their workmanship ability. Not having anyone else she could ask for recommendations, she hoped it wouldn't hurt to take some of George's advice to heart.

The following day Jamie MacKenzie called and furnished her with a quote to paint the house. His price was more, but he guaranteed his work and also could complete the project before the winter season. Furthermore, Craig Monroe had called upon her to see if he could tackle the plumbing issues and promised to have a bid to her by the end of the week. At the end of the day, she had been called by all the major tradesmen in town and they were willing to give her quotes and ensured they could get her work completed by no later than the end of November.

George Wallace visited Clarinda around teatime the next day. Not accustomed to stopping in the late afternoon to take a break, Clarinda was embarrassingly unprepared to received guests who typically expect some tea and biscuits. She was indeed eager to see George again and hurriedly prepared some tea and gathered some meager Walkers.

"Did you have some visitors today?" George asked with a gleam in his eye.

"Why, yes I did! Thank you so much! I can't thank you enough for arranging almost all of the men in town for giving me a call. Luckily they just wanted to persuade me to hire them for their handiwork and not all their services," she replied with subtle guile.

"No trouble at all, but make sure I take a look at those figures before you hire on. I ken when the lads are trying to take advantage of a sweet young lass."

Clarinda enjoyed George's quick wit and demeanor. She appreciated it, but she was also astonished how he was making such an effort to help her make the old house inhabitable again. Of course, she missed New York, and her friends there, but for the first time in the last three months, she felt as if she might be able to make a new life for herself in the Shire.

"So you will have the place looking spiffy in no time—when do you think you will take on some guests, or open for High Tea or supper?" he inquired.

"Well, the place may look the part, and although I am very skilled in the kitchen, I cannot run this place and do all the cooking. Since you know everyone in town, how about finding me a cook too?" she challenged.

"I just might hae the person you need, but let me ask ya' somethin': if ye are so skilled do you think you could help to train? What I mean is, I know of a great cook, but this person is not refined and would need some "upgradin'" so to speak. However, I am sure the wages would be favorable, and you won't have to provide board—the advantage hirin' a local Scot."

"George, I am flattered and I appreciate all you have done for me, so please don't think me rude by the remark I am about to make. I don't really want some person in my kitchen trying to tell me the way it should be and trying to revise and design new menus suited to their whim. I want to try this on my own, and I am not comfortable with the idea of my menus and specialties being changed or ignored by someone who thinks theirs are more suitable. Yes—I might be headstrong, but there are just some places where a woman's touch is superior to a man's, and

I think my kitchen is one of them. Thank you again, but I think on this suggestion I should try to find my own chef for the inn."

"Oh lass!" George smiled, " I hoped ye would feel this way, the cheef I have in mind is no a man! 'Tis a wonderful widow by the name of Janet Adams. In me humble opinion, she is the best in town—at least her pies and biscuits are the first to go at a bake sale. However, she is not well versed in any new culinary fancies from America, so you would have to show her, but if you are looking for the best cullen skink and stovies, there is no finer than the widow Adams."

He paused to let his sales pitch sink in and then continued. "If ya' want I could ask her, but again I was just haverin', sae I am not sure she wants to come and work for a "headstrong Yankee." Again his eyes twinkled and Clarinda knew she had been lured into this introduction—hook, line and sinker.

"OK, please do ask her if she would come and talk with me. Then we can both see what each other has to offer," Clarinda agreed.

"Brilliant. Thanks for the tea, but next time I hope ya' will have somethin' prepared more in keepin' with this inn. Tea from teabags and Walker's are not going to have them beatin' down ya' door." He winked again and strolled back to his car off to enlist the next townsperson into donating their time and services to Clarinda's new project. Yes—she felt she was lucky she did know George Wallace—and felt even luckier for the connections he knew.

chapter 5
simple life on the farm

"So—do they speak funny? Can you understand them?" asked Fran. Fran Humphrey was one of Clarinda's closest friends in New York. "I heard Robin Williams's skit and it was a riot, but I don't see how you know what they are saying."

Fran and Clarinda had met in college and became fast friends. They both joined the same sorority, Pi Beta Phi, and they both went into finance and marketing. Fran had the looks and was hired right out of college by Oligvy & Mather, but Clarinda had the brains and had spent the summer before her senior year as an intern, and this got her had a job with McKnowlton by the time she graduated. They found a small two-bedroom place in Bay Ridge, Brooklyn and enjoyed being young and living in 'The City'. Fran was always the person who would tell Clarinda to take chances. This suited Clarinda who was raised to be cautious, conscientious, and above all proper.

"Well once you hear it enough you pick up certain words and that helps, but sometimes I have a hard time." I heard some people speaking Gaelic (she emphasized the pronunciation and spoke the word as if she was a Bostonian pronouncing 'garlic' — without the "r"). "They sound like dogs growling or something. It is very had to understand and the spelling is not even remotely phonetic!"

"So how is the place coming? When do you plan to have guests? When can I come to visit — that is once all the work is completed? You know me — my idea of camping is a hotel without a hairdryer. I will state it for the record: I am your friend but I draw the line at manual labor." If nothing else Fran was an honest person; she said what she meant and didn't mince words.

"Well, I hope to have some guests before the beginning of the year. It would be nice to be open for Hogmanay."

"What the hell is Hogmanay? When you catch hogs, and as a prize, get a man? Would the man have a kilt on? What DO they wear underneath those things? Have you seen anyone wear one? Breezy, I have to think." Fran was letting her mouth keep time with her daydreaming.

"Well, for your information missie, Hogmanay is their term for New Year's only they do it right — it lasts for more than one night. And, yes I have seen some men in kilts and it is verry attrrractive." She emulated the Scottish trill. "And lastly no, I don't know what they wear under there, but it is told a true Scot wears nothing. I can only imagine when it is windy or midgey. I guess you will just have to come over here and find out for yourself. You can't expect me to do your research for you?" Clarinda challenged.

"I just might have to at that. But speaking of men — how are you getting along? I hope you are getting some time to recoup. I worry about you. It was terrible what happened to you. I know I shouldn't bring it up, but again, I worry. Are you OK?" Fran's voice was soft and comforting. She had an easy way of approaching uncomfortable subjects, and lulling one into feeling one could tell Fran anything and she would understand completely. This is one of the reasons why Clarinda treasured her as her friend so dearly.

"I am doing OK, but thanks for thinking about me. The inn has kept me so busy that I really haven't had the time to think about much else. I think I have been able to keep my emotions under control. Have you heard anything about him?" she queried, not really wanted to say 'his' name.

"Not really, but I did see all your stuff tossed out onto the street for the DAV to come and collect. I hope you have all you needed from that place 'cuz it is for sure gone now. As for David, I haven't heard much. I am not sure if he is still kanoodeling with that same tramp." Fran was not afraid to call it as she saw it, and she felt David was the lowest form of life on the planet after what he had put Clarinda through.

"Quite honestly, I rather not discuss it, I keep thinking about it and each time I wish I had had the nerve to really do some damage. I am such a wimp just to walk out. Remember the woman who ran over her husband with the Mercedes SUV three times? I wish I had had the courage to do that!" Clarinda was starting to get a bit riled about the subject again.

"Sweetie," Fran cooed, "I didn't mean to get you riled about this again. After all, you don't want to ruin a perfectly good automobile by getting his worthless internal organs splattered all over it."

Fran always knew the way to make Clarinda laugh. Sometimes she wondered why she needed to do sit-ups when a call to Fran would have her laughing so hard her stomach muscles would ache. They continued their conversation and Clarinda felt she may have convinced her friend to come for a visit.

"Hogmanay is supposed to be big fun, and you don't want to miss my opening night do you? Come on; book your flight now before the fares go up. Ask Uncle Rupert for some syrup and bring it when you come. I just can't stand anything else on my waffles. Thanks for calling. You really do make me laugh and feel better about life!" Clarinda hung up the phone and after a quick tally of the minutes she figured the call would cost her about seven pounds, but it was well worth it. She hoped Fran would take her up on her offer and visit Scotland. It would be nice to have some friends come for a visit. Her aunt and uncle were too old to travel, but she called them every week to make sure they were safe and sound. They were really the only blood-relatives Clarinda had left.

Uncle Rupert and Aunt Jilly once lived on a farm in a remote area of Vermont. Now they were residents at an assisted living facility. Sadly, Aunt Jilly had suffered several strokes and she had lost her speech and was confined to a wheelchair. Despite her frail condition, she maintained a smile on her face and seemed to be aware of conversations and her surroundings. Uncle Rupert continued to fare well, and he belonged to a woodworking group at the facility. It was nothing more serious than some whittling and carvings, but he strived to stay active and social. Clarinda was their only "child" and they shared a close relationship. Clarinda felt awful about leaving the country, but when Uncle Rupert had heard about what she went through, they both encouraged her to make a new start. They had felt there was no reason to stay and care for them when they had the best attention they could receive, and she was young and needed to live life to the fullest. She was glad to have their support, but she also missed not being near them. After all, there were her "parents" and she had become the person she was by their hand.

Clarinda Ann Tetrick was born on May 5th, 1975, to her parents, Madeline and Jeremy Tetrick in Stoneham, Massachusetts. The delivery was very standard, but afterward Madeline began to badly hemorrhage. Shortly after giving Clarinda life, Madeline lost hers while holding her small infant in her arms. This harrowing experience deeply affected Jeremy. They had been married for over five years, and both desperately wanted children. Now he had his wish, but without his wife to share the experience, Jeremy was lost. He began to find solace in alcohol. After six months of waking up at two o'clock in the afternoon to get ready for the next happy hour, he had lost most of the money the couple had saved for their future. The nanny was tending to the baby and taking most of the money Jeremy was making doing odd jobs when he was sober. Not even two years after Madeline's death, Jeremy Tetrick was found dead in a gas station garage, the victim of cirrhosis of the liver. Children's Services found the child at the home of the nanny. She realized she wasn't going to get paid, but she couldn't bear to leave the little girl under the care of a drunk. Not soon after, Rupert and Jilly Tetrick, Jeremy's brother and sister-in-law were asked if they could see their way to care for young Clarinda. Although, Rupert was almost fifty and Jilly only five years his junior, they were delighted. They had not been able to have children of their own and Clarinda was a beautiful child. They signed the required forms and left to head back north to their home in Salisbury, Vermont. The couple had a small farm; a couple of acres of vegetable gardens and some live stock. The animals consisted of assorted chickens and ducks, two large draft horses by the names of Bill and Bell, and two goats, Nanny and Billy, and of course the necessary farm dog named Megan, who was a Corgi. However, unlike most farm dogs, Megan was a homebody. Her short legs made her ideal for herding cows, but in the long distances she was not built for endurance. Despite her flaws, Megan was 'in charge' and made sure the other animals were safe, in their proper pens and if anything happened out of the ordinary, she would bark furiously to bring it to her masters' attention.

Rupert worked for a local farmer who had a chicken farm and sold eggs to most of the restaurants in the state. He was in charge of the business's operations. He helped to maintain the chicken coups, collect the eggs, inspect and grade them and get them in cartons, onto pallets, and finally load them into delivery trucks. He started his day very early, and ended it very late. Once he was finished at the egg farm, he returned home to make sure is own little menagerie was secure. In the spring he used the horses to plow the fields for corn, squash, strawberries, tomatoes, carrots, onions, cabbages and assorted herbs. Jilly would tend to the gardens the rest of the season and harvest them at the optimal time. Clarinda always loved simple suppers which consisted of nothing more than fresh sweet corn and sliced vine-ripened tomatoes.

Aunt Jilly also worked part time at the Town Hall. Because Salisbury was a very small town, there was not much civic administration needed to keep the town running smoothly. She was mostly needed to come in about two to three days a week to keep up the paperwork: filing of deeds, tractor registrations and issuing deer hunting permits. Not really terribly pressing matters, but she got to see many of the townsfolk on a regular basis. When she wasn't at the Town Hall, she was tending to the Tetrick's household—the regular stuff: cleaning, baking, mending, washing, and canning. Both Rupert and Jilly lived simple lives, but they worked hard, and laughed often. They raised their niece Clarinda with the same values.

Each season in Vermont brought new opportunities and the countryside would dramatically change its appearance. The year began in winter and the cold in Vermont is bone-chilling. Often the temperature would be as low as twenty degrees below zero for over a week or more. But the winter also brought skiers and since Vermont's major industry is tourism, everybody benefited from a cold and snowy winter. The Tetrick's did not ski, but they enrolled Clarinda in the lessons offered through the local school system. Clarinda loved the sport—she was not the fastest, but she had a natural grace and ability. Despite the chilly temperatures and heavy snowstorms, she would beg to go skiing as much as her aunt and uncle would allow. When she came home she would gladly help her uncle and carry stacked cords of wood to the house to keep the wood stove burning so she could sit beside it and thaw out. Her cheeks would be a ruddy color from both the combination of the cold and the warmth of the wood stove.

As spring neared, Vermont experiences two unique seasons. The first is "Sugarin' Season", and it is when the sap in the maple sugar trees starts to rejuvenate and bring about the new growth of leaves. Warm days and cool nights trigger the trees and the sap only runs for a short time. Often it is all harvested and boiled into syrup in only a few short weeks. It is not unusual for a 'sugar house' to be boiling for an entire forty-eight hour weekend. It takes a barrel of sap to make a gallon of maple syrup—thus the phrase "liquid gold". The lighter colored syrups are the most coveted grades and are called Fancy. Personally, Clarinda like the Grade B which was considerably darker, but had a richer maple flavor. The best thing about helping with sugarin' was to taste boiling hot syrup direct from the boiler's spigot. Some liked to drizzle it on snow so it would harden like taffy, but Clarinda loved the warmth of the sweet hot liquid as it made its way from her tongue all the way to her belly. It was a perfect antidote to make her forget about her soggy and frozen toes and fingers.

Once the snow begins in to melt in full force, the next season in Vermont is aptly called "Mud Season". This season tends to last longer than any other. Part of Vermont's charm is the abundance of unpaved roads. These roads become slick with mud and racked with washboard. Smooth summer rides on the same road are now a bouncy and jostling adventure. Also, the fields and barnyards are not able to drain the runoff quickly so they remain muddy for months at a time. Boots are not a fashion statement in Vermont; they are considered a necessary piece of equipment. Since Mud Season is not a popular time in Vermont, this is when many families will travel to warmer climates such as Florida, and try to cast off the gloom of winter hoping to return to a warm and green spring. Because Aunt Jilly and Uncle Rupert had Clarinda to care for and her education heavy on their minds, they often did not take a vacation, but would tough out Mud Season. Clarinda didn't mind. It was sort of fun to 'muck around' in the barnyard. There was no point in trying to keep clean—muddy feet were a given. Aunt Jilly was strict about boots and they didn't' go any further than the mudroom, but sometimes Clarinda found it great fun to tease her aunt and try to come into the house with her gloriously muddy feet.

Soon, the weather would warm and the mud would give way to grass and spring would soon paint the countryside with flowers and blooming trees and shrubs. Clarinda loved spring because everything smelled so good—the fresh grass, the flowers blooming in her aunt's garden and the sighting of the first robin. Trees would start to get leaves and everything seemed new again. The sun would allow short sleeve shirts to be worn. Clarinda would help her aunt and uncle ready the gardens. First all the leaves and twigs they missed from the fall would have to be gathered and collected before any planting could begin. Then Uncle Rupert would harness up Bill and Bell and plow and till the largest garden, which was for corn. Since it was a small garden by most Vermont standards, it was not worth the expense to buy a tractor and given that Bill and Bell had done this after so many years, Uncle Rupert felt they were more accurate and certainly more reliable. Tomatoes are planted the same week as Town Meeting, and corn three weeks before. The other vegetables were started in small seed trays and transplanted when they were hearty enough to survive on their own. Vermont could have late frosts, so occasionally Clarinda and her uncle would have to cover up the plants at night with some plastic to make sure they didn't freeze and ruin the crop.

Clarinda also looked forward to summer. It was a time to be carefree and easy. She would lie on the sweet smelling grass and watch the clouds drift by. Other times she would make a rudimentary fishing pole and go down to the pond on the egg farm and try her luck to catch a hornpout or steelhead. Her friends would meet at the swimming hole at the river and brave the icy water. Of course the summer was also a time for picnics and social gatherings. Her Aunt would make deviled eggs and the men folk would gobble them up. "The secret" her aunt would advise her, "is not to make them fancy. Sometimes simple is the best way to make Deviled Eggs." As Clarinda got older she knew how to make them herself and her friends would beg for the recipe. "Best to let them think about it," was her aunt's policy. "If they could make them on their own, why would they still want yours?" Aunt Jilly was not an unfriendly person, just practical. Clarinda didn't feel the same way. One day she shared the recipe with one of her friends, Carrie. To Clarinda's delight, Carrie still thought Clarinda's eggs were still better than hers, but just the same, she felt a small delight in making someone happy by sharing her talent. Summer was always very short. It seems school had not sooner gotten out when Clarinda was preparing for the next grade. Clarinda believed the old Vermont saying that describes summer as "a Tuesday in July between the hours of two to four" to be very true.

Fall was the most magical time in New England. The leaves of the trees turn from solid green to a kaleidoscope of oranges, reds and yellows. Some trees often appear to be sort of a peach color. It was spectacular. It also brought tourists to the state in droves. Some came in buses. Others drove their own cars—very slowly—to revel in nature's paintbrush. As a native it is frustrating to try to get into and about town due to all the misdirected people, but Clarinda's aunt and uncle reminded her that "they don't live in a place this beautiful and if by sharing it, we can prosper; than there is no harm." The foliage season is also a very short one. The trees typically start to "turn" the end of September and one short month later they are completely off the trees leaving them bare and spindly looking. Then comes the chore of raking them up into bunches and carting them to the compost pile behind the barns. This is tough work—especially on the hands; but once the pile is made behind the barn, it is the best fun to jump in the leaves and become lost in the flutter. Autumn is also the time to harvest the gardens—squashes are picked, onions braided and hung, herbs cut and dried, and tomatoes are made into sauce. Aunt Jilly would also make jams and jellies and can several vegetables and fruits. The small kitchen would take on the appearance of a chemistry lab with various pots steaming or bubbling and her aunt, the mad scientist, keeping track of all of them. By far, the best recipe was her aunt's applesauce. It was again, simple, but the rosy color and cinnamon flavor were irresistible.

As Clarinda got older she continually asked to have a horse she could ride. She loved Bill and Bell, but they were too slow and when she was astride their backs, they were so wide she felt as if her legs stuck straight out. The Tetrick's granted her wish, and on her thirteenth birthday she got a horse she nicknamed Sam. Sam was a Morgan, the state animal of Vermont, and although he was on the small side compared to other breeds, he was remarkably strong and agile, true to the Morgan standard. After chores Clarinda would pack a lunch, saddle up Sam and head into the Green Mountains. Megan would see them off and be the official greeter on their return. As with all other sports, Clarinda took to horseback riding as well. She had good balance and was even tempered when it came to understanding how to earn the trust and respect of an animal. To her, it was a pleasureable and idyllic way to explore the beauty of Vermont and to also gain independence and self-assurance as a rider. Clarinda would enter in competitions where she would ride for fifty miles or more over several days. She met several other girls during these rides and they formed a casual riding group. Many nights she would dream about riding endlessly over open fields, laughing with her fiends and Sam, her even and dependable steed.

Clarinda reminisced about her life as a girl and the simple, but rugged, beauty of Vermont. She looked at the hills and moors of Scotland and could see many similarities. This too was a wonderful place, the people were kind and practical, and there is a connection to the environment that made people wish to come and visit. Clarinda knew she could be happy in Scotland for many of the same reasons she loved living in Vermont. Life could be simple, but enriching.

chapter 6
witches brew?

Alistair's cell phone rang just has he was busy prying the shoe off a stubborn young filly. Before he could utter "Hullo", a voice on the other end began its outburst.

"You willna believe who came to see me today." This is Janet Adam's idea of fifty questions.

"Alright, I won't believe it," Alistair took the bait.

"Well it was himself thinking he can help everyone in this town. I doona think I need help, but there he was, in me very own home, asking me if I would go and speak with the American woman and ask her for a job. The nerve!"

"Janet, do ya' think his mother had the common sense to give him a name?"

"What do ya' mean—of course she did. What do you mean by that odd query?"

"Well so far ya' have been goin' on about this chap and have yet to identify him by name. When will ya' realize everyone in town doona gang by the names of 'him' and 'she? So who is this person who has gotten you to fash so?" Alistair tried to calm his sister with a soothing tone.

"Well it is that George Wallace. You ken since he sold his own business, he seems to want to be into everyone else's. I ken he means well, but now he thinks I need to be workin'. He came over to explain that the American woman is planning on openin' the old Cameron house fer guests and she is lookin' fer a cook. At me age—really! He must be haverin!"

"I think it's pure dead brilliant!" Alistair exclaimed. "Truly. Think about it—ya' spend ye whole day cookin' already—and fer who? Ye self mostly, and once or twice a week I join ya'. Now ya' could do what ya' love and get some money fer it. This would get ye out of the house. Ya' need a change. Gang and talk to her. How bad can she be?"

"Well I dinnae ken. At my age? Do ya' really think this is a good idea. I mean I dinnae ken if I could manage to cook fer all those folks. And I dinnae ken if I could work for the American woman, I mean, I do things a certain way, ya' ken, and I doona expect to change at me age."

"Janet," Alistair interrupted, "listen to what ye are sayin'. At your age—ha! Ye are not an old woman—yet, but ya' are startin' to rant like one. I am sure the American woman is about ye same age and will understand the advantages to consistency. Now ring her up and gang and give her a chat." Alistair wanted to be encouraging. This could be the change his sister needed and not only that, they both knew the money he made was not enough for both of them and what she had stored away was not going to last forever. Alistair had seen the American woman in the garden weeding and even though she had a nice slim appearance, he had seen these types before and they typically were single women, divorced from their husbands and looked the worse for the wear and tear. The American woman would not be any match for his sister—he would bet on it.

"Very well then—I will do it," Janet declared. "After all I am just goin' over for a chat, it is no a job just yet. I will ring ya' to let you know how it goes. Right-o."

"Right-o Janet—good luck. I need to get back to work now. The Kincaid's dinnae pay me to haver on me mobile."

Janet decided rather than phoning first, it might be best to make her first impression in person. The old Cameron house was a further distance than she typically walked, but she convinced herself the exercise would do her good. When she walked up the drive to the old house, she was slightly out of breath and she was also developing an angry blister on the back of her heel. "Blasted," she muttered under her breath. "I hope she likes round, sweaty, and lame old women."

When the weather was nice, Clarinda tried to spend it outdoors. She had cleared the garden and it was ready for planting when the time came. Today Clarinda was busy planting bulbs along the rock wall that ran up along the road in hopes for a fancy showing of irises and hollyhocks in the spring.

"Hullo there!" Janet called. "I am sorry to bother you, but George Wallace suggested I come to speak with ye. I am Janet Adams." She offered her hand.

"Oh—hi. Yes, George mentioned you. It's very nice to meet you. I'm Clarinda Tetrick," she replied, returning Janet's handshake. "Please come inside so we can talk. I have some scones I made today, and I hope you would join me for some tea."

"Lovely," replied Janet as they made their way into the house and through to the kitchen.

"Normally I would offer my guests tea in the parlor, but since you and I might be spending so much time in here, I thought it best for you to see the condition of my situation." Clarinda humbly smiled. She poured the tea and set the scones on a dainty plate with and a small crock of whipped butter. She gingerly placed a napkin and small knife near Janet's hand.

"It is very clean and tidy," Janet replied, but she could clearly see the kitchen was poorly equipped.

"Thank you—however I know I need more of the basic cooking essentials. I have only been preparing meals for myself, so when I need something, I get it; but the progress has been slow."

"Oh, sure," replied Janet now understanding this woman's situation. She couldn't help but look into those cool blue eyes and wonder how she ever thought Clarinda would be like her. This American woman was nothing as she expected. She was tall, but not gangly. She wore a simple shirt, with the sleeves rolled up, and jeans which were fairly snug. Janet could tell Clarinda legs were strong and she guessed her arms were equally able. She wore no makeup, but her skin was blemish free and had a healthy glow from the outdoors. She looked like those western cowgirls Janet had seen in magazines. She spoke with confidence, but was not assuming, nor condescending.

"So what are ye plans for this place? George tells me ya' want to be ready by Hogmanay," Janet continued.

"Well that is the idea," Clarinda explained. "I would like to get the place ready for that—I think it would be a good way to start the New Year, no?"

"Oh aye," Janet agreed, "but I think ya' have a lot of work to get this place ready in time. In the first place, what kind of fare were ya' plannin' to offer?"

Clarinda could sense Janet was probing to see if her skills were going to be sufficient for Clarinda's needs. "Here is a rough menu I have worked out. Of course I would only be serving this on just the one night, but I will have the inn open for guests, so they will expect a full Scottish breakfast the next morning. That is, the lucky ones who feel strong enough to keep their breakfast down." She smirked trying to make the conversation less serious.

Menu:
~ Boursin cheese and salmon curls with a Champagne toast
Starters:
~ Warm Goat cheese salad
~ Chilled Consommé

Entrees:
~ Chateaubriand of Aberdeen Angus with horseradish béarnaise sauce
~ Filet of Wild Salmon with a creamy dill sauce
~ Stuffed Cornish Game Hen with Rosemary
Sides:
~ Asparagus or Creamed Spinach
~ Garlic Mashed Potatoes or New Red potatoes with a chive and parsley butter
Enders:
~ Pumpkin-pecan pie
~ Cheeses, coffee, tea

"Well I hope ye will be chargin' a good sum for this, it is quite extensive. There are several dishes here I am no familiar, such as Pumpkin-Pecan pie. Is this an American treat? If so, I dinnae ken if it will go over big with the locals. How about Hot Sticky Toffee Pudding instead? I am known for mine, and I dare say it could be the reason for some of this." Janet smiled and indicated her round midsection.

"Well I can share my recipe for Pumpkin Pecan Pie with you, but let's add the pudding to the menu too. I think that is a great idea." She paused before speaking again.

"I am sure you may not know all of my recipes, and I certainly don't know yours, but I hope both of us would be willing to learn some new ones from each other?" Clarinda ended this is in the form of a question—hoping Janet might be open to this sort of arrangement.

Janet was silent for a moment as she thought about Clarinda's statement. "Well, I suppose it would be fun to learn some fresh ones. But I have to tell ya' that nae only am I a good baker, but me haggis is some of the finest in the Shire."

"Great," Clarinda enthused, "but can you make whisky sauce and serve it with tatties and squash?"

"Sure, I think so," Janet's reply as a bit sheepish. "I dinnae think I have tried that dish—with squash, you say? Instead of neeps? I guess I will have to try it before I pass judgment."

"So do we have a deal?" Janet asked.

"I think we might," Janet replied. "But I need to ask ya' two more things. First, how much will ye pay me to fill your dinin' room each night; and secondly, can ya' allow me a budget so we can rightly stock this kitchen?"

Janet Adams was satisfied with both of Clarinda's answers. Before she left, she began taking notes and making lists of the necessary supplies and provisions they would need to get the kitchen in order.

"I will see ya' bright and early in the morn, Clarinda?" Janet cheerily walked back to her house. With each stride, she continued to make mental notes and added to her lists and had completely forgotten about the blister on her heel. She had not felt this useful in some time and it made her chest swell with pride. To Janet, Clarinda Tetrick seemed like a fair woman, with a pleasant, but reserved disposition. *Sad,* Janet thought to herself, *she doesn't have a man to help her. She is very pretty and she doesn't deserve to be alone. Well, maybe I can work on that?* she mused. She got so caught up into her new assignment; she forgot to call Alistair to tell him the good news.

chapter 7
a call to dinner

"I feel sort of peelie-wally to be ye chef when you haven't really been able to sample me fare. I would like to invite ye to my home for supper. This would nd only be a good way for ya' to sample some of me dishes but I want to repay ya' in a small way for asking me to help ya' with the inn. It has been a long time since I have felt useful. Please say ya' can come over, let's say tomorrow?" Janet was almost giddy.

"Why certainly." Clarinda was a bit overwhelmed by this gesture and paused slightly before she continued. "I am delighted you are so enthused about helping me. However, I wonder after a few long days on your feet if you won't feel differently. You do know what you are getting into—right? I need to be able to depend on you." Clarinda wanted to give Janet ample time to consider this undertaking. She couldn't afford to replace a chef once she was close to opening. It was too crucial a position to the success of the inn.

"Aye, I do," Janet replied with confidence. "I have always had the unfortunate luck to have jobs that keep me on me feet all day. I am used to it and I fully understand ya' need to rely on me. Trust me—I promise I won't let ya' down. So how about dinner tomorrow night? I was thinking some fresh wild salmon—does that suit ya'?"

"I love salmon—that sounds delightful. I will accept and be there tomorrow night. What time would you like me to show up and is there anything I can bring…perhaps some wine?"

"Yes," Janet agreed, "wine would be nice. Why don't you come over around half-past six and ~~will~~ we will eat about seven-thirty. You can meet my brother, Alistair. See you then."

"Thank you—see you then. Bye."

"Right-o, bye."

As Janet hung up the phone, she was startled to see her younger brother at the door. "Speak of the de'il, were your ears burnin'?"

"No, why? What did you get me into this time?" Alistair winced.

"Nothing, but I was hopin' ya' could come o'er for supper tomorrow night. I'll be havin' Clarinda Tetrick over, and I didn't want her to think I am a sad lonely spinster. So I was thinkin' me brother would help me out and join us. Come on—what's the harm? Ye could even bring Lauren if ya' wish."

"Who is Clarinda Tetrick?"

"Och, are you daft?" Janet was dismayed. "Have you no heard anything I say to you? She is the American who owns the old Cameron house and is converting it to an inn. She offered me a job to be her chef and run the kitchen. I want to have her here for supper to thank her and to allow her to enjoy some of me superior Scottish fare."

"Oh yes, I know now—I just dinnae ken her name. So is she very American, or do you think she will be able to make a go of the place?"

"Aye, she is talented, and I think ye will like her too. So will ya' please come for dinner?"

"Fine—but just for me douce sister. When do you want me to appear? I suppose highland dress would be encouraged," he winked.

"Oh aye—that would be brilliant! And I suppose ya' will bring Lauren too? She is such as canny lass and I am sure Clarinda would love to meet your girlfriend."

"Yes—I better bring Lauren. If she were to find out me sister had a single American woman o'er for dinner and I was there without her, she would no be happy. Best to do the safe thing."

"Well it only makes sense. Soon the two of you will be married, and going to every social event as a couple."

Alistair rolled his eyes. "Jan, ya' know as well as I do that I will no be asking Lauren to wed me anytime soon. She is too young for me. I like her fine enough, but nae so much to make her my wife."

"Och—she is nae too young, and she is at a good age to have children. Why are ya' so stubborn about this? I don't want to argue about it, but I am glad ya' will be bringin' her with ya'. You both make a handsome couple."

"Yes, sis. I guess no good deed goes unpunished!" he smirked.

"Ye are so good to me. How did I deserve such a wonderful man to be my brother? Thank ya' for all ya' do for me." Janet knew a little praise would go a long way.

"I know, but right now I need to go do some other good deeds for ya' fowl or they willna survive the week." He gave her a kiss on the cheek and walked out the back door to care for Janet's chickens and ducks.

Janet watched her brother work in the coups and wished he would find true happiness with Lauren's love. The lass was young, yes, but she adored Alistair. Janet knew Lauren was hoping Alistair would ask for her hand in marriage—hopefully before the New Year. Janet had had true love once and it was glorious. Even though her bliss with Richard was short, she would not have traded the experience for anything. "I hope ya' find what ye are looking for," Janet mused, "ye deserve it too."

Clarinda was excited to go over the Janet's for dinner. It was the first time anyone in Inverwick had invited her over to his or her home. Even though Janet was her first employee, and she her employer; she still wanted to make a good impression. The first decision was her attire. She had plenty of "New York" outfits, but this was the highlands of Scotland and she wanted to try to fit in, and not seem austere. She chose a simple long black skirt, ankle boots, and a cranberry sweater. She also decided to bring a shawl to keep her warm along the quick walk down Telford Lane to Janet's small house on Rowan Road. She would abandon the usual ponytail, and leave her hair down to frame her face. "A small amount of make-up might be a good idea; after all I don't want to scare Janet's brother. It is not All Hallow's Eve just yet."

Clarinda went to examine the wine collection she had begun to store in her cool cellar. "Hmm, salmon, huh? OK, how about a Semillon or sauvignon blanc? Ah, here is a nice one—French burgundy grapes—lovely." She dusted off the bottle and took it upstairs to create a wine bag. After all, she was presenting the wine as a gift and wanted it to look the part. She was sure she had some sheer organza fabric and cording, and could easily come up with a simple drawstring sack that would look fancy enough. Janet wanted the evening to go well, so she focused on every detail.

I wonder if Janet would be willing to experiment and try my Dill Sauce to go with her salmon.

This sauce was very simple, but sauces where her specialty and she typically had one for every dish. She enjoyed salmon served with this easy sauce, whether it was grilled, broiled, sautéed or poached. It was very versatile and a nice change to the traditional plain lemon wedge or other heavier cream sauces. She took a small card and wrote down the four simple ingredients. She typically made it by look and taste, but since this would be Janet's first try, Clarinda felt the brief instructions would be helpful.

"There—I hope she doesn't take offence, but we will see."

Simple Dill Sauce for Salmon
From the kitchen of Clarinda Tetrick

Blend the following ingredients together in a small dish. Adjust quantities as desired.
- *~ 2 tbls sour cream*
- *~ 2 tbls mayonnaise*
- *~ 1 teaspoon of Beau Monde seasoning*
- *~ 2 teaspoons dill weed*
- *~ Sprig of parsley for garnish*

chapter 8
is this a place ya'd call home?

"So let's see where we stand on all these tasks." Clarinda reviewed her list.

~ Get the place painted—in progress (Jamie McKenzie)
~ Get the chicken house livable (and buy some chickens!)—Coup repaired, need to buy chickens.
~ Weed the garden for herbs (basil, dill, savory, rocket, rosemary and chives)—done, ready for spring planting.
~ Paint the rooms—in progress—5 done. 3 more to go.
~ Find a plumber to fix the toilets and add showers to each room (lots of $$$ there!)—in progress (Craig Monroe)
~ Buy new bedding for the rooms—done.
~ Find a chef to cook meals—done!!!
~ Find a maid to keep up the rooms—ask George
~ Find a friend—I now have 2!!

Clarinda was pleased with the progress she had made in a few short weeks. Both Jamie MacKenzie and Craig Monroe gave her fair quotes and Jamie was almost done. The house had been painted a new coat of bright white, but he still needed to paint the trim black. It was amazing what new paint could do to make a place look so much better. Craig was busy as well. Some rooms already had full baths, so he was working to get sinks and showers in the others. This was not so easy considering the age of the house and some rooms did not have easy access to the pipes carrying the water. He excelled at innovative ideas to solve these problems and Clarinda appreciated his attention to detail and his cost effective nature.

She was glad the outdoor work was done for the season. October had become cool and her hands were stiff when working in those temperatures. She had now moved onto indoor chores and she was single handedly painting the guest rooms. Like the exterior, paint really did help to improve the appearance of these rooms. She chose light colors to give the rooms some airiness, and had added wallpaper and chair rails to give them dimension. She had been able to find bedding and towels that matched, and purchased some fabric to make complementary accent pillows. The wooden floors had been scrubbed and waxed and she found some rugs to place by each bed. She didn't like trouncing on a cold floor with her toes first thing in the morning, and she felt her guests might feel the same. Each room was taking on their own personality. She wondered if she should 'name' them to make it easier for guests and staff to remember each one. She was going to consult with George about that idea.

"First ya' need a name for the inn itself!" George observed. Really—ya' can't go namin' rooms 'til ya' got that decided. So have ye got one in mind?"

"I was thinking about The Heather and Thyme Guest House. It sort of speaks to the spices we use in the food and also with this great view of the heather it seems appropriate. This way each of the rooms could be call a different spice, like Rosemary, Sage, etcetera. What do ya' think?"

George pondered this for a while and then smiled. "It like it—brilliant! The idea of namin' the rooms after the herbs in ye wee garden is very keen. Such a clever lass. How does New York get along without ya'?"

Suddenly Clarinda's face went dark, and George knew he had overstepped his boundaries with his new friend. "I am sorry—that was gruff of me to bring up ye past. Please forgive me."

"Oh no George, it is OK. New York is a far away place now and I need to learn to put those old feelings there as well." She smiled and willed herself to be sunny once again.

"So let me ask ya', can ya' recommend a chamber maid?"

After George left she thought about the comment he had made about New York. How did New York get along without her? Did anyone besides Fran miss her—specifically how was David faring? As she thought about him her mood changed from reminiscent to anger. "Never again!" she reminded herself. David was not good for her and she needed to let the past stay where it was. *However*, she wondered, *will I ever find that kind of passion again?*

David Kline was a master of marketing. As the proverbial saying goes, he could sell ice to an Eskimo. It was uncanny how he was able to predict consumer-buying trends. He was wizard-like at creating an emotional attachment to a product within someone's lifestyle. He had boundless energy and he was exciting to watch, as he would use his hands and his voice to evoke responses from his colleagues and clients. His reputation in the industry was legendary, and if a client wanted their product or service to be a household name, they sought out David Kline of Masters and Kline Associates.

When Clarinda met David for the first time she felt as if she had been struck by lightening. She had been hired by Masters and Kline as a Marketing Analyst and had worked for several months to prepare to bring on a new client. The company she was assigned to was a small, but promising, mail-order cataloger called Sand and Stone and they sought help to establish their brand and to achieve larger market share. Clarinda and her team were to perform focus groups and recommend a plan of action.

It is customary for the one of the founding partners of Masters and Kline to welcome new clients upon their first visit to the Masters and Kline headquarters. This demonstration is to reaffirm clients that Masters and Kline is one of the finest marketing firms, ideal for their business, and will take their company to the next level. Clarinda was spell bound as she watched David Kline strut around the conference room and with smooth, but broad hand gestures, demonstrated the power of the firm he helped to establish. He was at least six-feet tall and moved elegantly. Although authoritative, his voice was firm, slow and reassuring—it was almost hypnotic in nature. His well toned physique wore clothes well; today he sported black pants and jacket, and a cashmere V-neck sweater. The total ensemble was simple and although seemingly casual, it demonstrated power and self-assurance. Tanned skin contrasted by brilliantly white teeth, and black wavy hair graying at the temples, he was a most distinguished looking man. He never wore glasses and he certainly didn't look to be close to the forty-eight years of age the company annual report claimed him to be. He was one of the most striking men Clarinda had ever seen and she kept checking to make sure her jaw was not sitting in her lap.

When he finished with the introduction, David took a seat next to Clarinda to demonstrate his support of the team he had formed to work on this new client's branding initiatives. "Knock their socks off," he purred into Clarinda's ear. "Show 'em what you've got." Clarinda was able to smell his scent—clean, and very male.

Slightly alarmed by her own reaction, she took in a quick breath. She quickly gathered herself together and rose slowly to make her presentation, praying she didn't look as self-conscious as she felt. As she spoke, she had to train her gaze to focus on the clients—her inclination was to stare at David Kline. He sat back in his chair crossed one leg over the other, clasped his hands in his lap and sat back to watch Clarinda's presentation. When she made key points, he slightly grinned with satisfaction. She felt him analyzing her every move. Albeit nervous and excited, she wanted to 'perform' for this man who was not just her boss, but her boss's boss's boss. He was not only a man, (and an extremely handsome one at that), but he was The Man in her world—not only professionally, but he was the standard by which she would measure all others.

Once the presentation was complete and the clients left the building, Clarinda went back to her office to reorganize and plan her next day's work. The message light was blinking on her phone and she had fifty-seven e-mails to read. Although it was not her habit, she picked up the phone to retrieve the four new messages. The first two were her friends inviting her to lunch the next day. The next one was a colleague asking for some additional research on a project. Clarinda gasped when she heard the voice of the last one. "Clarinda—this is David. I wanted to call to commend you on a fine presentation today. I think the Sand and Stone folks will be very pleased with your attention to their brand. I also wanted to know if you would like to join me for lunch tomorrow. Say about one o'clock? Meet me at my office and we can go from there. See you then. And again—good job."

Click. Very slowly, as if moving through Jell-O, she placed the phone back in its cradle. "Did I just get a call from David Kline of Masters and Kline?" she asked herself. "And did he just invite me to lunch?" She was not sure if she should feel special because of his attention, or did he invite all of his marketing analysts out to lunch after a successful presentation. "Well, we will see, won't we?" she mused.

She quickly called her two friends and cancelled lunch with them. When they asked why, she vaguely told them she had to take a business lunch—she was not entirely lying. She immediately knew what she would wear the next day—her midnight blue suit which had a very short skirt and form fitting jacket. She would match it with some fairly high heeled pumps—she didn't wear them often, but this was an occasion. Her appearance would be conservative, but captivating.

At ten minutes before one o'clock Clarinda was in front of David's office door. His executive assistant told her to 'have a seat'. "He is still on a call and will be a few more minutes."

Clarinda sat and tried not to let her shoulders slouch—she didn't want to look dumpy and thick-waisted. The doors opened in a rush and Clarinda jumped to her feet like a perky cheerleader; smiling like one too.

"Clarinda, it's nice to see you again. Shall we go to Hibachi House and do some sushi?" David suggested.

"That sounds great," Clarinda agreed although she had never been there. He could have suggested a garage and she would have gone along with it.

When they got to the restaurant they were first instructed to remove their shoes. David confirmed they would need a table for two. As they padded toward their table, Clarinda could see it was a foot off the ground and floor pillows sufficed for seating. As supple as a greyhound, David removed his jacket, and sat on the cushion with his legs crossed and his back straight. He motioned to the cushion and looked devilishly at Clarinda. "Please join me won't you?"

Clarinda didn't know what to make of this. Clearly he had been to the Hibachi House before and he also saw what she was wearing and knew the two were not going to be a good pairing. But Clarinda was a sport and also did not want to offend this man—for several reasons. It may have looked awkward but Clarinda managed to take a seat on the cushion with her legs curled to the side. She thanked the heavens she did yoga twice a week in order to perform this seating stunt.

The lunch was one dreams were made of. The food was meager, but the David ordered some sake, and that was plentiful.

Although Clarinda wouldn't dream of drinking during working hours, she also didn't want to disappoint David. As they talked, she learned he had spent summers going to Vermont to camp and to ski in the winter. They reminisced about the towns and villages they both had visited and suggested they should take a 'road trip' to go and revisit them together. David told her about how he graduated from Vanderbilt and had always dreamed of his own company. He worked for one of the most prestigious firms in town and once he had enough clients of his own, he left and took them with him. To Clarinda it was clear this man was smart, capable, and could achieve anything he set his mind to. He was everything Clarinda desired. He was certainly very masculine, but also elegant, charming and well mannered. He was accustomed to the finer things in life, and although his family had wealth, he was not ostentatious and narcissistic. She was smitten and she knew this was dangerous, but could not stop herself.

David looked at his watch and indicated they needed to leave so he could take a three-thirty meeting and paid the check. As they got up to leave, Clarinda placed her weight on her leg, not realizing it had fallen asleep in the posture she had maintained, and she nearly fell to the floor. In an instant, David prevented her from suffering this embarrassment. "As Steven Write says—I hate it when my foot falls asleep during the day—now it will be up all night," he joked. She continued to balance on both feet, but still needed place some of her weight on his steady arm. She slowly lifted her head up to see his face inches from hers. She was transfixed and couldn't move; it was if she was paralyzed by the combination of his gaze and the sake. She was captivated by his brilliant eyes, long lashes which acted as a visor for his seductive stare. Slowly he leaned forward and gave her a kiss. Outwardly, her reaction was restrained; inside her she was combusting. Her heartbeat was like a trip-hammer, her stomach clenched, and her head swooned.

"I am sorry if I offended you, but you are enchanting," David whispered. She was numb and just nodded. Once they were outside the door, and walking back to the office, Clarinda decided not to let this opportunity slip by—whatever the cost, she had to have another kiss!

She stopped in her tracks. "David," she spoke. He turned and walked the few steps back. "Kiss me again," she half asked and half demanded. He wrapped his arms around her and leaned in to give her a kiss, but he lingered not letting her get what she so desired. He brushed his lips on hers and she was hungry for more. "Not so fast, my pet, just let me show you what a kiss from me is truly like," he smirked. He bent in softly and then touched his lips to hers, his tongue slipped onto her mouth and she loved the soft buttery feeling. She opened her mouth to receive him; his tongue darting and exploring. Clarinda didn't think her legs would hold her; her heart was racing, her stomach fluttery, and her tummy clenched in response to his unbridled passionate kiss. He then consumed her and she felt she was going to be swallowed up by a wave of desire. He then stopped and pulled away, leaving her breathless. "Shall we go now?" he teased. She was barely able to talk, and luckily David took her arm. Clarinda felt as of she was gliding along the sidewalk back to the offices of Masters and Kline.

"So tomorrow—the same time?" David inquired. Clarinda could barely focus on the present let alone the future, but was able to nod and mumble and affirmative answer. "Very well then—have a great rest of the afternoon and pleasant dreams tonight."

Clarinda was not sure if she was able to perform anything productive when she got back to her office. Her assistant asked if she was all right since she seemed distracted, but beaming. The remainder of the day passed quickly and she went home to think about the day's events.

"What WAS I thinking?" she reprimanded herself. "He is the head of the company and I am acting like a floozy. He must do this with all the assistants in the building—I am such a fool." Although she continued to chastise herself for her rash behavior, she did so while walking on air. She couldn't stop thinking about David, his smell, his taste, and the way he took her to new levels of passion. He was an all-consuming man and she was attracted to him with all of her desire.

The next day arrived, but time stood still until lunchtime. Again, she expected to be turned away when she went to his office, but instead he was waiting for her and they quickly left and headed to another swank restaurant. As soon as they were out of the building, David pulled her close to him and unlike the prior day's gentle and exploring kiss, this time he was pushing his lips to hers with a hard and powerful taking. She molded to him and could feel his passion jutting into her thigh. He was electrifying and she was his conductor and they both were lost into each other despite the busy street.

"I have been thinking about you the entire night and day. You have captivated me completely." His eyes searched hers to find reciprocal feelings. She, too, was falling for this man she hardly knew. As he looked into her clear blue eyes he saw warmth, trust, and a bright sparkle of life and love. Clarinda was a passionate, smart, witty and charming young woman. She was refined, but also empowered a great sense of humor and saw beauty in most things. David had not met a woman quite like her. Most of his past conquests had been beauties, but there was no substance to their emotions. They didn't strive to explore new boundaries or to embrace challenges. This woman was brave, confident, and breathtakingly lovely all in one person. "Let's go—I want to talk with you and find out more about you."

The rest of the week went much the same—lunch to get to know each other better and the end of their meeting would end with a kiss. The next day was Saturday and Clarinda was not sure if David's plans for the weekend would include her in any way. At Friday's lunch she decided to broach the subject.

"I suppose you have plans for the weekend?" she asked

"Why yes I do—I will be going up state to a small cabin I have right outside of Albany."

"All by yourself?" she pried.

"No actually, I plan to have a lady-friend as my companion," he stated without hesitation.

This was the moment Clarinda had dreaded. She knew she couldn't possibly be the only woman in David's life, but she didn't appreciate his cavalier manner of mentioning others in front of her.

"Well, then, have fun," she replied and began to get up from the table to leave. "I need to get back to the office." She didn't want David to see disappointment in her eyes, she needed to leave immediately before he could see her at such a vulnerable moment.

"Hold on a minute!" David reported and grabbed her arm. "Just where do you think you are going? When I said 'lady-friend', I was referring to you, silly. I was hoping you were free this weekend to join me?"

Clarinda felt sheepish. She had become spiteful for no good reason. She was learning to trust David more each day, but she still doubted that this magnificent man held so much interest in just her. Of course she had had other lovers in her life, but not someone who was so all consuming. The idea of spending the weekend together made her both giddy and anxious at the same time.

"Really? David, I am touched. I am sorry for acting so childish. I would love to join you this weekend. When do we leave? What do I need to pack?" Clarinda was having a hard time containing her joy. She envisioned a romantic getaway for just the two of them.

"Well, it is a bit cooler up there, and we will be spending some time outside—perhaps some hiking, so bring your boots. I will think of everything else. I will pick you up at your place at about 8:30 tomorrow morning, but I will need your address."

David arrived promptly the next day and it was a glorious one. The leaves of autumn were in full color, the sky was a bright blue and the air crisp. They rode in David's convertible listening to Van Morrison, shouting out the verses to be heard above the dim of the rushing wind.

When they reached the cabin, Clarinda was shocked. This was no average 'cabin' but a large log home. The front of the house featured a peaked roof and windows filled the span from floor to ceiling. David turned off the car and quickly got out.

"Wait here—I need to do a few things inside before you come in. It won't take me a minute."

Clarinda waited and looked around, taking in the view of a small lake not far from David's cabin; watching two men fish from their small boat. This place was special and lovely—ideal in Clarinda's mind's eye.

"OK, come on in now," David called. As Clarinda walked up to the door, David greeted her there. She stepped inside and the home was equally exquisite inside as it appeared from the exterior. The large windows beautifully framed the view of the lake and the Adirondacks in the distance. David had gone to the effort of starting a fire and lit candles so the room was bathed in a warm glow. There were woven rugs on the simple a hardwood plank floors and one made of sheepskin lay in front of the hearth. The fireplace was constructed of fieldstone and rose to the top of the cathedral ceiling and sported a massive mantel above which was the head of an eight-point white tailed deer. The couches were invitingly soft, chocolate-colored leather.

"David, this place is fantastic! When you said 'cabin', I certainly did not imagine something like this. It is wonderful. Thank you for bringing me here to share "

Clarinda didn't get the words out. David could no longer contain his need for Clarinda and kissed her with wild abandon sealing his lips on her and literally taking her breath away. "I am glad you like it. I wanted it to be special for you."

He eased her over in front of the fire. The room was not cold, but her skin turned to goose-flesh from the mounting excitement and anticipation.

"David," Clarinda panted, "I can't wait any longer—I need to be with you."

"All in good time my sweet, you cannot rush works of art." His hands started to explore her body as he continued to tenderly kiss her neck and move behind her.

"He slipped his hand into her blouse and ran his fingers over her stiff nipples. She gasped and let herself become the canvas on which David could paint his masterpiece. She reached behind her and felt David's muscular thigh and slowly ran her hand upward to find him ready and at attention. He had been unbuttoning her blouse and releasing her breasts from the confines of her bra. She turned to face him and as she did he slid her shirt off her shoulders and bent down to suckle her dark pink and erect nipples. Clarinda responded and pulled David's sweater over his head and began to unbuckle his pants. David lifted Clarinda up into his arms in a smooth sweeping motion and gently laid her on the devilishly soft sheepskin rug. The flames of the fire were growing in unison with the passion of the lovers in front of it. David removed his trousers and stood before Clarinda as if to allow her to take in his beauty of hard muscles and angled planes. He was obviously ready to take Clarinda, but she wanted to further delight him and extend his pleasure until he could no longer endure it another moment. She was impressed with the amplitude of his equipment and smiled up at him and he smirked with self-satisfaction.

"I will send you places you have not been before, my love," he whispered.

She reached up to take him into her mouth. He instantly gasped and involuntarily thrust with longing. She continued to tantalize him with her tongue and flicked at him in all the most sensitive places. David could barely stand this delicious torture any longer. He firmly grabbed her shoulders and gently forced her back onto the rug. He placed his mouth over hers and kissed her with such force and desire it sent shivers of delight along the length of Clarinda's body. He continued to kiss her neck, then her shoulder, and made his way to her breasts. He gently took one in his mouth and at the same time he was exploring her body with his hands—moving slowing up one of her silky thighs. His fingers found her moist cleft and started to manipulate her most sensitive erotic zone. Clarinda arched her back in reaction to his ministrations and cried out as she neared a new level of ecstasy.

She begged for him to come to her; he moved slowly and would not let her come down from her plateau of pleasure.

"Please, David, I need you now!" Clarinda demanded and dug her fingers into the smooth skin of his back.

The moment prime, David slid his legs between her thighs. He moved forward ever so slowly and began to enter her. "Now David," Clarinda pleaded. He continued to slowly rock and ease his way into her. She matched his pace and mirrored his rhythm. At long last he plunged himself fully into her soft loveliness and she gasped with delight. David continued his long strong thrusts until Clarinda began to cry out and shudder as she peaked in ecstasy. She had lost all inhibitions and was consumed by sensuality. David held onto her and could not contain his desire any longer and emitted a low groan of release as he exploded inside her. They were suspended in time as wave after wave of rapture washed over them. She was reduced to molten uselessness and remained intertwined in David's arms. A sheen of glistening sweat covered him, he smelled strongly of maleness. She beheld her nude conqueror—who was this magical man who could make her feel this way? She looked into his eyes to try to find and answer but instead he gently kissed her on the lips. She was afraid that if either spoke, this magic moment would be lost.

He held her face in his hands and looked fixedly into her eyes. "You are the most exciting woman I have known. I have not felt this way before, I have never met anyone who could take me to such heights of desire. You complete me."

The light of the sunset filled the room and Clarinda felt a peaceful heaviness after their strenuous engagement. Due to the culmination of these factors, she wanted to believe David with all her heart. She felt a severe loss of words but needed to say something, so her meager reply was: "I feel the same way." As soon as she said it, she wished she hadn't. How corny was that! David just smiled as if he understood the sentiment even if her words fell sorely shy of the feelings she wanted to express.

"Stay here, let me go and pour us some wine." He rose and began to walk to the kitchen. Clarinda watched him stride gracefully and was completely amazed by his trim hips, strong legs and smooth back (except where she had scratched him) and thought him to be the most stunning man she had ever seen, and just this visage of him rekindled her hunger once again. She sighed and watched him return with two glasses of red wine. As soon as she took a sip, her face flushed. This reaction could have been from the warmth of the fire, the afterglow of lovemaking, or the effect of the wine. Either way, she was living a dream and could not imagine a better way to spend a weekend. She reached down to stroke him again, and David was immediately eager to taste her. They began to kiss and explore each other's bodies and to what limit each other could withstand. It was evident to Clarinda the sheepskin rug was going to see a lot of action this weekend.

After some time their hunger for each other changed to that for food. They donned some robes and went to the kitchen to prepare something simple but filling. They had brought some homemade pasta and Clarinda volunteered to bring some of her pesto. "I am known for this stuff." She didn't want to sound immodest, but it was fair to say Clarinda was an expert at creating sauces and her pesto was one of the best. She began to sauté some mushrooms and onions in a skillet pan while the water for the pasta drew to a boil. It wasn't long before she added the cream and pesto and served the concoction over some flat square pasta. She could tell David was quite impressed—not because of his comments; but because he was not talking. His manners never deterred from perfect, but he was eating like he would not be fed again.

"This is wonderful," he declared as he smartly wiped the corner of this mouth with a napkin. "I have been to some of the finest restaurants in the city, and never have I had anything as wonderful as this. It is so unique but not heavy. Can you tell me the secret?"

She knew the recipe by heart, and was happy to share it with him. "The difference between mine and the next guy's is that I don't add Parmesan cheese to my pesto as 'filler'. This way the basil and parsley are not masked but really stand out." She found a piece of paper and was scribbling down the ingredients and preparation.

"Here you go" she offered the recipe to him.

Basil and Parsley Pesto Sauce for Pasta
From the kitchen of Clarinda Tetrick

Ingredients:
~ ½ cup white wine
~ 1 medium onion
~ 2 cups of sliced mushrooms
~ 2 cloves of minced garlic
~ Basil and Parsley Pesto (see below)
~ 1 c. heavy cream
~ Pasta of your choosing, but something with texture that will hold the sauce—spaghetti is not recommended.
~ Grated Parmesan cheese
~ Piñon nuts

~~~~~~

Basil and Parsley Pesto
~ 2 Cups of firmed packed basil
~ ½ cup of firmly packed parsley
~ ¾ c. of extra virgin olive oil
~ 1 tsp. of minced garlic
~ ¼ tsp. of salt
~ Pepper to taste

Blend the above ingredients in a food processor for 45 seconds. Place in containers and freeze for later use. Defrost at room temperature—do not thaw in a microwave.

~~~~~~

Sauté the onion, garlic, and mushrooms in olive oil and white wine until the onions are translucent and the mushrooms soft. Add heavy cream and stir until the cream is warmed and will coat the back of a spoon. Add 2+ tbls. of pesto and continually stir until the sauce is almost about to bubble. Serve over pasta almost al dente. Sprinkle with parmesan cheese and piñon nuts.

"Seems simple enough but I am sure my rendition will not be nearly as tasty. So what do you have planned for desert?" he teased as he winked at her.

"Why you, my sweet," she purred as she rose and came over to sit on his lap. "I think I have a tasty treat for you." Clarinda took her finger and ran it along David's lower lip. This time they were able to make it to the bedroom before they devoured each other in a frenzy of unleashed lust.

The weekend ended much too soon for Clarinda's liking. They could have stayed in the cabin for the rest of their lives as far as she was concerned. Sadly, there was a reality to face and they both needed to go back to work. Clarinda believed it would be hard to maintain a strictly professional façade at work as if they knew each other in only employer and employee roles.

"Shall we continue to meet for lunch or will that be too obvious?" she inquired.

"I think a few times a week will be alright—but I would caution you to be discreet. This is the first time I have ever had a relationship with an employee and I wouldn't want your reputation to be tarnished. Sadly, jealousy can breed nasty rumors. I wouldn't want you to be the subject of the water cooler discussions. Certainly, I need to be aware of my reputation as well, but I think we both know the rules are not the same for women as they are for men."

Clarinda mulled over his comment. He was being perfectly frank and he was right. He was a powerful and respected man, and she his employee. It would be fodder for the gossip hounds at work. While this relationship might be thought of as another conquest for David, it would ruin her reputation and dissolve her respect with her peers and direct reports. Yes—it was clear that they needed to be careful, but until they got into work on Monday, they had the ride home to pretend the weekend was not coming to an end.

Monday brought a new week, and Clarinda was so busy with the Sand & Stone account that quite frankly, she wasn't able to carve away any time to have lunch with David. They both worked late into the evenings, and spoke on the phone every night once they had gone home. David suggested another weekend in Albany and Clarinda leapt at the invitation.

"Fabulous—shall I bring my hiking boots again or will they sit in the car like last time?" she joked. They giggled like teenagers as they made plans. Clarinda could see a future of these weekends ahead of her as she packed a small bag of the essentials: perfume, corset and stockings, garter belt, and massage oil. "He is in for a stimulating weekend," she grinned.

Clarinda was awoken from her reverie by the phone ringing. It was Janet.

"We are still havin' ya' for dinner t'morrow night, right?" she reminded.

"Oh yes—I am really looking forward to it. Are you sure I can't bring anything besides the wine?"

"Och no—just ya' wee self, but ye might want to bring two bottles. I wanted to call to let ya' know that my brother and his young girlfriend will be joining us. I didn't think just the two of us would be excitin' conversation, so I have invited both of them too. I hope this is alright with ya'."

"Oh just fine—I would love to meet your bother and his girlfriend. Six-thirty, right?"

"Yes, see ya' then. Right-o." Janet hung up the phone.

"Missus Tetrick?" came a small voice. It was Emily Thompson, Clarinda's newly hired maid. "I have finished with the rooms ye wanted me to make up and I was gonna to leave for the day. Is there anything else I can do for ya'?"

"Not today, Emily. Thanks for all your help and I will see you tomorrow, right? I need to get the last room cleaned up from the painting and get it finished. This will thankfully be the last one."

"Very good ma'am, and I will see ya' in the morning. By the way, I overheard your phone conversation. You're plannin' to go over to Janet's for dinner, aye? Her brother, Alistair, is the town smithy and he is one of the most bonnie men in the Shire. He is datin' Lauren Lees, and some say she is too young for him. I could just watch him work all day—he is very fine and I don't think there is a lass in town who hasn't fanaticized about him. Anyway, have fun, and give my best to Janet. Good night. See ya' in the morn."

"Good night Emily."

"Very handsome, huh?" she spoke aloud to no one. "Well that is the last thing I need. I've had a handsome man in my life and what did it get me? Not happily ever after is for sure."

Clarinda went into the kitchen to make some dinner. Having thought about the pesto and pasta, she decided she needed to satisfy her craving. Fetching an onion out of the pantry, she began slicing.

chapter 9
no seasons of change

    After Clarinda made herself some dinner she decided to retire and read a book she had been trying to start, but her mind wandered. She couldn't stop thinking about David and how fun and easy their relationship had been when it first began. They would often visit his camp to be away from the hectic pace of daily life, each trip left those stresses and worries behind. It was just the two of them and nothing could infiltrate their world when they were alone together.
    During the week things were different. As time went on they lunched together less and less, but Clarinda looked forward to the weekends when they could make up for time spent apart. David was always very busy at work and often toiled late into the night so dinners together were not practical. Clarinda also submerged herself in work; as a result she was noticed for her diligence with Sand & Stone, and was offered another prestigious project. In the office they appeared like two dedicated marketing executives—always working and not much room for social life.
    Clarinda asked David one weekend where he thought their relationship was headed. "David, you know I enjoy your

company and I live for these two days when we can really focus our attentions on each other. But do you think there could be more? What do you want to see us grow into?"

David was silent for a while and then gave his reply. Clarinda could sense he was trying to be delicate and not say something that could be misconstrued as hurtful or over zealous. "Clarinda, my sweet," and he paused, "there is nothing that could make me happier than to come to this place and be with you—and I think you know I am completely sincere when I state this. But I know you are younger and would like to have someone who is completely yours and would be loving man to you and a caring father for children. Am I right?"

She nodded, "I really hadn't thought about children, but I suppose you are right—I probably would like to have a family some day."

"There you go—that is a noble goal and I don't fault you for wanting a family, but my firm is my family. I am past the age where I want to be tied down to provide for children. I like to travel, and as you know, I keep terrible hours so I would make a lousy father."

Clarinda could tell David was trying to soften his words so the sting would not be so sharp.

"However," he continued, "that does not mean we have to end what we have going on right now. I love being with you, I care for you deeply and if it makes you happy, I would hope you would want to continue to spend time with me."

"David, the time we spend together is wonderful—I agree, but it is not enough for me. I think about you all day and I would like to see you more than just two days a week. Why can't we try to see each other more during the week? I would like to propose a 'date' once a week."

"Clarinda—you know I often don't get home until nine o'clock, but I have a better idea. Why don't you come over to my place one night a week? We could enjoy a late dinner and you could spend the night and we could leave together for work in the morning? Let's just continue to take our time without creating rigid commitments."

Clarinda didn't think dinner out once a week was a 'rigid' commitment, but since David had been able to compromise on this lifestyle and include her more, she was satisfied.

As the months went by, they continued to meet at least once a week at David's spacious and modern apartment, but due to the change in the winter weather, trips to his cabin had all but ceased. Instead they would work part of the weekend, and Clarinda would join him for dinner. The next day they would spend at a movie, skating in Central Park, or merely window-shopping. She was happy to have him still in her life—every time she saw him he made her world light up like the tree in Rockefeller Plaza. As Christmas neared, Clarinda wondered if she could expect a special 'present' from David this season. She hoped as they spent more time together, her plans for a family with David might improve.

Christmas Eve was beyond her expectations. David picked her up at her apartment. He informed her they had reservations at Tavern on the Green. Clarinda could barely contain her joy. This would be it—this was the night David would propose marriage! As dinner ended, she was still hopeful, but perplexed. Then he announced they would be taking a carriage ride. OK – this was certainly going to be it! How romantic to be in a carriage in New York, with the man she adored and accept his proposal!

"Clarinda," David said softly and took her hands in his. "My sweet, you are wonderful and I care for you deeply. I have loved our weekends together and you have made coming home something special to ease a long day. I have something here I hope will express my feelings for you."

He handed Clarinda a small box and her heart began to race. "Go on—open it."

She untied the simple ribbon and opened the small white box. There was another small black leather box inside. She held the small box in her cupped hands.

"David, does this mean what I think it means?" she beamed.

"Go ahead—don't make me wait" he encouraged, "I want to see your reaction."

She opened the small box very slowly. "They are lovely," she whispered. The diamond earrings were at least a carat each. Granted this was not the ring she had hoped for, but gifts of jewelry were always a step in the right direction.

David helped her put them in her ears—not an easy task in a carriage drawn by a horse. They hugged and kissed the remaining duration of the ride. When they returned to David's apartment, they made love as if it was the first time. Both of them were tender, engaging, and took the other to new horizons of pleasure. Clarinda fell asleep in the arms of her handsome lover, and her dreams were of reliving the most wonderful night she could have ever imagined. She could only fantasize what New Year's Eve could be like, and that it couldn't possibly be any better than this.

A week later, New Year's Eve arrived and since the weather had been clear, David asked Clarinda if she would like to spend it in the cabin. "We haven't been there is such a long time, that I thought it would be special to get out of the city for the holiday. It can be crazy in Times Square, and I want to spend my time with you and not be distracted."

"David, that is a wonderful idea." Clarinda had always considered the cabin 'their place' and this was a perfect location for him to propose—maybe? Clarinda made sure she packed her sexiest negligee for the occasion. David took care of the rest of the preparation and made sure they brought plenty of Champagne. To Clarinda, these were all good signs.

Midnight came and although the couple had started the evening with fireworks of their own, Clarinda was waiting for the David to 'drop the ball' so to speak.

"David, my love, I want to be the first to wish you a Happy New Year!" she cheered. She leaned over to him and gave him a long and lasting kiss. "I hope there are many more to come in this New Year."

"Clarinda—my sweet, there will be." That was all it took for David to lure Clarinda onto the soft sheepskin rug in front of the fire. Their union brought them both to a deep and soul-branding zenith. Clarinda knew this year was going to be one she would never forget. She could not be happier; well yes she could—but she was sure David would ask for her hand in marriage before the year ended. She could adjust to that timeline. As they fell asleep, Clarinda spoke very softly: "David I love you." He made no movement and his breath was slow and steady, so she assumed he was asleep.

David did hear the words she spoke and his eyes opened but he made no movement to reveal what he had heard. He realized this relationship was terribly one-sided. He did not intend to harm Clarinda, in fact he cared for her deeply; but he did not have plans to become a husband and a father. She was expecting him to propose marriage, he was not blind to her plan. He wasn't ready for this commitment, but he didn't want to hurt this woman he so admired. She was everything he had wanted in a companion, but he wasn't the 'marrying kind'. He would have to try to find a way to make Clarinda understand; if she wanted to be with him, they already had the level of commitment he was ready to offer. He realized she was still a woman young enough to harbor plans for a family, but he hoped she would be willing to wait a few years to spend this time with him. He was as close to being in love as he ever could be—he just hoped it would continue to be enough for her. He fell asleep but it was a troubling night and he barely rested.

The winter season was a bitter one, but Clarinda and David made the most of it by taking weekend trips to go up to the cabin to go snow shoeing or skiing. The daylight hours were short, which made the nights longer which suited them just fine. They spent the days out in the cold and would come home to a warm fire and soon each would feel relaxed and sleepy. They each knew this was the essence of their relationship—they had settled into a routine and even though it did not vary widely, it was satisfying to both of them. David continued to be a passionate, caring, and exciting lover. Clarinda was able to provide him endless pleasure and at the same time she was witty, funny and strikingly beautiful. They each knew the boundaries of their partnership and for the time being, each was content to abide by these. Sadly, it would not continue.

As she relived these reveries in her mind's eye, she began to nod off. She got into bed and turned off the light. The time was eleven o'clock and she had a full day tomorrow and dinner at Janet's in the evening.

"It is a hard thing to put your feelings aside and act as if you never loved someone," she whispered to herself. Clarinda fell asleep, but she didn't rest easily—the ghosts of her past life continued to haunt her. She wondered why she couldn't have been the woman for David that would have made him devote himself completely to her—and only her. She had been a fool not to see the signs, but by that time she had invested too much into the relationship and couldn't turn back without seeing it through to the end.

chapter 10
a pair of kilts

Alistair Campbell met Lauren Lees when she came back from studying at Aberdeen. She had been raised in Inverwick, but Alistair did not remember her as a young girl. They had met at a summer picnic and Alistair thought her to be a fun, energetic, and cheerful lass. She was not a ravishing beauty, but she had good assets, better than most in the town, and she possessed a quiet and calm manner. This is what truly appealed to Alistair—he didn't care much for women who tried to manage the lives of their men, but rather let them be themselves. He was not planning on changing his lifestyle just now; he simply wanted to have a bonnie lass with whom he could enjoy movies, dinners out, and walks on the moor. For where Alistair Campbell was in his life's path, he longed for an uncomplicated and easy relationship such as the one he had with Lauren Lees. His sister pressed him to become a properly married man, but marriage was also not what he needed right now—he was still healing. At any rate, he wanted to please his sister in front of her new friend, so he decided to call Lauren to invite her to join them for dinner this evening. He knew she would not be busy; she was always available for Alistair when he called.

Lauren Lees was elated to be asked to come to dinner over at Janet Adam's house. Janet had always treated her like a sister and that suited her just fine. By New Year's she hoped to be betrothed to her brother. After all, they had been seeing each other for over six months. Even though they had not 'had relations' as her mother might say, Lauren found his restraint enchanting. "He's waiting to make our first night special and as man and wife," she considered.

Lauren was twenty-eight and worked as a bookkeeper for the lochs. The summer season was the busiest with the boats going from loch to loch, but in the off-season they prepared the county taxes. She was petite in stature which made her appear slightly plump, but she was not overweight. Her most stunning feature was her long auburn curly locks of hair. The mane would shine in the sunlight and she typically wore it down so dainty ringlets framed her face. Coupled with fair skin and green eyes, her friends and family would gently tease her and ask if she wasn't Irish rather than a Scot since she looked like she could be a leprechaun's sister. Lauren Lees paid them no mind, she was proud of her appearance, and she thought them just jealous since she had landed the finest man in Inverwick, let alone the entire Shire. She tried to envision what their children would look like; would they have red hair like her, or would they be dark like him? Hours of the day would pass by as she daydreamed about her handsome beau and the life they would create for themselves. She was certain Alistair would be asking for her hand in marriage any day—he was getting plenty of goading from his sister and other townsfolk. He was the age where he would soon need to choose a mate and since there was no one else in contention, Lauren was confident she would soon be Mrs. Alistair Campbell.

"So is this the American lady who is comin' to dine with us?" Lauren inquired. "I hear she is doin' a nice job on the old place—an inn ya' say?" Lauren wanted to know as much about Janet's guest as possible. She wanted to be welcoming and not ask any awkward questions to cause anyone to feel uncomfortable.

Alistair explained he really didn't know much about her sister's guest other than her name: Clarinda Tetrick. He also knew she had only arrived in the Shire about three months ago and hired his sister, Janet, to serve as the head chef for all the meals she planned to serve.

"Is she attractive?" Lauren pried. "I suppose if she came from New York City she has some fancy clothes and perfume." Lauren was already imagining Clarinda to be some sort of movie star who would arrive at Janet's house in a full length fur coat, smoking a long filtered cigarette, and looking like Myrna Loy from an old black and white movie.

"What should I wear? Should it be something fancy or will a plain dress be suitable?"

These types of questions were out of Alistair's element; he didn't know the difference between a frock and a dress, and he felt Lauren had always attired perfectly for any occasion.

"I told Janet I would wear the tartan. Ya' ken she likes me to wear it when there are folks comin' to visit who are not Scot."

This gave Lauren some pause. She knew what she would need to wear to compliment Alistair's fashionable dress. She had seen him sport the traditional Dress Campbell tartan and its deep green and blue hues were complementary to his dark features. He was a striking man when adorned in his ancestor's native dress.

To ensure he didn't look overly formal, Lauren decided she too, would wear a full-length kilt of her clan. The Lees family was part of the Clan MacPherson and the red tartan highlighted her hair, and the green and navy background complemented Alistair's tartan. The length of the skirt made her appear taller and thinner—always a good thing. Adorned in their respective tartans, they would be the quintessential Scottish couple.

"Well that will make ye sis happy, and ya' always look bonnie when ya' wear it. I shall wear mine too, aye? Is there anythin' I should bring?"

"I dunno—why don't ya' call Janet and see if she has somethin' in mind. I am sure ya' could bring a sweet of some sort.

Shortbreads, maybe?" Alistair had to admit that Lauren's baking skills were almost as keen as his sister's and he had a special fondness for her cookies.

"At any rate, I will come and fetch ya' tonight so ya' won't be danderin' alone on the road. I will be by about six o'clock. I want to be to Janet's by the time her guest arrives at half past."

As soon as she hung up the phone, Lauren rushed to prepare her ensemble. Luckily she had made some cookies this past afternoon, so she would bundle them up in a cloth-covered tin. She was excited to meet the new American woman and learn of her plans for the old Cameron House.

Alistair had some cleaning up to do himself. He had come back from shoeing six horses and he smelled like it. He also needed a good shave. He pulled is kilt, sporran, and belt out of his wardrobe and turned on the water to take a long hot shower. Once out, he felt revived. He towel-dried his hair, ran a comb through it and began to shave. He wrapped his kilt around him, pulled on his socks with flashes, and laced up his boots. A cable knit sweater of cream-colored Scottish wool would keep him warm during his walk but not too hot for inside temperatures. He gathered up his personal items like his wallet and other essentials and buckled them inside his sporran. Quite frankly, he didn't mind wearing a kilt—he was a Scot and proud of it, and it was simple and comfortable to wear. The only caution was on windy days. He felt he looked presentable, he headed out to collect the young miss Lees.

Clarinda prepared to dress for her evening at Janet's, and continued to ruminate on the ruin of her relationship with David.

The weather had begun to warm and spring was struggling to cast off the gray gloom over New York City. By this time, it seemed to Clarinda their relationship had fallen into a rut. David had made it perfectly clear that he didn't want to marry — even Clarinda. She tried to make concessions and offered they not discuss children; she tried to convince herself she could be happy without them as long as she was with David. David stated they had that already, but Clarinda wanted a ceremony to make the union legit.

One day Clarinda decided to add some spice into their lives. One or two nights at his place and a weekend-night was not enough. She decided to surprise David by creating an impromptu night of pampering. She would greet him at the door offering wine, a full-body massage and dinner. She would stop by a favorite Italian restaurant and get some ziti to go. Simple.

As she walked up to the front of his building she sensed something was amiss. A long time visitor of David's apartment, the doorman didn't hinder her arrival, but he gave her a curious look. Stepping off the elevator she felt unnerved. She stopped as she came to the door of David's apartment. Could she smell of something already cooking? David rarely made his own meals when he worked late — he typically would arrange delivery at the office and eat before he left. This change of routine was certainly out of the ordinary.

Clarinda rang the doorbell and waited. Nothing. She rang it again, but with much more conviction. She knew he was home. Finally she heard him yell. "Just a minute — I'm coming. Hold on!" The hurried sound of thudding footsteps was all she could hear. When he opened the door it is not clear whose jaw hit the floor first.

"Clarinda! What are you doing here? You didn't call. Tonight is not one of our nights."

She was awe struck. There was David, in his dark gray jacquard silk robe and it was clear he was wearing nothing else. Immediately Clarinda's head filled with all the retorts she wanted to say: "After all the sacrifices I was willing to make " or how about "I should have known that you wouldn't make a commitment. How could you—and still keep your sluts on the side," or better yet, "I hope that thing gets whittled down to a nub. You didn't want to make any rigid commitments, but look who's rigid now!" They all sounded good, but they really weren't speaking to the feeling of betrayal, deceit and disappointment she was experiencing. She had invested all her love into this man—and didn't hold back; and for what? To be this badly hurt. She found she really couldn't say anything. She just shook her head slightly, placed the food and wine at her feet, turned and walked back down the hallway to exit the building as soon as humanly possible.

"Wait, Clarinda, let me explain!" David shouted after her.

"My God, did he actually just say that?" she steamed. "How perfectly unoriginal."

"What's going on? Who's that?" Came a squeaky voice behind him. "Never mind," he replied and it gave Clarinda some consolation, as she knew his evening could not be salvaged after her unannounced 'coitus-interruptus' visit.

She held back the tears until she reached the street. Then the sobs broke out uncontrollably. She could barely see the cab when it pulled up to accept her fare. When she got in, the cabbie could clearly see her distress and wanted to know if she had been attacked and needed to go to a hospital. She shook her head, and utter one word: "Bastard". The cabbie was sympathetic and said all the right things. Her sobbing was uncontrollable and the cabbie pulled over to turn around to look at her and make sure she was going to be all right. "He didn't deserve such a nice lady as yourself. It's his loss. There, there now. Try to pull yourself together. Here's a tissue. You got someone you can talk to about this?"

Clarinda knew what she needed to do at that point. "Please take me to 925 E 65th Street," she sniffled. She got out her cell phone and called Fran to make sure she was home. The minute Fran heard Clarinda's agony over the phone she insisted her friend come over immediately and began to ready her small guest room.

When Clarinda arrived, she could barely hold herself up. It

seemed as if the weight of her grief was sapping the strength from her legs. She nearly collapsed before she reached Fran's couch. She curled up into a fetal position and continued to wail with total abandon. With Clarinda in this state Fran would not be able to get anything out of her, but then again, she knew what had happened. Her role was to be Clarinda's friend and to try to administer triage to the broken soul shaking on her divan.

When she could finally speak, Clarinda told Fran of the awful episode at David's apartment. Fran didn't know what advice to give her other than to try to restore her friend's self-esteem. At long last Fran introduced the subject of the supposed situation Clarinda would face back in the hallowed halls of Masters & Kline. "Do you think you will loose your job?"

Clarinda hadn't really thought about it too much since she was busy trying to flush the poison from her ruptured heart. "I don't think he'd dare. After all, it would become public knowledge he had an affair with an employee. It would damage his reputation."

Clarinda then recalled what David had advised her so many months ago: "I wouldn't want your reputation to be tarnished. Sadly jealousy can breed nasty rumors. I wouldn't want you to be the subject of the water cooler discussions. Of course I need to be aware of my reputation as well, but I think we both know the rules are not the same for women as they are for men."

It was clear he was not going to let his reputation be associated with this affair. Clarinda realized she had been used. Was there anything David said to her that wasn't a lie? The more she thought about it the more her ire replaced her sadness.

"He is not going to win this so easily." She planned out what she could do. It had to be simple, not self-serving, not overly vindictive, but enough so he would not escape his digressions with and employee unscathed. She asked Fran for her laptop and began to scribe her resignation letter.

When she had finished, Fran asked her what she planned to do. "You will have no job, but you are so talented. Why don't you do something you really love to do? I am sure you made enough with that marketing gig to get you by for a while. Do something you really love." Fran was open and supportive. Rather than looking at this disaster as a bad thing, she was trying to turn it into a new opportunity for Clarinda; to find her true calling.

"You have always wanted to travel and open a small inn—so why don't you do it? If not now, then when will you take the chance to give it a try?" Fran was answering all of Clarinda's questions before she even could form them in her mind. Clarinda welcomed the opportunity to get her thoughts off of David and the anguish he caused, and think about something else. "You were never devoted to marketing, were you? Didn't you really just continue to do it because it paid the bills? Well you have the bills covered now—go out and become what you always wanted to grow up and be. You are not a 'spring chicken' and you won't have many more chances to make a clean break. I am sure your aunt and uncle will agree with me on this one. You don't know what you might find unless you ~~don't~~ give it a try."

Clarinda knew she was right. This was the time, but where was the 'place'? She had always wanted to go to the UK—the B&B business was strong there and she loved the quaint idea of a proper guesthouse.

"Wait a minute—hold on. Let's not get carried away," sounded Clarinda's voice of reason. "Let's just think about this for a minute. Tomorrow I am going to go into Masters and Kline and resign my job and attempt to besmirch my boss. You then think I am going to simply pack a bag, get on a plane, take off for the UK, buy a place, fix it up, and open a guesthouse?"

"Yup" was Fran's simple answer. "I do."

Well come to find out, Fran was right after all. Clarinda did go and deliver her resignation. She made sure she filed a claim of sexual harassment with the HR department, but declined to press charges. There was no denying it was consensual. She took her time to explain to her colleagues and direct reports her version of the escapades she had with ~~the~~ one of the namesakes of the company. By the time she left every jaw was flapping and she was certain productivity would hit an all time low at Masters and Kline for the rest of the day. She predicted the memos and press releases that would be published all in an effort to make this digression on the part of one of the senior partners disappear. Despite her sorrow, her ability to wreak havoc on David's life was giving her some small amount of solace. It was all going well until she hit the ground floor to walk out when a security guard caught her arm.

"Just a minute Miss Tetrick, I have been asked to have you wait here for just a moment. Mr. Kline is on his way and wants to have a word with you."

This was exactly what Clarinda wanted to avoid. She couldn't be sure she wouldn't literally melt in front of him like the Wicked Witch of the West when doused with water. A few minutes seemed to last hours while she waited for David to arrive.

"Clarinda." She heard her name coming from the far elevators. He walked over to her and pulled her into a small alcove off the main lobby to evade prying eyes.

He got within inches of her face and calmly asked, "Why did it have to end like this? I understand you're upset about last night, but is that any reason to take it out on the company you work for, let alone what you have done to me by these vindictive actions?"

"Done to you? Done to you?" Clarinda could barely believe her ears. "David, it is over! You had your chance with me. I loved you—with all my heart and I would have done anything to be with you. But you didn't care—you couldn't even keep it in your pants. I can't bear to look at you any longer for two reasons. One, for fear my heart will break, and two; I might throw up at the very sight of you. Good bye, and I hope someday you might realize what you lost."

David tried to stop her and offered another shallow excuse. She turned and broke the grip he had on her arm, held her head high, and marched out of the large shiny doors. She was finished with Masters & Kline, and she was finished with David. She fumed as she marched back to her apartment, and with each step her anger grew. By the time she opened the door to her spacious and bright apartment she was in a full rage. Looking back she realized she would not have had the courage to make such a bold move to come to Scotland had she not been braced by her fury. She was able to keep it under control enough to pack and head to the airport without being thought a terrorist. She wanted to call Fran to tell her she was glad she had her friend's support. Sometimes it is good for the soul to thank those who don't expect it.

"Nice to hear you are going over to the neighbor's house– I am glad to hear you are making friends." Fran cooed. "So this woman, Janet, is going to be your chef? That is super. Clarinda, I am so happy to hear you are fitting in and you are doing what you want to do. You seem to be content."

Before Clarinda hung up the phone, she begged Fran to visit hoping she could come and see Clarinda's efforts and because she missed her friend. She finally said her good-byes and realized she was smiling.

"Yes," she agreed, I am content. "I may have lost the love of my life, but I think I will be happy here."

A quick glance at her watch confirmed if she didn't hurry, she would be tardy to Janet's. She hastily pulled her clothes out of the wardrobe and began to change. She looked forward to getting out of the old house; weary of cooking meals for just herself. A side glance in the mirror to ensure her appearance was suitable, and she was off. "So let's see how the Scot's throw a dinner party."

Chapter 11
Good Food, Good Wine, Good Company, and Good God!

Clarinda banged the knocker on Janet's house and waited.

"She's at the door, Alistair, please let her in, will ya'?" she heard Janet chime from another room.

Solid footsteps approached and Clarinda prepared to greet Janet's younger brother. She quickly thought about Emily's comment—Janet's brother was 'fine'. Reflecting on Janet's features she could only imagine 'fine' had a different meaning here in Scotland than it did in America. She supposed blacksmiths may be considered 'handsome', but probably more for their handiwork than for their physical appearance. She was sure he would be a gentle and kind person, but certainly only suitable in the 'looks department' to take to a tractor-pull.

The door opened and the light behind the figure was bright so Clarinda was not able to clearly make out the features of her greeter, but it was clear from his silhouette his figure did not suffer from the same softness as his sister's; he stood over six feet tall.

A deep and smooth voice spoke to her. "Please come in. Ya' must be Clarinda. I'm Alistair, Janet's brother. Me sister is in the kitchen. May I take yer wrap?"

Clarinda stepped into the house and focused on disrobing her shawl and adjusting to the brightness of Janet's home. She gathered her scarf and handed it to the outstretched hand. She then looked up to reply to Alistair and was taken aback. This man was certainly no farm hand. He had a face like no other — deep dark brown eyes, high cheekbones and an angled and strong jaw that stopped at a dimpled clef. The most striking part of his appearance was his shoulder length silky dark hair. It shone in the light and framed his rugged and savage features. Clarinda let her eyes scan down this figure and could see rippling muscles under his sweater and he wore a kilt that was not donned like the bagpipers on the corner. This was a causal approach to the traditional dress and it ~~not only~~ suited him; wild and untamed.

Clarinda forced herself to speak before she seemed rude. "Yes — I am Clarinda. Here you go." And handed the shawl to him. "What a dolt." she chided herself under her breath. "You have a tongue in your mouth — why don't you use it?"

"Pardon?" Alistair questioned. "Did ya' ask me something?"

Oh this is getting better by the minute Clarinda thought. She quickly jutted out her arms presenting the two bottles of wine. "No, only here is some wine I thought we would enjoy. Janet is in the kitchen?" Clarinda not only wanted to hide in the confines of Janet's undersized kitchen, but she wished she could crawl under its floorboards.

Pull yourself together, girl, she coached herself. *You have seen many handsome men before, so why is this guy throwing you so? After all, he isn't even available — besides you don't need another male distraction after the last disaster. So try to pretend he isn't there and have a good time — for Janet's sake.* After giving herself this small mental pep talk, she went into the kitchen to greet Janet and meet the Adonis's girlfriend.

"Clarinda, sweetie," Janet gushed and wiped her hands on her apron and gave her a casual hug. "So glad ya' could come. I suppose ya' have met me brother, Alistair." She gestured to the figure completely filling the kitchen door.

Clarinda could only nod to Janet and back again to Alistair. One side of his mouth curled up and he nodded in return. *He must think me a moron*, Clarinda thought.

"This is Alistair's girlfriend, Lauren," and Janet turned and motioned to the young lady standing behind her.

"Hi there, I am Clarinda." She offered her hand to the diminutive lass. *This must be the house of tartan*, Clarinda thought when she beheld Lauren's lovely full-length kilt. "Nice to meet you, you look lovely. Is that a family tartan?"

"Why yes!" Lauren exclaimed, glad she went to such detail for this outfit to be noticed. "It is, I am a Lees. Our family is part of the MacPherson Clan which hails from the area just east of the Great Glen. This is the dress MacPherson tartan."

"It is stunning on you and the red sets off your hair." Clarinda felt if she could continue to babble to this young lady, she wouldn't have to turn around and resume her retarded manifestation in front of Janet's brother.

"I have brought some wine," Clarinda announced again and presented the bottles this time to the madam of the house. "Would you like to open one now, or do you want to wait for dinner?" Clarinda hoped Janet would vote for the former—a drink was certainly in order!

"Why not open one now? What a bonnie idea," Janet declared and Clarinda was thankful for one small bit of luck.

"Alistair, why don't ye and the lasses go into the parlor and I will join ya' soon. Perhaps ya' could assist Clarinda and decant the first bottle?" She handed the bottles to her brother standing behind Clarinda. He gladly accepted them, turned and strode toward the parlor with Clarinda and Lauren falling into line of this small parade. Alistair's kilt swayed with each step and it was hypnotizing to Clarinda even in the small distance they marched.

"No, a true Scot doesna wear anathin'," he announced when they reached the parlor.

"Huh?" Clarinda asked stupidly.

"I suppose ye were wonderin' what I had under me kilt, no? Well, as a true Scot, I can assure ya' there is nothin' but me under there." Lauren giggled after he made this remark. "All travelers to Alba always want to know about the proper underdressin' of the honored tartan, and it is quite simple really." He was not really taunting, but Clarinda was not sure if he was trying to tease or offend.

"Well, I am glad to know this interesting fact, indeed, but I really wasn't thinking about that," she lied. "Quite honestly, I was wondering about the music you have playing." Clarinda was glad she could at least conger up this awkward segue to redirect the topic away from what was under Alistair's kilt to something less thrilling.

Lauren jumped to answer this question and join in the conversation. "Aye, that is Karen Matheson and her band Capercaillie. The word 'capercaille' means large grouse in gaelic. The band is known for singing many of their songs in the gaelic dialect. They are very popular, it is hard to get tickets to their shows—they sell out very fast. Have ya' heard them before?"

"No" Clarinda explained, but she made note of the band. The woman's voice was hauntingly beautiful. She sang with reserved passion, resonating the pride and turmoil of the Scottish people.

In the meantime, Alistair had opened one of the bottles of wine and presented glasses to the ladies. "A toast?" Clarinda offered.

"Yes—here is to meetin' new friends," Lauren volunteered.

God bless this girl, Clarinda thought, *for keeping the conversation going.*

"Yes," Alistair agreed, "to meeting new friends. Sláinte mhath!" Then he took a small sample of his wine. Clarinda noticed he held the glass by the stem as customary with white wine to prevent it from warming.

Hum, will wonders never cease with this one? Clarinda thought.

"Lauren, sweetie," Janet chimed, "can ya' assist me in the kitchen for a spell?"

"Sure," Lauren replied, set her wine glass down and headed straight for the kitchen. She was happy Janet considered her to be part of the family to be called to assist in the kitchen.

Oh Lord, thought Clarinda, *now how will I further embarrass myself?* She felt decidedly uncomfortable to be alone with this man. Alistair was not an average man, he was surrounded by an air of mystery, and he was so stunning it was hard not to grasp.

"Lovely name, Alistair, is that a family name?" Yes—she had done it again. She had made another dumb, dumb, dumb question.

"No, it isn't, but it is the most popular of Scottish names, so I guess I am one of a thousand."

Yeah, right, more like one in ten-million, Clarinda thought. "At any rate, I like it. It is not a popular name in the States, so I guess it is unique to me." She attempted to be flattering.

"Ye are tryin' to open an inn out of the Cameron house, I hear? I'm glad ya' hired my mum for a job. She is a bonnie cook and I think havin' an occupation will do her well."

"Yes, yes I am. It's been a lot of hard work so far, but I think it will pay off later. I'm delighted to have Janet helming the kitchen. I couldn't do it all myself. I think we will be able to learn from each other too, which I think will be exciting." At that moment Clarinda remembered she had brought the card with the Dill Sauce recipe. She wanted to join the other women in the kitchen, but she didn't want to be rude so she continued to remain with Alistair in the parlor and continually sip her wine to give her fortification.

"Are ya' no winchin'—by that I mean ya' are no seein' someone?"

This seemed quite a forward remark from a man she had just met. "Yes—I am a single woman. Is it customary in Scotland to ascertain one's marital status early on in the conversation?"

Alistair realized he might have overstepped his boundaries with this woman, but he saw her eyes were twinkling; God love her, she was trying to keep the conversation lively.

"No—just I am not one to engage in town gossip, but I heard your husband had left ya'."

"Well, that is news," exclaimed Clarinda, "since I was not married! No, my husband didn't leave me…I was cheated on by my lover—who was also one of the founding partners of the company where I worked. So you could say I really made a big mess of it."

"Have ya' no heard of the sayin' 'don't shite where ya' eat'? I guess it is too late to tell ya' that now. Anyway, I hope ye are able to make the Cameron place a go. We could use accommodations of that sort here in Inverwick—with the Way so close and the anglers coming to our wee town."

"It's my hope too. I think Inverwick is perfect, and there is a severe loss of inns and B&B's around town." Clarinda continued to talk about the old house, the status of all the refurbishments, but it was clear Alistair was not fully paying attention to every word. Clarinda's bright blue eyes, her soft shiny hair, and the elegant way she moved her arms and hands had transfixed him.

She was not at all what he had expected. She was sophisticated, but not pretentious. She was tall and slender, but Alistair ascertained from the work she was performing at the old house, she was stronger than she appeared. Typically women her age who lived in Scotland were not this well persevered. Her skin lacked the weathered and wrinkled texture so common from the harsh weather. She didn't smoke; her teeth were straight, white and all accounted for. She dressed stylishly, not flashy—but practical to keep the damp chill of the evening at bay. Alistair liked 'no nonsense' women; he was not fond of those who pretended to be helpless so their men folk would have to perform every chore for them. He also was not fond of those who were overly concerned about their looks so they could not walk in the misty moors or would require two hours to ready themselves for a football game. This Clarinda Tetrick was the kind of woman he would like to associate with—a natural beauty, self assured and very capable.

"So tell me what you do. You're a farrier, right? Do you ride yourself?"

"Yes—I am the town smithy, and I do ride on occasion. There are times when I ride some of me client's steeds, but mostly I just work on 'em. I don't have a ridin' mate, which would make it more fun. And you? Do ya' ride? Ya' doona have a horse at the house, do ya'? At least ya' haven't called for me services."

That's a loaded statement, she was thinking about his 'services' and decided not to be so brazen. "No, I don't, but if you are looking for a riding partner I would love to join you. I haven't ridden since I was in college, but as a young girl I had my own Morgan, so I consider myself a reasonably skilled horsewoman. It would be lovely to go for a ride and see the sites of Scotland on horseback."

"'Tis beautiful. I will see what I can do. Let's check on the hens in the kitchen and see if they are ready. I'm famished and the wonderful aroma is makin' me stomach growl." This time, he directed the way and followed Clarinda back to the kitchen.

"What can we do to help?" Clarinda offered as they entered.

"Here, make sure everyone has water and wine poured at the table, here are the rolls, and let's see…oh, please make sure the napkins have been folded." Janet listed off the last minute preparations.

"Janet, do you mind if I made a quick sauce as a garnish to your wonderful salmon. I hope you won't be offended, but it really is a nice accompaniment."

"Och, no! Go right ahead lass. What do ya' need for fixin's?"

"Got them right here." Clarinda found the spices in a counter rack and the other ingredients in the refrigerator. In a jiff she had whipped up the easy recipe.

"Everyone—let's sit and eat!" Janet declared. Everyone took a dish to the elegantly set square table, Janet facing north, with

Alistair to her right, and Clarinda to her left and Lauren faced her. "Alistair, please give the blessing?"

Alistair first glanced at his sister and then at Clarinda before lowering his eyes. Clarinda had never seen such long and thick lashes—like those of a child, but very alluring.

Once Alistair finished the blessing, he offered wine to refill everyone's glass.

"This looks just wonderful, Janet. Thank you for inviting me. This is such a treat to not have to cook for just myself, and salmon is one of my favorites."

"Not much to it really." Janet was pleased to receive the admiring comment, but didn't want to make a fuss. "The wild salmon is the delicacy; the new red potatoes and carrots are simple fare. I just like to add some parsley and butter to the tatties and some curry to the carrots to make it fun."

"It is superb—I have no fear you'll have a waitin' list for diners at the guest house every night," Lauren concurred.

The rest of the night's conversation was light and lively, each getting to know the other. Alistair often stole glances at Clarinda, but these distractions did not go unnoticed by the watchful eyes of Lauren.

"I wanted to let ya' all know, Alistair has agreed to help me at the Holiday Bazaar. Isn't that kind?" Lauren announced and placed her tiny hand on his. It was striking how pale her skin was compared to the large tan hand under it; as if they were two different species. Alistair continued to keep his eyes trained on his plate, looking somewhat ashamed to be associated with his girlfriend's endeavors. Clarinda surmised this affair was not something with which he wanted to be associated. Perhaps Lauren had sprung on him at this very moment, so he was unable to decline.

"That's my caring brother, for ya'." Janet beamed. "Always helpin' others. Ya' ken ye got a good man there, Lauren." Lauren nodded in agreement and sat up straighter as if she had won him as a prize.

"So when are ya' goona to make an honest woman of her, my dear?" Janet redirected the conversation to her brother."

"Need to get some air," he declared and looked at his sister, then to Clarinda. "Please excuse me." He slowly stood up from the table and walked out to the front of the house. Janet and Lauren waited until they heard the front door open and close before they released their pent up giggles.

"Child, ye are makin' progress, but it is just so slow," Janet grinned.

Lauren nodded, "I know. But to see the expression on his face is priceless when the subject of marriage is brought up."

"All right," Janet cheered, "let's get these dishes cleaned up and have some tea and pudding in the parlor. That should give the man enough time to come back into the hen house. I know me brother; he willna stay mad long." They took the dishes into the kitchen and each took up a chore; the crockery was loaded in the dishwasher or wiped dry, and put away in no time. Janet had some tea brewing and the pudding warming in the oven.

"Let's call him in and we can have some pudding to satisfy our sweet tooth's. Lauren, go and see if ya' can bring him back inside," Janet instructed.

Clarinda took the tray of tea, cups and other condiments into the parlor and left Janet to prepare the Hot Sticky Toffee Pudding in the kitchen. She could barely hear the conversation taking place on the porch but it was clear to Clarinda that Alistair was still hot about the comment his sister had made during dinner. He was making it perfectly clear to Lauren she should not expect an eminent marriage proposal and his sister's remarks were in no way to be considered a reflection of his own plans.

"Feg! Now I don't want to have to have this conversation again, ya' ken? When I'm ready, I will be ready. If ya' want to wait -that is fine. But I willna be forced into doin' somethin' which is no in me heart."

Lauren was keeping a stiff appearance, doing her best not to look defeated. "I understand," she softly replied.

He gave her a hug and kissed the top of her head. "Ye are a douce lass, and I care about ya', but if ya' care about me as ya' claim ye do, than ye have to let me be me own man." She closed her eyes and buried her head into his chest and nodded. "Now let's go in and have some of that puddin' me interfering sis has fixed us. I feel bad to have walked out and leave her guest alone."

Clarinda made herself look busy as the couple returned ~~inside~~ and reentered the parlor.

"I'm sorry for me behavior, Clarinda. It was uncalled for. Please accept me apologies." Alistair was very calm and his voice even.

"'No worries'—as we say in the States." Clarinda tried to rekindle the lightness of the earlier conversation. "Your sister's pudding smells heavenly. You've come back in just in time." As if on ~~queue~~ cue, Janet entered the room, with four small bowls of steaming desert. The warm aroma of toffee filled the room.

"Please sit, and I will serve ya'." Clarinda and Lauren sat on the couch as per Janet's instructions. Alistair continued to stand. "I have ice cream so if anyone would like there's 'a la mode'."

"Please!" Lauren and Clarinda cheered in unison and smiled at each other. Once Janet had given each person their serving, she took a seat in the corner chair. Alistair walked over to the mantel place of the fire, carefully spooning his pudding.

Clarinda wanted to make sure the elephant in the room did not enlarge. "Janet, I see now why you suggested we add this great concoction to the Hogmanay menu. It is divine. I will have to walk home twice to take off the pounds this is adding to my waistline."

"Ye should talk—yer as slim as a rail."

Once everyone had nearly finished their confection, Alistair spoke. "Would anyone like a wee dram of the water of life?"

"Water of life?" Clarinda inquired. "What exactly is that?"

"'Uisage beatha' is gaelic for whiskey. It literally means 'water of life'. When the English first heard it, they turned the word into 'whisky'—spelled without the 'e'. Of course, as an American I am sure ya' refer to it as 'Scotch'. So would ya' like a small dram? I have a nice twelve year-old Tamnavulin I keep here for such occasions."

Lauren and Janet both still had their mouths filled with the pudding, but both gestured that they would join him in taking a nip.

"Janet, with water, right? Lauren, ya' would like both ice and water?" Alistair asked to confirm their order. "So Clarinda, some whisky? It will put some hair on your chest, especially if ya' take it neat as I do—as I can certainly attest."

Clarinda got the impression he was teasing her, or was he? She was never very fond of 'scotch', but she wanted to fit in and she decided 'when in Rome' was a good policy; she decided to be game and give it a try. After all, this was the birthplace of the liquor and perhaps what she had tried was inferior to the private selections of the Scots.

Alistair promptly returned with four glasses—two were rocks glasses, which he handed to Janet and Lauren. He then handed one of the two snifters to Clarinda and took one for himself. "Try it neat first to get a true sense o' the flavor. It used to be unthinkable to add water and ice, but it is now considered a way to lengthen the enjoyment without getting' pissed as a fart—if ya' doona mind me English!"

Clarinda took a small sip of the amber colored liquid. A warm and slightly burning sensation made its way to her belly. The feeling was not unlike drinking boiling sap in Vermont, but the flavor was distinctly different. There was the overwhelming flavor of alcohol, but beyond that was a rich, earthy flavor.

It was as if Alistair was reading her mind. "The key ingredient in whisky that makes it unique is the peat. As ye know, the moors are almost fully comprised of peat, and that water is what gives whisky the unique flavor that can only come from our fine country. So do ya' like it?"

"Yes—I think I could get used to this. It is different, but it is not overpowering, and actually quite enjoyable. This could become a bad vice." Clarinda laughed.

Before another round was offered Lauren felt she needed to leave. She only drank the stuff because Alistair enjoyed it, and she wanted to please him by pretending to enjoy it. But one shot is all she could muster, and that needed to be diluted with both ice and water. She thought she must be the only born and raised Scot who did not appreciate the country's official drink. "Alistair, it is gettin' late and me Da wants me to help him in the morn before I go off to work. Could ya' walk me home now?" Lauren requested.

"Sure, where is yer cloak?"

Lauren went to the foyer and grabbed her cape and came back to thank Janet for her hospitality giving her a quick hug, and kiss on the cheek. "Thanks again, and I will see ya' soon." She waved as she and Alistair walked out into the night.

Alistair ducked his head in before completely closing the door. "Janet, I will be back in about fifteen minutes, so please do not let me whisky run away a'fore then."

Janet and Clarinda sat across from each other and sipped their drams. Clarinda broke the silence. "Your brother is very attentive. It is clear he cares, and watches over you."

"Aye, that he does. We only have each other, and I am a widow, ya' ken. It is a comfort to have him look in on me once in a while. He thinks I'm helpless with my chicks and ducks, but I let him do it. It guarantees he will stop by once a week, and I can give him a good hot meal. I dinnae think he cooks much for himself. It's a wonder he is nae just skin and bones." Janet paused. "I saw him once like that, and I dinnae want to see it again."

Clarinda didn't really know what to say so she remained silent. After a while Janet continued with her train of thought.

"He is a bit of a loner, but I was hopin' he would wed the Lees lass. She is bonnie, no?" Clarinda nodded. "But I think after tonight she may be afraid to come around again so soon. He is always gentle with her, but he cannae be forced into anythin' he doesna wanna do. I was hopin' for a spring weddin'. He may still propose at Hogmanay—so we will have to wait and see." Janet was obviously trying to be optimistic about the situation as if her positive attitude might dissuade her brother's stubbornness.

Clarinda continued to remain quiet, sip her Tamnavulin and reflect on Alistair's manner when he and Lauren were sequestered on the porch. She sincerely doubted he would propose to this girl before Hogmanay. It seemed he was not enthusiastic about the idea at all. In fact, Clarinda believed she could win big money in Las Vegas if she could place a bet on the man. He would most definitely not be getting married even in the following year. Clearly, Lauren was a lovely girl: sweet, petite, well mannered, cheerful, and every bit a Scottish housewife-in-training. But it seemed she was the exact opposite of the type of woman who would best suit Alistair. Clarinda imagined he probably needed a woman who in fact did not need a man. Someone who was self-sufficient, independent and was not going to try to change him into something he could not become. *Someone like me*, she thought. At that revelation she gasped and tried to scatter the thought from her head.

"Is something wrong, dear," Janet asked when she saw Clarinda start.

"Oh no, just thinking about all the work I still need to do—sometimes it even wakes me up at night. Will you be coming over tomorrow?"

"I would love to help you organize the kitchen with the supplies you have purchased, of course, that is if you need a hand."

"Yes, I was thinking about comin' over. Ya' know it will be November next week and there is so much still to do in two short months if we wanna be ready for Hogmanay. I would love yer assistance. Ya' ken, many hands make light work."

Alistair walked back into the door. "I'm back and Nessie dinnae get a scratch on me!" he winked at Clarinda.

"Let me tidy up the kitchen a bit. Ye two get to know each other a little bit better." Janet got up and took the sticky dishes to the kitchen. Alistair took his sister's seat across from Clarinda. He stretched his legs out in front of him and crossed them at the ankles. His reached for his whisky and took a sip. "That takes the chill off, no?"

"Yes, it does. So I assume Lauren is home, safe and sound. You certainly were not gone long."

"Yes, the wee lass is home. No, I dinnae tarry when I have a whisky waitin'. I also wanted to get back to see ya' home as well. I cannae have ya' traipsing home in the dark. Who knows what dangers lurk. I know me sister would have me heid if I dinnae see ya' back." He was very serious in his delivery, but Clarinda had the impression he had ulterior motives.

"OK, very well then, I will accept your company on the way home," Clarinda replied acting 'prim and proper'. "After you finish your whisky. I couldn't deny you from enjoying it."

"Wait, let's have another to fortify us before we go? Ye only had a verra small amount."

Clarinda didn't think this was a good idea, but before she could protest, Alistair had produced the bottle which he had stashed under the table and neatly poured them another sampling. "Ya' ken the pubs will only serve ya' twenty-five milliliters at a time, which wouldn't even get a mouse stocious. This is not much more, so don't fash. You'll no have a hangover in the morn."

They sipped in silence, but every once and again they would look up and glimpse at each other. The music had changed and Clarinda was enjoying the easy, but liveliness of it. She didn't realize she was lightly tapping her foot in time.

"Do ya' know of the Peatbog Faeries?" Alistair inquired. "They are a band from Skye. That piper is braw, no?"

"Yes—I am really discovering a lot of the new music. Often there are songs are sung in gaelic. Do you speak the language?"

"No, not to well, but I ken enough to get by."

THE CELEBRATION OF HOGMANAY

After the song ended and the tipples drained, Clarinda felt it was time to go. She got up, turned to Alistair and indicated she was going to see if Janet needed any further help in the kitchen. Janet had fallen sleep in a kitchen chair, with a linen towel still in her hand. The kitchen was spotless and all the dishes from the dishwasher had been put back in their cupboards. This hour was far past Janet's typical bedtime. Clarinda touched her on the shoulder and Janet awoke with a start.

"I'm leaving now," Clarinda whispered. "Why don't you go to bed and I will see you in the morning? Alistair will walk me home. Thanks again. Good night."

Janet patted Clarinda's hand and in a half-sleep, nodded and smiled. She waved good night and began to get up from her chair and make her way to the stairs up to her bedroom. As she passed the parlor doorway, Alistair waved her a good night. She blew him a kiss continued to her bed as if in a sleepwalking trance.

"Well, I think me sister is done for the night. Let's turn off the lights, and I will lock up and take ye home. Let me fetch yer shawl." Alistair handed Clarinda her wrap and then toured the house to turn off lights, check windows, and ensure the house was closed up for the night.

"Are ya' ready?" he asked when he returned to the foyer where Clarinda stood waiting. She nodded and they walked out onto the porch, he shut and locked the door behind them and started down Rowan Road back to the old Cameron house, otherwise known as Clarinda's new inn. The air was cool, and Clarinda was thankful for the comfort of her shawl. They walked for a spell in silence.

"I hope ya' had a good time. I ken me sister likes ya' quite a bit and I can see why."

Clarinda let this comment sit a minute before responding. She figured the dumb-blond technique had its uses sometimes, and this was one of those times.

"Really? What is it that you find appealing?"

"Well, I doona know if I can explain, but I like yer wit, yer demeanor, and that ye ken who ya' are. Ya' don't put on airs and make yourself into somthin' yer not."

"At my age it is not as important to try to impress. I am not one to waste valuable time applying make-up and fancy clothes. It's not that I don't like to try to look my best, I do; but I am not a young filly. It's not as if I need to try to lure a man to my bed."

"Clarinda, if ya' don't mind me sayin', but I dinnae think ya'd ever have trouble attractin' a man. Yer nae what I imagined, but trust me, once the men folk in town meet ya', they will be captivated."

"I appreciate your flattery, but most of the men folk in town have seen or met me, and I hasten to say they were not 'captivated' as you put it. Of course, when they have met me, it is usually when I have been painting or digging, so I suppose my first impressions where not what they could have been."

"Aye lass, right ye are on that. I suppose if I had met ya' under the same situation, I wouldn't have thought ye to be as bonnie."

"Well, Alistair, I think the same may be said for you. I don't think you wear your kilt everyday—do you? Because I have to admit, you clean up pretty good."

"I am glad ya' like it. Me sister likes me to wear the highland dress when she has guests. She may be me sis, but I guess she has seen the reaction of the ladies in town. So she has me parade around in it. I doona mind, really. It is me heritage, and I'm proud to wear me family tartan. And besides; it is very comfortable."

"I can well imagine, but isn't it cool on a night like tonight?"

"No really. The wool is quite dense so it traps in the heat."

Hm, heat, really? Clarinda thought to herself but offered a less beguiling response. "I guess that's why it's so suitable for the climate of Scotland."

"Aye, that's why there are so many versions of the Campbell

tartan. There's patterns fer huntin' and also for the different branches of the clan. This plaid is pleated sett which keeps the pattern of the tartan even though it is pleated. The military pleat their kilts on the line, so each pleat has a bold stripe in the plaid at the edge."

"I didn't realize there is so much to the kilt. It is really quite fascinating. I'm glad you continue to honor the Scottish tradition by wearing it."

"Aye, there was a time in Scottish history when owning any sort o' tartan could be punishable by death. Do ya' ken much about Culloden?"

"I know it was the last battle fought on English soil, but other than that, I guess I would have to study up on it."

"Blasphemer—English soil! No, lass. Scotland never was and never has been English soil. However, ya' are right that it was the last battle fought in the United Kingdom." Alistair's voice became very soft as he continued. "It was a massacre. The bloody English led by Cumberland the Butcher slaughtered the Scots on that April day in 1746. They even lingered to see if family members would come to bury the dead, and if they did, they too were killed. Even women. After some time the British lost interest and left so family came back to bury their dead. By this time they could only be recognized by their plaids, so they where buried in mass graves—just the wee gravestones indicating the clan. If ye ever go to Culloden, ya'll see the graves. They are still mounded to this day, and no heather will grow on 'em. I have always felt it is the souls of the brave Scots who lost their lives that day who want visitors to clearly see the graves and to remember how they were brutally slain.

After Culloden the British condemned the Scottish clans. They passed the Dekilting Law. This meant the tartan would nae be worn for any reason. If even a scrap of fabric was found in a home, all family members could be sent to prison. The bagpipes were also banned. They were originally used in battle because the sound carries even in dense Scottish fog. After then, nae were allowed to be played. Gaelic could no be spoken or taught. Basically, anything considered Scottish was outlawed by the British swine. It was no until the nineteenth century the Scots were able to take up their honored traditions. As a Scot I am glad I can wear the tartan, and speak my native language again."

"That is a horrible story," Clarinda said softly. The manner in which Alistair told this bit of history it was as if he himself had personally been in the battle, seen the horrors and lost loved ones. It was clear to Clarinda the Scots still harbored resentment toward their neighbors to the south for such abominable treatment of their countrymen. Obviously, the Scots were a proud nation and held fast to the old customs of their country.

"Aye, it is. There're many atrocities in Scottish history, but that is one of the worst."

They continued to walk in silence and Clarinda noticed they were almost to her home. Time had passed quickly, taken up by Alistair's story.

"Here we are," Clarinda indicated as they turned to walk up Telford Lane. She could see the hallway light left on through the narrow glass panes on either side of the door.

"Let me see ya' in. I want to make sure yer home safely."

Clarinda thought there might be other motives on Alistair's mind, but she reminded herself that he was almost engaged (even if he was against it), and he was very sincere in his statement.

She walked up to her door and tried the key. The door opened easily, and Clarinda turned to thank Alistair for escorting her home and found him standing directly behind her. She could smell his scent, and it stimulated her. "Thank you for walking me home," she whispered.

Alistair nodded and lowered his head toward hers. His lips were full and softly inviting. *Is he going to kiss, me?* Clarinda wondered. She was too mesmerized by the excitement of the moment to sort out her emotions. He continued to come closer and Clarinda lightly bit her bottom lip and ran her tongue over the upper. She didn't want to feel like an old dried up woman if this strong and mysterious man was about to kiss her. Her excitement and anticipation grew as he continued to near. She could hear her heart pounding in her ears. She closed her eyes to receive his lips on hers. She felt a sigh upon them and opened her eyes to see Alistair walking back down the path toward the road.

"Good night!" she called. He didn't turn around, but waved and kept walking.

"There is no way I am turnin' around now," Alistair said to himself. "I couldn't let her see me with this massive cock stand."

Clarinda's heart was still racing when she turned off her lights and slipped into the cool sheets of her bed. She fell asleep thinking about the enchanting evening and the thrilling man she had met. She had not felt this exhilarated in such a long time, and she felt heart coming alive again. "I know this is not the right thing to do—but sometimes your heart leads the way and leaves the brain by the wayside. I just hope I don't make a fine mess of things again. Good night, Alistair; I hope to see you soon."

chapter 12
so, do ya' come here often?

The riotous clashing of pots and pans drew Clarinda from her slumber and into the kitchen; perhaps a bull had been trapped in there and was the cause of the deafening clamor. It was Janet who had arrived at the guest house early and cheerful as ever. She had some organizational plans in mind and was getting the place into shape with a fervor that would make a military unit envious.

"See here, we need the sauté pans near the knives so small bits can be easily scrapped into the pan from the cutting boards." Clarinda wasn't sure she saw the logic of this orderliness, but she was not the commander of this battalion any longer—Janet was the new general and getting her troops in order.

"Sweetie, it is so nice that ya' came over last night. I am sorry I didn't have the legs to stay up later, but I am best early in the day. I trust that me brother walked ya' home safely. I'm so glad ya' were able to meet him."

At the mere sound of his name, Clarinda went into an immediate daydream and tried to relive the interlude at her front door the night before. *What would that kiss have been like?*

How would he taste? Would he have been soft and teasing or strong and alluring? The questions poured into Clarinda head.

"Clarinda, are ya' alright? I said I hope my brother walked ya' home. I hope he obliged me."

Oh, he was obliging, thought Clarinda. "Oh yes, your brother was a proper gentleman and saw me to my door. Last night was wonderful. Thank you for having me over to your home. You are a wonderful cook. I have been thanking George all day. Thanks to him…that he thought of you to be my chef. I hope you are as excited about this arrangement as I am."

"Yes, dear, I am, but we have so much work to do in just two short months. I ken the rooms are almost done, I was wonderin' if we could have some 'dry runs'. Ya' ken, with some actual guests so we can iron out any kinks. I don't want Hogmanay to be a time to hold a dress rehearsal."

"Great minds think alike. I have a lot of bills mounting and it would be nice to get some guests in here so I could get some cash flowing. I would like to see if we could open next week and take in a few guests and slowly work up to capacity. Do you think we could be ready to serve breakfast by then?"

"A full Scottish Breakfast is me specialty. I typically serve some eggs, black puddin', bacon, sausage, mushrooms, broiled tomatoes, and off course, toast, marmalade, and tea and coffee. Traditionally tea is the only beverage to drink in the morning, but ya' Yankees prefer coffee so we should make sure we have what they want. I will review the costs and show it to ya' so ya' can make sure we are makin' it back in the room tariff. I have established an account at the butcher's so we'll be able to get fresh meats when we need 'em."

"Janet, thank goodness for you! I appreciate a woman who is good with figures and able to understand what it takes to make a profit." The two women started to giggle. Clarinda gleaned a partner such as Janet was not only a financial benefit, but her sensible, and fun, approach to running her kitchen made this guest house a labor of love.

"So what have ya' been busy with today?" Janet inquired. "I don't mean to pry, but is it somethin' that I could assist ya'?"

"Well, I am sort of taking a day off so to speak." Clarinda confessed. "I have been working on small pillows that will hang on each of the doors to identify the rooms. As you know the guest house will be called The Heather and Thyme Guest House, so I think we need to refer to it by it's proper name, don't you think? We don't want the tourists to be directed to the 'inn' and most certainly get lost, do we?"

"No, of course not. Yer right; I have been callin' it the 'inn' and not really thinkin' 'bout what it would be officially called. We're so used to the 'old Cameron House'; for some old dogs it is hard to learn a new trick. So let me see the wee door marker ya've been stitchin'."

Clarinda showed Janet the small five-inch square pillow she had started. It was only half finished, but Janet could see she had a good eye for cross stitch. "Aye, this is lovely. Ya' should sell the pattern for others to try."

"Spoken like someone who used to work in a shop!" They began to laugh. "I think that is a great idea. It is not hard to print the pattern and cut some floss and offer a needle. So during what free time will I take on this project? Tell you what, let me get this one finished and I will keep the pattern and if they are requested, we can spend some time putting up some kits."

This one is Savory, and I think the next one might be Basil."

They were both so engrossed by the topic of cross-stitch they didn't hear the door knocker. When there was no response, a voice called out "For goodness sakes, is this guest house or a vacant house?" After his grandiose introduction, George Wallace entered the main foyer.

"There are me lasses! Well can ye no hear me beatin' down the door?" Clarinda laughed; she was charmed by this man who acted so much younger than his years. "I have no been by recently so I wanted to check in and make sure the place is still standin'. I trust the lads have finished up and the place is near ready to welcome pound-paying guests."

"Yes, Janet and I were just discussing how best to open the place. We were thinking we would invite some guests to come stay with us—as guinea pigs. Perhaps you could come and stay a night with us? It is on me since you have done so much, but I expect you to be a harsh critic. So what do you say; are you free some night next week?"

"Well let me see…" He looked at the floor and quietly pulled at his chin. "Yer asking me, the most handsome and available lad in Inverwick, to come and stay at the guest house knowin' two available lasses will be here to make me stay comfortable? Hmm, I guess I could fit somethin' like that into me busy social calendar." George looked up at Clarinda with that twinkle in his eye. She liked his beguiling sense of humor. It probably was Clarinda's imagination, but when he looked at Janet, she began to blush. Although Clarinda did not know Janet very well it was clear her life was very structured and a man would only upset her routine. She envisioned Janet's idea of a romantic evening would involve a paperback romance novel, soft music, a candle and some tea—but not a man. And especially not someone as *lively* as George Wallace.

"George Wallace, now ye get yer mind out of ya' trousers!" Janet chided with a small smirk on her face. "This is a proper guest house, not a cat house, ya' clotheid. Besides, ye know well enough I doona live here, I have me own home. The only lass to see to yer whims will be this fine Clarinda here. I am sure if ya' made any advances, I would have to place me money is on her to be the victor in such an altercation."

This has the makings of a lovers spat, thought Clarinda. "OK you two. So George what do you say? Next week, plan on getting the royal treatment? And Janet, you know you will have to serve him breakfast even if he doesn't earn it!" Clarinda elbowed Janet and she grinned despite herself.

"Oh I ken, and it will be a pleasure. Now what still needs to be done to get the place ready?"

"Today I am doing some inside work, enjoying some rest actually, but I need to get your opinion on the sign I am planning to erect out front. Do you think it should be just text or should there be some sort of icon or logo?"

"Why are ya' askin' me? Or 'us' I should say?" He gestured toward Janet to include her in this key decision. "Weren't ya' the marketing professional—doona ye already know the proper design?"

"If this was Anytown, USA, I wouldn't hesitate to go with a logo that speaks the name regardless of the words, but here that might no be so good. Drivers and hikers might need to have large words to guide them to the place as they are nearing town."

"I agree," Janet concurred.

"Boy, her instincts for marketing are great." Clarinda realized.

Janet completed her idea. "I think the words are the key thing, but ya' could add some branches of thyme and heather for charm so it is not stark."

"Alright then, I can design something, but is there someone in the Shire who can make a sign to the fit the image of the house? I am looking for something where the words are a slight engraved script, but painted in black and gilded on a white background."

"Clarinda, have I let ye down yet?" George quizzed. "I will take care of this. Please bring me the design and I will see to it. I suspect my stay next week would not be considered proper until the shingle is hung, so I better get on it."

"Look at the time, already tea time, no?" Janet pointed out. "George, will ye be staying for a wee bit?"

"Lasses, nothin' would warm me heart more, but I do need to be gettin' to the rest of me chores. Nae only that, but I might need to go to Inverness to fetch meself a proper set of pajamas. After all, I don't think ye would want me wanderin' about the house in me all-together."

"I don't think I would be afraid, but then again, you Scots have a reputation for not wanting to confine your nether-region." Clarinda knew she was just egging him on, but she enjoyed George's clever conversation. "So yes, some pajamas are a good idea, especially if you feel you will be "wanderin'" about the house. I am not sure if you think you will be checking in on all the guests in all the rooms, but I can assure you that if you do, this will not be one of the room service highlights I plan to feature."

"Oh lass, if I was only ten years younger," George whispered wistfully. "Ya' ken how to engage a man in conversation. Much like a geisha. Well enough for today, I will see ya' later this week. Right-o! He tipped his forehead and walked out the door, shutting it quietly as if not to disturb any sleeping patrons.

"That man!" Janet protested. "He has some gall. Really!" Janet wanted to protest more, but her lack of specifics were eluding her. "Insulting ye that way!"

"What way was I demeaned?" Clarinda hadn't felt insulted, but then again she was still struggling to understand everything spoken in a Scottish accent.

"Callin' ya' a geisha, yer certainly nae a loose woman."

"No, I am not Janet, you are right about that." Clarinda didn't want Janet to think that she was small minded so she was careful how she phrased her next words. "Janet, I don't know if you are well versed in the Asian culture, but a geisha is not a woman who is solicited for sex. She is hired by men, sometimes even married men, because of her conversational skills. I think George was giving me a compliment of sorts since we both seem to enjoy bantering with each other."

"Oh, well, I guess that is alright I suppose. He is very quick witted, indeed. Well, I must be gettin' back to me kitchen and readin' ready for the lord on high to come and visit us. I know one thing, he willna complain about the food. He is always one of the first to purchase my goodies at a bake sale. I'll check back with ya' before I leave."

Clarinda walked back into her small apartment and noticed it had become cool. The day was damp and raw and had a sharp chill in the air. The fire had almost gone out so she added some more coal to the small stove. She was not used to the smell of a coal fire. Growing up in Vermont, wood was so readily available there was not need to search for other fuel sources for stoves. Hard wood was the most sought after; it burned hot and with little creosote buildup. Pine smelled great, but it would tend to create creosote which could lead to a chimney fire. Coal had much more of an industrial smell, but it was cheap and burned slowly and evenly. No sooner had she tended to the stove, when the phone rang.

"Darling, how are you? I hope you are enjoying the balmy weather of Scotland!"

"Fran!" Clarinda was delighted to hear from her dear friend.

"So guess what? I'm coming to Scotland! I decided I have some time off, and since you and I really don't have family to speak of I am coming to Scotland to share Thanksgiving with you."

"Fran—that is terrific! When do you get here?"

"I fly out from JFK on Saturday which means I will be arriving the Sunday before so I can help you shop and thaw out the turkey."

"Fran, this is great and I can't wait to see you. But I hope you won't change your plans when I tell you this news flash: they don't celebrate Thanksgiving here. It is an American holiday only. Remember your history lessons—the Pilgrims decided to celebrate because they escaped European persecution."

"Oh, silly girl, I know that! That doesn't mean we can't have our own private holiday. I guess the next thing you are going to tell me is that they don't have turkeys over there. Will I have to stash one in my carry-on?"

"You might have to. However, they do have pheasant and that is very tasty. Enough about the food, we can certainly whip up a fine feast. I want more details about your trip; how long are you planning to stay—just one week?"

"Yepper, I gotta be back to work the following Monday. Luckily, the day I lose on the way out is gained coming back. I can leave on Sunday and still be to work the next day. Ah, the marvel of time zones. Is there anything else I need to bring?"

"Yes, your wallet. Remember the dollar is weak so it doesn't go very far and I know you will want to do some shopping in Edinburgh. The weather should be about the same as the Big Apple—damp, cold, and miserable; so the same attire will do nicely here. But remember, I now live in a simple town. Sequins are not needed on everything."

"Anything else?"

"Like what?"

"Well, I didn't know if you missed anything from the states and you can't get it there."

"Nope—nada. I think I am good—except bring some maple syrup. That is a must! We will need it for the squash I plan to serve with haggis."

"You don't expect me to eat THAT do you? I mean I am not about to eat the innards of a sheep," Fran protested. Clarinda grinned.

"Fran, first of all you will place a man's member in your mouth, but you won't eat haggis? You have had a hot dog at Nathan's, no? Trust me, haggis is far better than that death tube and far tastier."

"Alright, I will bring you the syrup, but I will reserve my judgment of haggis for later. As for what I place in my mouth—that is NONE of your business, even though I might tell you anyway. After all, a woman's prerogative is to change her mind." They both heard peals of laughter coming over the other end of phone line.

"I will roll out the red carpet for you, and put you in my best room. At least it has running water," Clarinda joked. But don't expect the electric to be able to maintain the voltage needed for your blast furnace of a hair dryer."

"Clarinda, don't worry. This voyage is quite a change for me, so to be a more organized and ~~more of an~~ on-the-go traveler, I was planning on shaving my head."

"Well, won't that be a bonnie look?" Clarinda replied and tried to imitate the highland drawl. "I will be anxious to be seein' that!"

"OK, enough for now, I will see you in a few weeks. Meet me at the station, won't you? I don't want to have to walk through the village and look like its idiot."

"Yes," Clarinda reassured her friend. "I will meet you at the train. Have a great trip and let me know if you need more advice as to what to bring. Remember to pack light, only one steamer trunk ought to do for a just a week," she mocked. "In truth, please pack a small bag; it will be better through customs and on the train. Whatever you need that you may not have brought, I am sure I can supply you with something. Travel safe and I can't wait to see you."

They said their good-byes, and when she hung up the phone Clarinda was both excited and petrified. She not only was trying to open the guest house, but she now had to create a Thanksgiving dinner to boot. Until Fran had mentioned it, she had completely forgotten it was November already. Hogmanay was only eight weeks away; there seemed to be so much to do and not enough time to get it all complete. Delighted her friend was coming for Thanksgiving, but Clarinda knew this was not a holiday celebrated in Inverwick. She didn't want to go to all the necessary effort for just Fran—not that Fran wouldn't be worth it. But it was just that she didn't want her friend to make this courageous voyage out of the comfort of NYC and have to share the holiday looking at just one face. It just didn't seem right. Who else could she invite and not offend by the very mention of the holiday?

Clarinda first considered George. After all, as a widower she was hoping he would be available. Additionally, he would be thoroughly enamored by Fran and her quick humor. *If he thought I was witty, wait until he meets Fran,* she thought. She wrote his name on a piece of paper and planned to invite him.

Other than George she was at a loss for additional guests. Janet and Alistair were already a family and although Thanksgiving may not be a Scottish tradition, it was a family one. Clarinda had to admit that after her encounter with Alistair at her front door, she somewhat considered the young Miss Lauren Lees her competition, in a strange way. The girl was kind and sweet, but it is a golden rule that love and another woman make poor combinations. Thus, if Janet were invited, she would in turn invite Alistair, who would then invite Lauren. Not good. Besides, Fran would eat Lauren alive. She despised 'helpless women'. These were women who defined themselves but the image and status created by their men. So, it seemed the group would be a tiny, but fun-loving. She began to list the staples she would need to pull off this impromptu holiday dinner. She would handle this meal herself; Janet already had enough to do. More importantly, she didn't want to be rude and have her help with the preparations if she was not going to invite her.

chapter 13
a welcome guest

The next weeks were a blur. With Emily's help, Clarinda had been able to get all the rooms in order. She was diligently working on door hangers for all of them, but those projects were taken up only when she could spare a few moments of quiet time.

George Wallace had come over for a 'test run', and Clarinda was sure it was one of the few times he had left his own home in over a decade. Even though he was only staying over for a single night, and the guest house provided guests with the basic necessities such as shampoo, mouthwash and the like, George arrived with a satchel which could have afforded him to stay at least two weeks.

"George, you are only staying for one night, not a fort-night, right?" Clarinda teased when she saw him lumber up the stairs straining with his bag's bulky weight.

"Aye, only one night, but I was no sure which pair of pajamas I would want, the silk ones or the flannel," he replied in his typical dry wit. "Ya' ken I am quite stunnin' in both. Shame ya' won't have the privilege of seein' me in either."

"Yes, and I know you don't believe me, but I am gladdened by that small comfort," came her retort.

Clarinda and George dined together, and Janet joined them for tea after they had finished.

"Janet, yer meal was superb. I loved every bit of it. I found the salad to be most refreshing. Can ya' tell me what is in the dressin'? Do I taste some basil and marjoram?"

"Why, yes you do." Janet replied. "But it is nae me recipe, but Clarinda's."

"Really?" He seemed surprised. Clarinda wanted to put him back at ease, so a compliment was in order.

"What a good sense of taste you have. It is the guest house's 'signature salad'; and to keep things simple, it will be the only dressing we serve on the house salad. I will make the recipe available to guests in the form of a postcard so they can take it home with them or send it to their friends. Would you like me to give it to ya'?"

"Typically I would say yes, but knowin' I can come here and get it fresh will be good enough for me. On second thought, I ken me niece in Aberdeen would like it so if ye could give it to me when ya' have the time, that would be nice."

Clarinda got out a piece of paper and starting writing, but still continued to remain in the conversation. "So please give us more feedback. We need to know the bad as well as the good. In fact those are the things we need to fix first and foremost."

"Well, the most disappointing thing was that Janet couldn't join us." George plainly stated. It seems a shame the woman who created this fine supper was hidden behind the kitchen doors."

"George, please don't be daft," Janet scolded. Ya' ken I hae to be in the kitchen mindin' to the sous chefs and other staff. Of course, tonight it was just the three of us, but when we have guests I can't be greetin' and meetin'."

"Of course I know that," George rejoined. "I was just hopin' since it was just the three of us, ya' would have joined us. That's no matter is it?"

Clarinda was surprised to see George not his cheery self, but she was glad Janet didn't chide him too badly. She thought perhaps this night was something so unusual for George that he may be feeling a bit out of sorts. Maybe just a little lonely even though he was sharing his company among friends.

Janet rescued the awkward moment. "George, I want to thank ya' for the compliment. It is greatly appreciated."

"I dinnae give ya' a compliment. I just said I missed ye at the table." George shook his head.

Janet had lured him into a trap and snapped it shut. "We asked ya' to tell us what we needed to improve upon and all ye could come up with is that ye wanted more women at yer table; I say that is a pretty good praise, for sure." That sent everyone into giggles.

B&B Buttermilk Salad Dressing
From the kitchen of Clarinda Tetrick

Blend the following ingredients together in a bowl with a whisk. Reduce size if only serving a few, and not a houseful. Store refrigerated in an air-tight container.

½ gal. Mayonnaise
½ gal. Buttermilk
½ cup Marjoram
½ cup Basil
2 Tbls. Celery Salt
2 Tbls. Granulated Onion
1 Tbls. Minced Garlic
¾ Tbls. Brown Sugar

"Here ya' go, George." Clarinda handed him the simple recipe scribed on a recipe card. "Well, I think I might get some more tea, retire to the parlor, and put my feet up and watch a *McCallum* rerun. Anyone else game?" Clarinda offered.

"I must be goin' so I can come back here in a few hours," Janet replied and started to gather her things, and wrapped her shawl about her shoulders.

George took Clarinda up on her offer. "Yes, some tea and telly sounds verra good. I will join ya' for the first half. I am an early riser and that doesn't come from burnin' the midnight oil."

They bade Janet a goodnight, poured some tea, and settled into the soft chairs and sofas in the parlor. Before too long George was drowsy. Clarinda presumed it was due to a combination of being in unfamiliar surroundings, and the glass of wine he had with his supper. He rose to say goodnight to Clarinda, but she had already fallen asleep in her chair. George didn't wish to disturb her—she looked so peaceful and lovely. *That man was a fool,* he thought to himself. *He had no right to hae such a fine woman and throw her away with no care in his heart.* He took his leave and stepped gently on the stairs so as not to wake her with any creaking floorboards. He was not as successful to keep the door from squeaking. He pulled on his trusty flannel pajamas—he had only brought one pair anyway—and once he was settled in his bed of crisp linens he fell fast asleep.

Clarinda heard George's guest room door creak shut, but she didn't move. She watched the fire, enjoyed John Hannah's lyric accent on the television and spent some time self-reflecting. She felt more confident about the guest house, the appearance of the rooms, and the menus she and Janet were finalizing. She was hopeful the guest house could be successful, but there were still so many uncertainties. The premier main event of Hogmanay was just a little over a month away and she made a mental note to get the word and flyers out early next week. And she was looking forward to seeing her good friend, Fran. She had created a brief itinerary of sights they could go and explore near Edinburgh and knowing her friend would want to shop, so that excursion would take up at least an entire day. She hoped Fran might also want to see what the small town of Inverwick had to offer. Clarinda was becoming quite fond of her neighbors and friends in this small town—even Mrs. Fitzrandolph was charming in her own way.

The fire died down and Ian McCallum had gotten his man. Clarinda wanted to avoid a stiff neck in the morning so she reluctantly uncurled from the coziness of her chair and made her way to bed. She too, chose her flannel pajamas—for quite different reasons. They made sense in the winter months when there was no man to warm her bed and body. In this stage in her life, it was not about finding passion, but about finding herself. "Why can't they share something?" she sighed. In minutes of her head hitting the pillow, she was dreaming of the sound of bagpipes, dressed in white and tartan.

The next morning she was the last one to the breakfast table. Janet and George had already finished most of their Scottish breakfast, and were enjoying each other's company. Not that they were really talking, but just looking at one another and smiling to themselves. When Clarinda joined, they noticeably changed their demeanor and became more formal.

"I trust everyone slept okay," Clarinda inquired with the traditional American expression. George merely nodded, his mouth filled with black pudding.

"Aye, I did, in me own home and me own bed," Janet reported. "I trust there were no shenanigans over here," winking at George. George looked surprised but said nothing and kept his attention focused on the remains in his plate.

"Yes, we were on our best behavior. I think I was the first who went down for the count," Clarinda confessed as she helped herself to the plentitude of breakfast items Janet had fully prepared for George to sample and rate.

"Well, I see ya' both aren't crabbit or I would know something was fishy," said Janet as she smiled at George.

Clarinda decided it was best to take her breakfast into her quarters and begin her day eating and reading emails. She was hoping by leaving they would revert to the intimate moment they shared earlier. "Well at least someone is finding love while discovering a new vocation." She was happy for Janet and George, but she finally admitted to herself that she was lonely. An intimate relationship to weather through the dark and cold winter months was appealing. "Just best to stick to making a go of the guest house," she reassured herself. "Keep focused and you won't lose focus." God, she was so deep.

chapter 14
a reason to give thanks

"Fran! Over here!" Clarinda was waving and trotting down the tracks to greet her friend. Unknowingly, Fran had boarded the last car of the train, so the walk along the platform was a long one.

"Franny!" Clarinda continued to holler as she made her way to greet her friend. Once they were close enough, they embraced each other with lung-compressing hugs.

"God, it is great to see you," Clarinda uttered into her friends hair knowing her ear was in there somewhere. "And you smell great too!"

"Well, *you* smell like the country, but I am glad to see you anyway," Fran joked. "You look wonderful. I have never seen such a healthy person in all my life."

"Of course not, everyone in New York is tanned to a nice light green shade by the florescent lighting in their cubicles, and any walking is done underground in the subways." This started a full weekend of puns, jokes, and endless laughter.

"We ourselves, would have a quick walk over to the guest house, but I brought the Mini instead."

When Fran saw Clarinda's Cooper she was like a kid who saw a marvelous toy. "I can't believe you drive something like this. Is it safe to leave the driveway and use this on actual roads? Where is the trunk? Oh, I guess I need to place my luggage in the back seat. This is so CUTE. But, honestly, don't you need a truck?"

"Not really, George is really helpful with his, so I haven't needed one."

"George—who is George?" Fran was leading with raised eyebrows. "You didn't mention George."

"George is a hottie alright, especially if you were about twenty-five years older. No really—he is a wonderful man and has really helped me out in so many ways. He lost his wife a few years ago, and I think having something to do, and helping others, keeps him young and sharp."

It was clear to Fran Clarinda thought highly of this Scottish gent, but he didn't sound like the type of man Fran had in mind. She came to Scotland to see lads in kilts, and any pleats should only be on a tartan, not on the midsection.

"Are you terribly jet-lagged from the trip? Do you have a head-ache? Do you want something to eat, or take a nap?"

"What is this—a medical version of twenty questions? I am fine, but I do wish to take a shower, change my clothes to rid myself of the scent of 'airline'. But now that you mention it, I could go for a 'cocktail'—the trip left me verrrrry parched." Fran tried to make the word sound like a Scottish brogue, but failed miserably. Her Noo Yauwk accent was too ingrained.

"Well as soon as we get to the Heather and Thyme Guest House, I am sure the proprietress will be happy to set you up with whatever you may require."

"But, I thought I was staying with you?" Fran protested.

"You are silly—the name of MY guest house is the Heather and Thyme." Clarinda looked over at her friend's wild and sly grin and knew she had been prey to her trick. It was the first of many she would endure this week, and she looked forward to each and every silly moment.

"I need to stop by Janet's house first. I just want to give her a list of the provisions we need this week." She realized she could have done this earlier, but she wanted Janet to meet her friend at the first possible moment—regardless of Fran's demeanor or appearance resulting from the long voyage.

When she turned into Janet's drive she instantly regretted her decision. She could see a panel truck in the drive and it looked like it would hold the equipment of a blacksmith. She guessed this was one of the days Alistair visited his sister. This could be a disaster, but she was committed now. When Janet heard a vehicle turn into her house, she was at the door and waving to Clarinda who was reciprocating with one hand out the window and the other barely managing the wheel from the uneven gravel driveway.

"Halloo," Janet cried. "Please come in."

"This shouldn't take long," Clarinda prepared. "Please come and meet my friend Janet. She is also the head chef at my guest house, so you better get on her good side if you want to be fed while staying in Inverwick."

Fran rolled her eyes, but in truth was excited to meet an honest-to-goodness Scot. She also had a feeling this woman would truthfully tell her how her friend was faring in this land far from her roots. She climbed out of the cramped car and made her way to the woman's porch. Janet was already giving Clarinda a light hug and a kiss on the cheek when she turned to Fran.

"You must be the lass from New York who is me Clarinda's bonnie friend?"

Not really sure she understood all the words, Fran still nodded her head figuring this conversation was going to involve some charades to be understood.

"Please come in, I was just tryin' a new recipe for banana scones—they are warm and fresh." The smell caught Fran and her stomach rolled in hunger. Before she knew what had happened, she had accepted the invitation and was eagerly making her way into this jolly woman's house to hunt down the smell that was making her so ravenous.

"Please sit here lass, and I will get ya' some tea. Clarinda, have ye no compassion to feed yer friend. Dinnae ya' no see she is already waistin' away and then not feedin' her when she arrived." Clarinda knew there was no use to explain that she had just claimed Fran from the train station and was about to take her to her house to get her some food. But upon reflection, she was glad she stopped by; Janet's scones were by far better than whatever Clarinda would have had for tea. She still hadn't gotten the habit to have treats ready at that time of the day, so she was delighted Janet could offer them some.

"Me brother, Alistair, will be joinin' us as soon as he is done seein' to me fowl." At Janet's remark, Clarinda felt anxious. She wanted to see Alistair again—who wouldn't? But she also was feeling somewhat embarrassed about the last time they met. Lastly, she was in jeans and a sweater, and really not prepared aesthetically to encounter him.

The ladies were enjoying their tea and Janet was asking Fran the standard traveler questions when Alistair came in the back door. Not realizing his sister had guests, he spoke his mind. "Those geese are good for nothin' craiturs. I dinnae ken why ya' insist on keeping 'em. Those scones better be bonnie fair—I can eat about six."

Janet and Clarinda looked at each other, but kept their giggles to themselves. They waited to see Alistair's reaction when he would realize there were guests he was unknowingly addressing.

He came around the corner speaking at full volume. "Where are ye? I dinnae see the scones in the kitchen!" He then stopped short and was fully surprised to see three women in his sister's dining room. "Och! I am sorry I dinnae ken ye were all here. Clarinda…nice to see ya' again, and who is yer friend?"

When Fran looked up at Alistair, she was not prepared to gaze upon such a fine example of the male species. Her reaction was an audible gasp. That was enough to make some of the scone she had been chewing lodge in her windpipe. She held out her hand to shake his, but had to retract it to cover her mouth to hack and cough up the dislodged morsel. *Great*, she thought, *I'm sure I'm making a great impression!*

"Are ya' alright? Have ya' got some water? I think a wee bit went down the wrong pipe." He turned his attention to Clarinda while Fran was getting her coughing under control.

"Clarinda" he smiled. "How have ya' been? I have been meanin' to stop by the guest house to see how the place turned out. After all, when I walked ye home, I was no invited in to see it." He slyly looked at his sister certain Clarinda would vouch for his propriety.

"Well stop by anytime. We are happy to welcome guests. We entertained George last week, and I know will have my friend Fran stay there for a whole week." By this time Fran was able to speak and tried to recoup some grace and offered a greeting to this Adonis of a man standing before her. He was tall, broad shouldered, and grubby. He looked as if he hadn't showered in a couple of days; his hair was uncombed, his jeans and sweatshirt were filthy and he smelled of stables. He was rough, wild, and above all alluring.

Fran stood to introduce herself. She stood five foot nine, and she noticed he still stood a good head above her. "I don't usually greet most people by choking. I hope I can get a second try to introduce myself. Hi, I am Fran." She stated and extended her hand.

"Hullo Fran. After meeting Clarinda, I believe any friend of hers is worthy. I hope ya' enjoy yer stay to our fine Alba."

"Alba?" Fran looked confused and looked at Clarinda and Janet for clarification. "I thought the town was called Inverwick."

This brought a chuckle to Janet and Clarinda. "Alba is gaelic for Scotland," Alistair explained.

"Garlic?" Again Fran was getting lost in the common

THE CELEBRATION OF HOGMANAY

language separating Americans and the peoples of the United Kingdom.

Clarinda interjected before her friend could further offend the Scots. "Gaelic is the Scottish pronunciation for gaelic," pronouncing the second utterance of the word as 'gay-lick'.

"Oh." Fran stated sheepishly. "I am sorry; I am trying to understand your accent and I am sure you are equally confused buy mine."

"Och. It is no bother, we enjoy meetin' folks from other places, don't we Alistair?" Janet was trying hard to make Fran feel welcome.

Alistair came around the table and sat next to his sister across from Clarinda and helped himself to the scones, butter, and honey. His sister, as if an automaton, poured him a cup of tea and added the milk and set it next to him.

"So what made ya' decide to come to Inverwick at this time of the year? I am sure ya' don't find the weather very hospitable and the heather is no longer loamin'."

Fran didn't understand most of the words, but she thought she got the meaning and not wanting to make her visit a vocabulary comparison, she decided she would answer the question as best as she could given the information she knew.

"Well, I didn't want Clarinda to spend Thanksgiving alone, so I decided to come and join her and see her new guest house to boot."

Now it was time for the Scots to look at each other inquisitively. "Thanksgiving?" They asked each other than turned to the Yankees for an explanation.

This was a subject with which Fran was familiar. "Well, Thanksgiving is an American holiday celebrated on the third Thursday…"

"We ken what it is." Alistair interrupted.

Janet in turn stopped him. "What Alistair means is, we ken the holiday, but we completely forgot ya'd be celebratin' it. I ken it is quite similar to a Hogmanay feast, but I need to ken right

125

away what I need to get for ya'." Janet was up out of her seat and looking for some paper and a pen to take notes and make lists.

"Janet, please don't do anything. I realize this is not a UK celebration, so I have made most of the preparations myself. I didn't want to trouble you since you have enough to do."

"Don't be silly. What is it I can do? I am sure there are lots of wonderful goodies ya' make only for this feast so I could learn a few more recipes—like pumpkin-pecan pie?" Janet's eyes were large and lit up.

"There is a big problem if you help." Clarinda was trying to be subtle and she hoped her trap might work.

"What?" Janet was alarmed.

"Well, I can't rightly ask you to assist in the preparations if you don't come to join us. After all there will be plenty of food, and the more the merrier."

Janet thought a brief second and then resoundingly responded. "Of course we will join ya'—won't we?" Giving Alistair a poke to elicit a response from him.

"Huh? Oh, yeah, sure." Focused on adding honey to his scones, he was not sure to what he had just committed but seemed agreeable to it at the moment.

"Well dinner will be on Thursday, obviously. Why don't we plan to eat at six o'clock, but we can have some appetizers beginning at four. Sound good?" Clarinda queried.

"Clarinda, I am sure it will be a fine feast." Alistair finally speaking. I am honored to attend and share one of yer traditional holidays. I will wear the tartan again, if that is agreeable to ya'?"

"Of course." Clarinda was almost panting when she recollected what Alistair looked like in a kilt. "I would feel privileged if you would." She thought to herself, *that is not the only privilege I would like to feel.*

Fran could see her friend slipping into a daydream and gave her a jab in the leg underneath the table bringing Clarinda back into the present.

"We need to be going. I am sure Fran is quite tired from her travels and would like to settle into something more comfortable," and Clarinda rose to leave.

Alistair may have been dressed to work in a barn but he was not raised in one, and also rose from his seat to see the ladies off.

"It was a pleasure to meet you both and thank you so much for the scones and tea. They were delightful," Fran offered her praises to Janet and her striking brother.

"Let me see ya' out," Alistair offered. "Are yer coats by the door?" He assisted them each with their garments and walked them out to the Mini.

"Fran, nice to meet ya'. Enjoy our wee country. It may not look it, but it is bonnie on a good day, and we Scots are a great lot."

Fran took the easy way out and nodded and merely said "Thank you'."

Alistair walked around to the right-hand side of the car, bent and to address Clarinda. "I will be seein' ya' Thursday. I look forward to it," and winked.

Clarinda started up the car and backed down the gravel drive to reach the main road and travel the short distance to the guest house.

Fran was now a live wire. "Did you see that man? Do you not have a pulse? What red-blooded woman wouldn't want to ravage that man? I don't care what he smelled like today, I am sure he cleans up verrrrry well! My God, Clarinda, there is a perfect man in your wee town and you didn't tell me about him? What are you thinking?"

"Look missy," Clarinda jokingly chided, "he has a girlfriend and they are about to be engaged so he is off limits. I can see just as well as you, but he is already taken so do not even think of going there."

"A fiancé has never been an insurmountable obstacle before, so why is it now?" Fran was gesturing with her hands to try to illustrate her point. "My God, he is like a cross between Sean

Connery and William Wallace—raw, but sophisticated. What did he mean by he would wear the 'tartan'.

"'Wait until you see me in a kilt', is what he means. I am sure he was fully aware you were drooling all over him—it was clear you were choking. We almost needed to get you a bucket of tea. He is just trying to egg you on. And it is working!"

Fran could sense a touch of jealousy in her friend's voice. "The old Clarinda is BACK!" she cheered.

"Whatever do you mean?" Clarinda asked beguilingly. "Back from where?"

"You are back, sistah! You came here to heal from the atrocities of the past, and to rid yourself of men, but after seeing that man and hearing the tone of your voice, I know he has gotten to you, too, and you want him."

"I do not!" She unconvincingly protested. "I will admit he is very attractive, but for the reasons I stated earlier, he is not available. I have just moved to this place and I don't want to make a mess of things here, too. It is a very small town so I have to be careful. I can't afford any enemies."

Fran decided to let the topic slide. Her travels had finally caught up with her and she needed a shower and a nap before dinner. She was grateful when they pulled up to the guest house.

Clarinda showed her to the Savory Room, checked it to make sure she had enough towels and left her friend to make herself at home and relax. She had enough to do elsewhere. Fran would reappear when she was rested, bathed and hungry. As Clarinda made her way down the stairs she heard a vehicle pull up. Not expecting anyone at this hour, she padded down the stairs to greet her unexpected guest. When she spied her visitor she would not have guessed in a million years—Alistair. *What in the world is he doing here?* she wondered to herself.

She walked out to greet him as he was getting out of his lorry. He had his head down so he didn't see her approach and walked head-long right into her. "Oooph," Clarinda exclaimed. He was equally off guard. "Oh I am sorry, I didn't see ya' comin'. Are ya' alright?"

"Oh yes. I am fine. Sorry about that. I wasn't expecting you either." That was all Clarinda could come up with and felt pathetic in the art of casual conversation.

"Well I came to talk to ya'."

"Well that seems clear. About what?" At that moment Clarinda felt she might appear to be terse and sought to be more inviting. "What I mean is, what can I help you with?"

"I heard what me sis wants to do for yer Thanksgiving dinner, and I think it is a bonnie idea. In fact, I am glad ya' invited us. But there is somethin' I need to discuss before I can attend."

"What is that?" Clarinda thought Alistair might renege on their acceptance of the invitation; he seemed very serious.

"Ya' ken I hae been seein' Lauren Lees, right?" At that moment Clarinda knew the problem. She had been rude and not invited Lauren to join the dinner and Alistair saw this and was going to make Clarinda invite her—just the very reason she didn't want to invite them in the first place. She had to admit the sight of Lauren and Alistair together made her uneasy.

"Yes, I know. I am sorry I didn't mention her before, but I welcome her as your guest, so please extend to her my invitation." Clarinda knew this was feeble—too little, too late.

"That is no really what I was tryin' to say, but I thank ye for yer warm thoughts. No, exactly the opposite is what I wanted to let ya' be awares. I hae broken with the young Lees lass. She is a fine girl, but she is lookin' for me to be her husband, and I cannae be that for her. So I wanted ya' to know I will no be bringin' Lauren to join me. I hope I am still welcome to yer table. I hae never had a Thanksgiving feast and I would like to give it a go."

Clarinda was near tears. She was astonished by the open and honest approach of this rough looking man. Despite his typical appearance and demeanor, it was clear he was mannered and thoughtful.

"Of course you are still welcome. By no means would being single exclude you—in fact it makes you one of the group!" Clarinda tried to make light of his break-up with Lauren, but wanted to show more tact. "What I mean is, I am so sorry it didn't work out with you and Lauren, but the rest of us are all single too. As they say 'misery loves company', so you are more than welcome to join our little group. Please do come."

"I will, thanks again for havin' me. I guess I was no polite to yer friend, so I hope we can try again on Thursday."

Clarinda's protective fire started to flare again. "I am sure she was not offended. I believe you have charmed her already." She tried to act nonchalant, but the sight of him was making her heart pound and her pulse race. He was a single and available man now, so there was no reason not to . *Wait a minute!* she scolded herself. *This is not what you need to be thinking! Step away from the man, and keep your hands high,* the police officer in her head was cautioning her.

"Well, I guess I might be goin'," he stated, but it sounded more like a question. Clarinda had to think fast if she was going to keep him from leaving. He just got there and she had not had her fill of him yet.

"Why don't you come in and see the place? You are here now, so why not come on a tour?"

"Och, no. That would no be the proper thing. If I see it now my reactions will no be true when I see it on Thursday, me and sis and Fran will ken I was here afore to see it. I best wait till then."

"Okay," Clarinda knew he was right and felt defeated she couldn't think of anything else to keep him from leaving.

He opened the door to get in his lorry and Clarinda was right behind him so when he turned around he could barely avoid her. She didn't know what she was doing, but she was trying anything to keep him in sight. He started the lorry and leaned out the door.

"See you Thursday," he called and waved as he drove out the driveway. Clarinda waved back. She knew she would think about the man she was watching drive away for the rest of the evening. She liked the tight sensation in her chest, but at the same time she knew it was not the right thing. After all, her inn depended on a good chef, and this man was her head chef's brother—younger brother as well. Yes, this was a good feeling, but a bad idea. She just couldn't help herself—she was becoming overwhelmed. She walked back up the drive to prepare dinner for when Fran resurfaced.

"Was that the fine man we saw this afternoon? Alistair, isn't it?" Fran inquired with a twinkle in her eye.

"I'm not going to say," Clarinda toyed.

"I think you are sweet on him," Fran stated and looked at the driveway not really offering a glimpse at the smirk on her face.

"I am not."

"Are too."

"Not"

"Too!"

"Na, na—na—na, na." Clarinda thought she might have won the argument. "Come on, I have dinner ready. Let's go so you don't alarm the neighborhood with that scary post-nap sleepy face."

"Tell me you have made pesto and pasta. I can't get anything like it in NYC. I have had a craving for it since you left."

"Lucky for you—I have become a mind reader and have prepared the very same. But right now I would like to have some wine to preserve this giddy feeling."

Fran smiled at her friend and knew the cold area in her heart was warming up to the prospect of a potential new lover. Fran felt good to see her friend healing right before her very eyes. She was not a match maker, but she was glad she could be in Scotland to see a new love begin to blossom.

"I am so hungry; I hope you made a ton. Can I help with the garlic bread?" Fran put her arm around her friend and they both walked back into the house to enjoy a cozy evening together, have some food, and share a bottle (or two) of wine.

After they enjoyed Clarinda's dinner, and the wine had broken down her inhibitions, Fran decided she needed to tell her friend about David.

"Clarinda," Fran spoke with a cautioned voice. "I have some news about David. Do you want to know or is it better off brushed aside?"

Clarinda wanted to hear what the shoe-heel of a man had been up to, knowing it would be emotionally challenging nevertheless. She was curious, alright; but she could see this evening becoming a big 'wine fest' and with the both of them professing to each other to be their 'best friend' and then having a wicked headache the next day.

"Alright." She bravely squared her shoulders. "Tell me the awful truth. I'm ready."

Fran took a sip of wine, held it in her mouth, and then gulped it down. "Okay here it is and I warn you I have censored this for only your audience.

"He called me," she began with a steady voice, "and then he wanted to know where you went. I told him you were out of town and could not be reached. That just made him madder. I finally told him you had moved out of the country to start over. I told him really nothing, but I let him know you were doing fine, despite the emotional train-wreck he had caused."

Fran paused and took another sip. Clarinda was quiet, and her features did not reveal any of the emotions and expletives she wished to reveal. "Is there anything else?" she asked tersely.

Fran continued her report. "He wanted me to give you this," and handed her friend an envelope.

Clarinda opened the envelope which contained one piece of paper and a short handwritten note. She instantly recognized David's penmanship.

Dear Clarinda, I know I treated you horribly. For that I am deeply sorry and ask for your forgiveness. I was foolish to think I would happy with anyone else. I want to talk to you and ask you to come back to New York to be with me. I want you and need you. Please call me.

P.S. You also will always have a position at Masters and Kline.

Clarinda felt anger, sadness, and vindication all at once. "What a dirt-bag son of a bitch," she muttered under her breath but Fran still heard it. She looked up at her friend and Fran could see tears brimming in her friend's eyes.

"He is not worth it, Clarinda. He wants you back because he realizes he threw away the best thing he ever had. He has never been denied anything, and he can't stand the fact you are not where he can manipulate you. He is a son of a bitch. You don't need him. You are better than he is and he doesn't deserve you." Fran ended her diatribe with a satisfactory sigh and crossed her arms.

Clarinda shook her head in disbelief. "I can't believe this: 'I want you and need you'. Really! What a load of crap. 'You will always have a position and Masters and Kline'. I can't believe how truly shallow he is! As if I could be bribed by offering me my old job. I couldn't bear to look at that man in the hallways—I would rather cut off my right hand than go back to him and beg for my job! I have more dignity than that!"

"That's right you do!" Fran was trying to rev-up Clarinda. She didn't want to see this letter make her friend remorseful; she wanted Clarinda to take stock in herself and realize she was better off without David, The Cad.

"Fran, can you remind me again what I thought I saw in him? I can't believe it was just the sex, and his looks? Was I that shallow, too? I can't believe I made a ruination of my life just to get some once in a while? Was I that desperate?"

"No, girlfriend," Fran counseled her friend in a soft voice. "You couldn't be more wrong. He was very charming, and in the beginning I truly believe he was devoted to you. But he is the type of man that knows he attracts women; and once he has made his conquest he needs to find another."

"I spent so much time thinking I would have made a good wife for him. I was just kidding myself. I invested so much time, emotion, and effort into making the relationship work. I have to tell you—I will not do it again! This time I will not be the pursuer, but rather the pursued. Next time—ha! As IF!"

"Clarinda—how quickly you forget. I think you are already being chased." Fran raised her eyebrows at her friend. "I think that strapping Scotsman is already in the hunt for you."

"Yeah—right!" Clarinda guffawed. "He is certainly not interested in the likes of me. His latest girlfriend was almost half his age. I am too old and used up for him." She stood up firmly and placed her hands on her hips. "So, on that note, I am going to clean up the kitchen and wash the dishes."

"OK—you've won. You know the best way to win an argument with me is to threaten manual labor. I will come and watch, so at least you will have some company."

The two of them resumed their earlier reminiscent conversation. Fran caught Clarinda up on the welfare of most of their mutual friends, and they shared just general girlie silliness. They didn't realize the time until Fran yawned. "I think I need to get some more sleep to adjust to this time zone. I'm spent. See you tomorrow." She trundled off to seek the warmth and fluffy coziness of her goose down comforter.

"Good night, Fran. Oh, and if I didn't say it a hundred times earlier, thanks for coming to visit me. This has meant the world to me."

"You are SO welcome. It is wonderful to see Scotland. It is lovely for as much as I have yet to see. See you tomorrow and you can show me more." Fran yawned again, waved to her friend and plodded up the stairs.

Clarinda heard the door to Fran's room close. Once she knew her friend was down for the count she reopened and reread the letter David had written to her.

Clarinda spoke directly to the piece of paper. "You are a worthless human being. I gave you everything you ever wanted, and what did I get? You cheated on me, fired me, and humiliated me in the lobby of your pretentious building. I hope you are holding your breath until I call—at least I will know you will die a horrible death."

She couldn't help it. Her words were harsh but her heart was aching. Her face began getting warm, and try as she might, she couldn't hold back the tears. She curled up on the couch and wept. Sobs racked her until she couldn't breathe. She finally stopped when she ran out of energy. She had let her tears cleanse the sting from the salted wound David had cleaved. He was thousand of miles away, but she felt as if he had personally tried to squeeze the agony out of her heart with his own hands. He had no right to intrude into her life! She was starting over, and didn't need or deserve his half-hearted attempt to 'make nice'. Swine!

As her tears subsided, they were replaced with dignified resolve. She was better off without him, and she was making a new life in Scotland, and she was happy here. She may not ever find the love she had with David, but she also could do without the hurt and grief when the relationship ended—as they always do. No, she was not going to call him. David Kline was dead to her and had no place in her life any longer. Once she felt better about herself, and realized sometimes a good cry can purge toxic emotions, she too decided to catch some sleep. The next days would be busy ones with lots of cooking and sight-seeing. She needed to be well rested to be a good Julie McCoy.

chapter 15
the big feed

On Wednesday Fran and Clarinda took the train to Edinburgh so Fran could see the Castle and do some shopping. They enjoyed a wonderful lunch at The Witchery and caught the 4:07 train back to Inverwick. The next day was Thanksgiving and Clarinda needed to make sure everything was ready and in order for her guests. Thanksgiving was an exhausting day, all the cooking and once the tryptophan kicked in, she dreaded KP. She had always been able pawn off the clean-up to her family, but with guests, she knew she would have to shoulder the task herself. She wanted to make her famous Pumpkin Pecan Pie in advance so it was one less thing to do. As she pulled into the drive she tried to solicit Fran's assistance, "Wanna help?"

Fran looked at her as if she had been recruited into the Black Watch Regimental Army. "Help? I can cry for 'help' if you need it. As for assistance, I think you are doing a fine job without me. I don't want my influence to screw something up."

Clarinda smiled at her friend. Just Fran's company was enough to lift the glazed-over feeling she had this morning from her 'good cry' of the night before. Fran suspected Clarinda kept up a good front in front of her, but when she was alone, Fran knew her friend well enough to know Clarinda had purged her heart of the pain David's letter had brought.

"Clarinda, there is nothing I can say to make you feel better, but at least I can keep the whisky coming so we loose our inhibitions and you might reveal your thoughts to me."

"Fran, I appreciate that—I really do. But I have already tried to exorcise my psyche of him. I am sure you understand the cleansing effect of tears."

"I do my friend, but sometime tears shed alone do not have as much of a healing effect as those shed with a friend offering a comforting shoulder, a strong hand, and a soft stuffed animal."

Fran pulled a floppy plush dog from the paper bag she had been hiding at her feet.

"Oh—I love him—he is sooooo cute," Clarinda cooed. "You know I love these things. Thank you so much for my new cuddly friend."

"What will you call him, 'Alistair'?" she winked.

"You may never know—but I can assure you he will rule the kingdom of my bedroom." They both giggled.

OK, now back to my pie making. Where is that recipe?

Perfect Pumpkin Pecan Pie
From the kitchen of Clarinda Tetrick

3 Eggs, slightly beaten
1 c. Pumpkin
1 c. Sugar
½ c. Maple Syrup (or Dark Corn Syrup/Molasses if REAL Maple Syrup is not handy)
1 Tsp. of Vanilla
½ Tsp. Ground Cinnamon
¼ Tsp. Salt
1 Unbaked 9" Pastry Shell
1 c. Chopped Pecans

> *Combine eggs, pumpkin, sugar, syrup, vanilla, cinnamon & salt until smooth. Pour into Pie Shell (adorn edge of pie crust with leaves or fork tine indentations). Top with the Chopped Pecans and Bake at 350° for about 40 minutes until a test knife pulls clean.*

Clarinda baked the desert, and then boiled the yams and potatoes, and peeled the pearl onions. Fran was the dutiful supervisor and sipped wine while Clarinda acted as her own sous chef. The onions stung her eyes, but nothing like the smart from David's correspondence. She was thankful at the end of the evening that she was completely exhausted. This meant a welcomed night of uninterrupted slumber—no dreams, no nightmares, and no tears—only renewing rest. Lord, she was glad Fran was here—it kept her mind off David's disturbing note; and who could ask for better company?

Thanksgiving Day she awoke early to get the pheasant in the oven and to finish the rest of the side dishes. It seemed odd not to watch the Macy's Thanksgiving Day Parade on the telly followed by the Detroit Lions and/or the Dallas Cowboys football games. Yet, sometimes traditions were meant to be broken. She decided most Europeans would not eat a large dinner in the middle of the day like many Americans, so Clarinda decided to have her guests come over about four o'clock and serve the bird about six thirty. She hoped since she would have so much time between waking and eating, she might even be able to sneak in a quick nap to energize for the long evening. Since Alistair was going to wear his clan tartan, she thought she might want to compliment his attire. The last thing she wanted to do was to dress like the Lees girl and attempt to match him like life-sized Barbie and Ken dolls, but she knew navy and black were continually appropriate, and those colors were plentiful in her closet.

Fran had already chosen her attire. She always chose some sort of black ensemble accessorized with something black, and then set the whole thing off with some black footwear. It sounds stark, but she was always able to avoid looking like a mortuary owner by her bright red lipstick and reflecting dark eyes. At about three o'clock she awoke from her nap to hear a ruckus happening downstairs. "What could be making that infernal noise?"

She ventured down the stairs to find her housemistress hammering a nail into the front door. "What in Sam Hill are you doing?" She asked with a bite of acid on her tongue from being roused so abruptly from her deep slumber.

"Look at the wreath I made from juniper clippings. This will not only be fragrant, but I hope it will last through Hogmanay. Here hold the hammer while I hang the thing." Clarinda stepped back to admire her handy work. Perfect—and it smells so wonderful! OK, back inside before we congeal where we stand."

They stepped back into the guest house the smell of the food made their stomachs' grumble. "How many hours 'til dinner?" Fran asked and looked at her watch. At this realization Clarinda burst into high-gear.

"I have so much to do, and so little time. Can you help me get organized? You seem to be dressed so if I give you some chores can you get them done while I go and change?" Fran numbly nodded and Clarinda showed her how she wanted the table arranged and to pour water and open wine bottles.

When Clarinda returned downstairs she was dressed in a simple white blouse and long black watch kilt she had purchased from Hector Russell in Edinburgh. She figured she didn't have any Clan to claim and navy and black were always fashionable. The Black Watch tartan seemed appropriate and universally appealing. She placed a strand of pearls around her neck and put her hair up in a simple, but elegant French twist. She looked stylish, not too ostentatious, and practical for final dinner preparations. As she came from her apartment, she neared the front door and the door-knocker uncannily sounded.

George Wallace was at her threshold, smiling, and thrusting a bottle of Talisker in front of her. "Happy Thanksgiving," he cheered. He looked to be about as happy as a five-year-old on Christmas. "I hope I am nae late."

Clarinda smiled. She was charmed by this wry elfish-looking man, and she couldn't be happier to see the joy in his eyes this simple dinner party had given him. "Oh no, you are not late! In fact, you are early, but come in anyway."

"Brilliant," he retorted, "put me to work. What can I do to help?"

"First, why don't you come in, let me take your coat, and I want to introduce you to my friend, Fran. She has traveled all the way from New York City and I have told her all about you."

A frown passed over George's face. "Only the good parts, right me lassie?" Then his somber look passed and he gave her a bright wink. "Is the Adam's widow here yet?" he inquired cheerily.

"No, not yet," Clarinda ushered George in through the door and into the foyer holding the whiskey and waiting for him to offer up his rain coat. "Actually, I am glad, so I have some time to get everything done before they arrive. You know Janet: if she sees something to do she will not hesitate to do it herself. Come into the kitchen where the action is." She gestured for George to take the lead.

"George Wallace, I would like you to meet my best friend, Fran." Fran held out her hand to welcome a handshake, but George gently raised it up and acting most debonair, gave her a graceful kiss on the back of hand while his eyes delivered a winking glimmer. "My dear, I am George Wallace. It is a pleasure to make yer acquaintance."

Fran smiled, tilted her head, charmed by the elderly gentleman. "Thank you kindly, sir. The pleasure is clearly all mine."

The two of them began a comfortable conversation of their worldly visits, the wonders of the Big Apple, and the ordeals of travel. Fran continued to mildly assist in the pre-dinner preparations and George aided without being told as if both of their hands were directed by some sort of outer forces. Clarinda continued to bustle about the house to make sure all the details were considered.

The door-knocker thudded again and Clarinda rushed to the kitchen to shed her apron, wipe her hands, pat her hair, and check her lipstick in the mirror hall. Seeing her obvious jitters, Fran and George looked at each other and smiled. "So who is coming, the Maharaja, or what?" Fran teased.

"Och no!" George replied. "The newly available Alistair Campbell."

"Available?" Fran sounded credulous. "Really this is news from a few days ago."

"Ye have met the man, I guess?"

"Yes. Yes I have." Fran looked at her hands so George would not see her blush.

"I guess ya' have by the look of ye. He is a brawny lad, no? I think his sister would like so see him settle down, but it seems he is not quite done lookin' at all the lasses in town. By the looks of our dear friend Clarinda, it seems she would like to have a go at him, too."

"I don't know about having 'a go', but I think she would like to be in contention before the final match is decided. She is a little bit gun-shy, so she is really not pouring on the charm in her standard fashion. You might have heard about the troubles she had with her past boyfriend?"

"Well, not from the source, no; but I understand she is reeling from a bad time of it. Shame. She is so lovely, and I am sure she did no deserve the pain she got. Perhaps she is not trying so hard because she might actually care for this one?"

"Perhaps." Fran smiled, but was careful not to be too encouraging. She didn't want her friend to be considered too 'easy'. After all, Alistair was a fine specimen, but Fran was sure the line of conquered women was long, and didn't want her friend to end up being just one more of the rank-and-file that she imagined to be lined up outside his bedroom door.

"Janet, so nice to see you, please come in." When they heard Clarinda's welcoming comments coming from the foyer, they almost tripped over each other in their rush to come and greet the new guests. Fran let George have the lead — she didn't want to trip him and give him a broken hip, and besides he was spryly swift for a man of his age. Given she was in her highest heels; and he barely topped five-foot-seven, she could easily view the scene over his semi-bald head.

"Here let me take your shawl," Clarinda guessed. Janet wasn't falling for it.

"Ya' silly girl, I come here everyday and ya' have yet to take me shawl; I ken where I'm gang."

Clarinda was not going to be out done. "Janet, this is not any other day. You are my guest so please let me treat you as one." Janet acquiesced to this truth and allowed Clarinda to welcome her quests properly. Janet released her shawl, walked in and took a fragrant inhale. "I have no had Thanksgiving before, but by the aroma of it, I think I will enjoy it very much." She spied George and Fran blocking the kitchen and rushed over to make her greetings.

"Hullo, Clarinda." Alistair was polite, calm and beyond stunning as he made his way through the doorway. "I hope ya' will find this wine suitable for the meal."

"Thank you!" Clarinda was stunned and stared at the remarkable man standing on her porch. He was wearing his Campbell kilt again, but this time, he wore a light, solid black, mock-neck sweater. Clarinda thought his would be the very same David might wear, and instantly wiped the thought from her mind.

"Clarinda, are ya' feelin' alright tonight?" The phrase brought Clarinda back the current moment.

"Oh yes, I am fine. Thank you for the bottle of wine. This is perfect and so thoughtful," she gushed. "Please come in and get out of the cold."

When Fran saw Alistair in his kilt, she nearly choked again.

Astonished at his appearance once more—she couldn't understand how everyone in this town could be so ordinary and yet this man was so outstanding? She had never seen any man wear a kilt so comfortably. Sure, she had seen the pipers in Edinburgh dressed for the tourists, but this man was dressed only for himself and wore his heritage with comfort and ease. As he stepped into the house, Fran noticed his shiny black laced shoes, black socks and a hint of tartan coming from the tops of his socks. His sporran was trimmed with some sort of fur, and the silver chain that disappeared around his waist sparkled.

"Thank you for wearing your kilt, again," Clarinda blurted out without realizing what she had said. Once she had, she fell silent and could only smile. It seemed the more she saw of this man the more her refined and distant persona eroded which was designed to protect her from moments such as these.

"Me pleasure, Clarinda." His voice sounded as if he was purring, or was it just her imagination? "I am proud to be a Scot, and I am proud to be a Campbell. But since I am wearing it in the cold, I think I would forfeit some of my family pride to come into the warmth of yer guest house. Thank ye." He took a long step forward and slid by Clarinda who seemed to be anchored in cement. He made his way into the foyer and Fran was extending her hand to be greeted once again.

"I am Clarinda's friend, Fran. We met at your mother's house last Monday? It is wonderful to see you again." Not sure if every man in Scotland greeted women with a kiss on the back of the hand, she offered hers at an ambiguous angle, so Alistair's greeting could go either way.

"Yes, cheers. Nice to see ya' again." He took her hand and gave it a firm shake. "I hope ya' have been enjoying our wee country?"

"Yes—I have. Edinburgh was wonderful! I hope you don't find me tactless, but I must say I have not found any man in a kilt as dashing as you."

"I dinnae find ya' rude, and I thank ya' for the notice of our Scottish style. I am proud to wear the highland dress, nae only is it comfortable, but stylish, no?" He somewhat looked at George for an answer to the question.

By this time Clarinda had returned to the kitchen and was ensuring everyone had their proper beverages. They continued to converse until dinner was ready. Clarinda commandeered everyone to the table.

"Are there assigned places?" Janet asked.

At this point Clarinda realized there was a kink in her plan. She had not even considered this small, but very important detail. "No, but I would appreciate it if you would allow me to sit here, near the kitchen, and Clarinda grasped the back of the chair at the side of the table closest to the kitchen.

"George, why don't ya' take one end, and Alistair, ya' take the other," Janet suggested.

"I'll sit here, if that is OK." Fran took the seat between her friend and George, and Janet filled in taking the last seat on the far side of the table, alone, but between her brother and George at either end.

Clarinda continued to stand behind her chair. Once everyone had quieted, she started to speak. "I want to thank you all, my closest friends, for joining me to enjoy this special holiday. I realize this is an occasion not openly recognized by the peoples of the UK. In fact, I am sure you realize it is a holiday which might be considered an offense to some of your countrymen. Because of this, I want to thank you all for coming. This is my blessing at Thanksgiving. I want to thank you all for your friendship, help, support and belief that I can make a success of this place." She paused, looked up and swept her arms open. "A welcoming guest house so gainful it can support not only me, but my loyal staff." She beamed at Janet. Janet returned the smile, then looked down and smiled at her plate.

Clarinda then looked at Fran and asked if she would like to share any blessings. Fran was thankful for her health, her friends and her family, whom she admitted to missing terribly; but was thankful to be able to visit her friend in Scotland, and to make new friends.

George went next and was thankful for his health, and that he was still able to live each day to the fullest. There was a lull, and Alistair and Janet looked at each other trying to decide who should go next. Janet opened her mouth to speak, but Alistair was already beginning. "I want to thank Clarinda for havin' me and me sister over to enjoy this fine celebration. I also want to thank Clarinda for givin' me sister a new look on life—I have no seen her this happy in a long time. I also want to thank God for me health and to thank me sister for helpin' me get it back."

There was a somber quiet about the room. Janet broke the spell with a few softly spoken words. "I want to thank God for giving me brother back to me. Amen." The other four responded in unison, "Amen."

Clarinda didn't know what to say or what to do. The moment seemed so serious. She was flattered her guests were honoring her holiday by offering true thanks for their blessings, but Thanksgiving was meant to be a joyous holiday, not depressing. She was glad George broke the silence. "I hope we are no gang to gawk at this wonderful food all night. I dinnae ken if the rest of ya' are hungry, but I am!"

"Yes!" Clarinda chimed. "Let's dig in. Cheers." She raised her glass to toast her guests.

"Cheers," Fan echoed.

"Sláinte mhath," replied George, Janet and Alistair.

This brought the smiles to everyone's faces and the food was merrily passed around the table. Janet asked about the ingredients on several dishes and Fran decided next year she would break with tradition and have a pheasant instead of the turkey because it was so tasty. Wine was poured and drank, and toasts of good cheer were offered time and again. Clarinda was delighted to see her guests happy and enjoying themselves. Even the room seemed to emit a warm golden glow of gaiety.

Alistair turned and leaned, and motioned for Clarinda to come closer so he could whisper something in her ear.

"I am glad I came, thank ye for thinkin' of including me sister and me in yer plans. I especially like yer choice of music." His smile was brilliant and lit up his face. Clarinda had to listen intently to hear what she had placed in the disc player. She realized the Peatbog Faeries were supplying the background ambiance to the festivities. "If ya' ever get to Skye, ya' should try to go and see them play. Their piper is good, no?"

Clarinda smiled and nodded her head. "Thank you for coming. I am glad that I could share one of my American traditions with you and your sister. I truly treasure her hard work, dedication, and friendship. I don't know what I would do without her."

"As I said in me blessin', it is ye that deserves the credit. Before ya' gave her some pride in herself, she was becoming an old spinster before me very eyes. She was becoming too set in her ways and dinnae want to look outside her small world and embrace life. Now she comes here, she is out and about town to stock the pantry, and she couldn't be happier. Look at the rose on her cheek—and it is not all from the wine." They both glanced at Janet and she spied them doing so.

"What are ya' two up to? I hope yer are no schemin' up something.'" She lifted her glass to take another sip of wine to hide her smirk.

Alistair and Clarinda looked at each other and shrugged their shoulders and snickered. "Och, ya' never know," Alistair confessed. This brought another round of chuckles about the table.

The conversation began to quiet and Clarinda could see her guests were starting to feel the effects of full stomachs of food and wine; she began to clear the dishes into the kitchen. "Why don't you all move into the parlor and I will bring in some desert and tea. I have made a wonderful Pumpkin Pecan Pie and I have fresh tea ready to pour. I think the furniture in the parlor will be more accommodating to our expanding figures."

Her guests agreed and moved into the parlor and Clarinda took another round of dishes to the kitchen. As she turned to ~~return to~~ retrieve another supply she was surprised to find Alistair holding the very same. "I thought I would help ya'. I would much rather stretch my legs than to go and sit some more."

"Great." Clarinda felt utterly stupid for that remark. He was Scotland's version of a Greco statue and all she could say was 'great'.

"I really appreciate it. I don't mind the preparation, but the clean-up is never very fun. Thank the Lord for the modern conveniences of dishwashers. Load and go."

"Why don't ya' load the miracle machine and I will bring the rest of the crockery in for ya'." And with that statement he was off to fetch another set of dirty dishes.

Because Alistair did not join them in the parlor, Janet could not keep the curiosity from getting the better of her. She had to see what was brewing in the kitchen. Clarinda was equally surprised by her entrance. "Did my brother happen to get lost? It is no like him to venture into a kitchen when it is clear help is needed." When Alistair appeared with the next armload of dishes from the dining room, it was had to tell who was more surprised. Janet, Clarinda, or Alistair. Clarinda was hoping to get some time alone with Alistair, so she acted quickly to try to clear the scene.

"Janet, I am so glad you came. I hate to abandon my guests like that. Would you be a love and take the pie and tea into the parlor?" With that she loaded Janet up with a tray of the tea, cups, saucers, dessert plates, napkins and the pie. *That ought to keep them busy for a few moments*, she thought. Now she would have time to get her business in the kitchen fulfilled.

Back in the kitchen, Alistair was sitting on the table swinging his legs, his hands tucked under his legs looking very boyish. "I am sorry, but I dinnae want to break any of it and I have to say I am no the best organizer when it comes to these things. I thought it best if I let ya' handle the delicate procedures. I will keep ya' company, though."

Clarinda was sorry she had to turn away from him to continue working in the sink.

"I heard from the MacDonnell's and they would be willing to let me bring a friend to go ridin' their horses. They have several, but there are two that are gaited and a pleasure to ride. Would ya' like to join me sometime? I was thinkin' if the weather holds, we could go next week. The days are cool, but not too cold. Would ya' be free?"

Clarinda hadn't ridden a horse on almost ten years or more, but to be outside would be great and since her riding companion would be the fine mister Campbell, what red-blooded woman would pass up an invitation such as this? "I would be delighted. It sounds wonderful. How about Wednesday, is that enough notice? Do I need to bring anything?"

"No, I have taken care of everythin'. Just remember to wear boots since the mud in their paddock is terrific this time of year, and gloves so yer hands to stay warm. I will knock ya' up around nine thirty or so on Wednesday."

"I think our job is done for now; why don't we go and rejoin the others. I think George would like for me to open his whisky. Let's not disappoint him." Clarinda grabbed the bottle of Talisker, some sifter glasses and went into the parlor. She found George, Janet and Fran in a debate about which was rougher, American football or rugby. It seemed the two-against-one offense was winning although Fran was offering some good points to help her side of the debate.

"I see you all have enjoyed the pie, but I thought we should open your bottle; what do you say George?"

George instantly perked right up when he heard the mention of whisky. "Of course, let's have a wee dram to settle the stomach."

"Settling the stomach is not what I usually associate with

hard liquor, but if you insist." It was clear Fran enjoyed toying with the senior Wallace; he was just as pleased to become her fair verbal opponent.

Clarinda took a seat on the settee next to her friend and prepared a slice of pie and handed it to Alistair. "I am afraid it is not as warm as it was, but I hope you will like this. It is a great way to spice up the blandness of pumpkin pie and tone down the sweetness of pecan. A perfect union.

"Well, I have searched for a perfect union, so I guess I have to give this a try to understand what it would be like." Alistair directed this last comment to his sister, and Janet shook her napkin and huffed.

"I am sure ya' wouldn't see the perfect union, if it were to hit ya' head on," she muttered under her breath.

George in the meantime poured some drams of whisky and was raising his sifter to share a toast. "May the best ye've ever seen, be the worst ye'll ever see, May a moose ne'er leave yer girnal, wi' a tear drap in his e'e, May ye aye keep hale an' he'rty, till ye're auld eneuch tae dee, May ye aye be jist as happy, as we wish ye aye tae be."

"Here, here," replied Fran, not sure of what was just said, but she understood the basic gist of it. She was hoping it would certainly be true and took an enthusiastic sip of the amber-colored liquor.

"Easy me lass," George cautioned. "This is for sippin' so it will last. At yer rate ya' will be smeekit in no time. Are ye' wantin' me to take advantage of ye?"

While the banter continued Alistair needed some quiet time and decided to go into the kitchen and add some ice to his dram. As he was there he spied an envelope on the kitchen table that looked out of place. The return address was from Masters and Kline in New York City, but the address was a simple handwritten word: Clarinda. He spied the enclosed note was almost out of the envelope and also handwritten. Alistair was not one to snoop, but he was curious to know if

Clarinda was corresponding with her previous lover in New York. He was beginning to take an interest in her, but he was not going to attempt to steal away another man's lady. He opened the letter, read the contents, and quickly replaced it as he had found it. He could hear footsteps coming and went to the icebox to get some ice for his drink.

Clarinda cleared the dessert dishes and started toward the kitchen to start a new load in the washer. As she entered she was surprised to find Alistair in her refrigerator. She hadn't noticed him leave the parlor. "I am gettin' some ice for me dram," he explained but he seemed to harbor more guilt than just absconding some ice.

"That's fine. Ice is only frozen water, help yourself." She wanted to know what he was up to.

"Do ya' need help?" he offered. Now she really knew something was strange. Earlier he had stated he was not keen for this sort of thing, and now he was suggesting his assistance. Very odd.

"No, I am fine. I wanted to empty the last load, and start another but actually I came in here to get a bit of peace and quiet. I love to have company so don't get me wrong; but sometimes a breather is good. You know?"

"Aye, I ken. The same goes for me. I guess I needed a break too. I like yer friend; she is a fiery thing, but she and George were beginning to wear me out. I can't keep up with that type of banter."

There was a peaceful silence and Alistair liked the fact he could spend time with this woman, enjoy each other's company, but not have to talk. He felt the timing was right for him to get something straight with this woman, so he knew where he stood.

"Clarinda."

"Yes."

"I need to ask ya' somethin'. Are ya' planning on going' back to America?"

"No, why would ya' ask that?"

"Dunno. I guess I wondered if ya' missed yer man, and ya' might go back to him."

"Alistair," Clarinda turned and walked up to him; her hands on her hips. She was tall herself and boosted by her simple pumps, but even as she stood close he was still a good four inches taller. She turned her face up to him and looked solidly into his eyes. He noticed her lips were glossy and soft and at the perfect angle for an easy kiss. He wiped that thought out of his mind—he needed to focus on what she was saying.

"I want to make something perfectly plain. I am not going back to New York, I am quite happy here. I also have absolutely no desire nor inclination to ever speak to, listen to, or see David Kline, ever again. That is a closed chapter in my life. Are we clear?"

It seemed to Alistair he had hit a nerve. He couldn't admit he had peeked at the letter, but until this response, he didn't know if she would somehow have the same feelings he was beginning to feel for her.

"I think I am clear, but I want to ask ya' one more question to be certain."

Clarinda nodded for him to proceed.

"So the way I see it, this David won't mind if I do this."

Clarinda was about to say "do what", but in the span of a second, Alistair bent over, moved his arm behind her back and tenderly kissed her lips. Clarinda felt herself become weak as her strong legs instantly became the consistency of crème brulee. In response, Alistair tightened his embrace. She was awestruck, continued to look into his eyes and didn't say anything but hoped he might do it again.

Alistair was not about to let this moment pass. It was too perfect. Here was this fascinating woman, in his arms. She was alive and exciting. Her eyes brilliant with mounting passion. Her lips were parted as he had left them. They had a smoky and sweet taste. He bent to kiss her again.

Clarinda felt his tongue search for hers. His lips were soft, but his kiss was demanding and urgent. It was as if he needed to release all his desire with just this one kiss. She opened up to him and then slowly pulled away. He pulled her in tight again, and his kiss was more powerful and his embrace stronger. Clarinda was melting. She had felt passion before but nothing as unbridled. She was in the arms of a powerful man, one who was aware of his masculinity and was not afraid of its rule. He was gentle but forceful, soft yet unyielding. Clarinda was captivated by his wild rawness and felt his hardness bore into her thigh. He was as enflamed with their current ardor as she. And damn, he smelled so good!

Alistair didn't want to crush this indescribable woman, but he was unable to control his desire. He had wanted her from the first time they spoke, and now she was in his arms and yielding to his desire. It was too much for him to take, and his body was speaking for some needed release. He couldn't stop but if he didn't try, it was not going to be pretty. He gently pulled away and lessened his embrace. As he did so, Clarinda lightly bit his bottom lip. A low moan of longing came from the very core of his being. They stood and looked at each other for some time. Neither one wanting to speak for fear they might break the spell, and shatter the bubble of warmth and wonder they were floating within.

"Alistair," Clarinda whispered. "I didn't know."

"I know." He nodded.

The precious moment ended when George wandered into the kitchen. "Clarinda? Clarinda? Where are ya' me love?"

"Hey there, George," said Clarinda hazily. She continued to hold Alistair's hands; she just couldn't bring herself to break contact with him, no matter who might see.

"Oh, there ya' are." George seemed a bit surprised, but not overly so. "I need to be on me way, but I wanted to bid ya' a good night. Thank ya' again for yer wonderful hospitality. I will join ya' for Thanksgiving anytime!"

Clarinda finally stepped away from Alistair and turned to give her dear friend a hug goodnight. "My pleasure. I am so glad you were willing to come. I hope my friend Fran did not talk your ear off."

"Och no!" I think I am fancyin' to marry the lass. She is a bonnie quine!"

Janet and Fran then entered the kitchen. "Now ya' are just haverin'" Janet retorted. George waved her off and smiled. "I too, need to be aff. Alistair, ya' can stay with the lasses, George here has offered to take me home." George winked at Alistair. The younger man smiled and winked back. He was glad to see his sister willing to let a man escort her home. It was part of her new renaissance.

George Wallace was harmless, but he could see the older man liked Janet's company. It was good for both of them. Clarinda had produced Janet's shawl and the couple waved goodnight and slipped into the sodium light of the yard to get into George's car.

"Well, I am going to bed. I know we didn't have turkey but I feel like I have just downed a full bottle of tryptophan. Good night." Fran waved and it seemed she would barely have the energy to make it up the flight of stairs. After all, she knew there was something cooking in the kitchen and she didn't want to spoil it by being just another cook. She was bone weary, and wanted to have a good night's sleep.

The couple was once again alone. "Okay, now where were we?" Clarinda toyed. She was still reeling from Alistair's kiss and wanted to resume the fervor.

Alistair, too, wanted to take advantage of their privacy, but he didn't want to take advantage of this woman. He knew if he continued to kiss her, he would want to make things further and he didn't think he had the discipline to stop himself. He knew she had felt his growing desire and where it would lead. She was something to be treasured and he wanted to savor every wanton moment. "I think I need to say good night too, Clarinda."

Clarinda was crushed by his declaration of his eminent departure. "I'm sorry. Have I done something to offend you?" She often felt she was separated by the same language with these Scots. They spoke English, sort of, but their styles and customs were so different.

"Och no lass, on the contrary. I have enjoyed yer meal, yer home, and especially yer hospitality. But I ken I need to use some reserve and not burden meself on ya' any longer." He thought the statement sounded very grand and gentlemanly.

What a load of crap! Clarinda thought. *I know men and they never leave when there is something worth staying for.* "Well, I am glad you have enjoyed yourself, but I guess I thought a man of your age could stay up later than ten o'clock, but I guess you are running with the older crowd now." *This ought to set him straight!* she thought.

"Clarinda, I don't want to be rude, but I really must be going. Again, it is nothing to do with ya'. I would love to stay, but I know it would no be proper. After all, everyone in town knows yer a single woman, and I, a single man. But often these simplicities are forgotten when the woman is an American and the man a Scot. I don't want people to think ill of ya'."

What you mean, is they will not to think ill of you. Clarinda had a dialogue going in her head. *After you have been seeing a much younger woman it could harm the reputation to be associated with a woman your own age. It would be scandal for Alistair the Conqueror.*

What she actually said was: "Right, I appreciate your consideration for my reputation, but I think at my age, there is really not any need to behave so guarded. After all, there is no secret I have had previous lovers so I am not a young debutant flower who needs have her proper social engagements arranged."

"Clarinda, I can tell by the tone of yer voice I have upset ya' in some manner. I guess ya' think I do not desire ya', and for that ya' assume it is because of yer age which makes ya' ashamed. Nothing could be further from the truth. I would very much like to stay here and continue to get to know ya' better, but that is not the way I want to our relationship to go. I want to know more about ye—the real ya'." He poked her upper chest with his finger. It was not taunting, but it did take her by surprise. "And as for our age, I think it is better to act it rather than snoggin' like a couple of teenagers." All of this was a complete lie. He wanted to stay and fervently kiss the woman, but he was glad his sense of reason was winning over his preternatural drive.

"Alright then." She knew she had lost this argument and he was indeed going to make his leave. She needed to salvage the evening so the last memories of the night were not of arguing in her kitchen. "You are right. Thank you so much for coming; and for helping me in the kitchen. I am sorry for my harsh words. I guess I still think the worst when I sense rejection, even if it doesn't exist. On a happier note—I can't wait to go riding on Wednesday. Give me a ring if you think of something I need to prepare."

"Good night Clarinda." He gave her a quick peck on the lips, but didn't get close enough for her to touch him. He stepped back to see her with her eyes closed, as if in a trance not wanting to let the brief moment dissolve.

At last she opened her eyes. He had already stepped out the door into the dim lit night and made his way to his lorry. She watched his kilt sway as he walked and then waved as he drove away. She turned out the lights, and walked to her small apartment, disrobing as she went. She was in a reverie even though she was fully awake, and didn't want it to stop because of sleep. She crawled into her bed and lay there. Her mind replayed the whole night over and over again, but it seemed her interlude with Alistair in the kitchen was on the short loop.

Alistair was thankful for the coldness of the night. It helped to cool his blood and bring his heart rate back to normal. He hoped he had not terribly offended Clarinda, but he needed to leave her house tonight before he lost control of his gentlemanly composure. Lord, that woman was stimulating! She was bright, independent, smart, and alluring. The combination was intoxicating and he was beginning to understand the virtues of women his own age. They didn't need to be told things about themselves; they already knew these facts. They were self-assured and comfortable with their own sensuality. They welcomed desire, and didn't fear it. Alistair made the quick drive to his small cottage. When he walked inside, he dropped his kilt, and then took off his shirt and walked into his bedroom. He lay in bed a while and reflected about the evening. He recalled what it was like to hold a woman—not a girl, but a real woman—in his arms. He recollected how Clarinda tasted and how she smelled. He could almost feel her lips upon his and her tongue engaged with his. As his thoughts continued to ruminate in his head, he found his hand moving down his torso near his groin with a mission to alleviate the pent up passion he so desperately needed to release. It had been a long time since he had been with a woman, but he was a man after all, and sometimes matters needed to be taken into his own hands. Once tired, he slept peacefully, and dreamed about riding horses with Clarinda by his side over the heathery moors.

chapter 16
taken for a ride

On Sunday, Fran need to catch her plane back to the States so Clarinda joined on her train ride back to Glasgow. It seemed the time had gone by so fast. Of course, Fran talked most of the time. As they rode she verbally relived her experiences in the Highlands. She recanted the sights they saw, the people she had met and of course the best shops where she had surrendered her legal tender. Clarinda was going to miss the liveliness of her friend. Her guest house would seem empty without the energy of her most vivacious guest to date.

By the time the train pulled into Glasgow's Queen Street Station, Fran was somber. She knew she would have to say her good-byes and they were very hard. Clarinda helped her maneuver her bags to the taxi line, they had a tearful good-bye hug and Fran sped away to the airport. Clarinda decided to do some shopping while she was in the city. Christmas was only a short month away, and she needed to be able to have time to send packages to Aunt Jilly and Uncle Rupert. Glasgow was getting into the seasonal spirit and Buchanan Street was decorated with lights, wreaths and banners. Shoppers were bustling to and fro and the chill in the air put Clarinda in the holiday spirit. She got some ideas from the merchants and made a few purchases, and got the 5:23 train back to Inverwick. When she got home, the guest house was cold and dark inside. This was the first time since she had come to Scotland she truly felt alone and lonely.

"No time for self pity, Tetrick," she told herself and went about the house to start a fire and turn on the lights. She picked up her cross stitch to keep her hands and mind occupied. She was working on a Thistle—the Flower of Scotland, to be used for a coaster. The next couple of days she was in a fog. She missed Fran and her effervescent conversation.

Janet was also not in town; she was purchasing the food for Hogmanay in Glasgow. And oddly enough she hadn't been called upon by George either. Most of all, she wondered if Alistair would pay her a visit. Not that she would have been prepared. Her daily uniform consisted of jeans and a Fair Isle sweater over a turtleneck. She didn't have guests yet, so she didn't feel she needed to dress for them. She passed her days reviewing the menu, making some minor changes and checking her room bookings. She planned to be open for the Christmas holidays when guests would be coming to town to visit relatives. It was a good way to get some money coming in and rev the kitchen into high gear. It appeared she was almost going to be full. Just one room remained vacant for Christmas Eve, pretty good for just opening and not really advertising.

Wednesday finally came and the day appeared to be glorious. The air was cool and crisp, the sky was clear blue with a few puffy clouds. Perfect for riding. Clarinda wore jeans and the old pair of Ariats she wore when she rode in Vermont. She put her hair in a pony tail and pulled on an Aran sweater, gathered her gloves and she was set. She performed some household chores while waiting for Alistair to arrive. Just before nine, the phone rang. Clarinda hoped it wasn't Alistair calling to cancel. She picked up the receiver and greeted the caller.

"Thank you for calling The Heather and Thyme Guest House. How may I help you?" There was a long pause and still no reply. Clarinda tried again to engage the caller. "Hello, may I help you?" Clarinda could hear slight breathing on the line, but still there was no reply. Her voice was firm, "You have called the Heather and Thyme Guest House. How may I assist you?" Still there was no answer. She decided not to let this go any further and allow this caller to continue to be so secretive at her expense. "I am sorry, but I think you may have reached a wrong number," and promptly hung up. "That was strange," she thought aloud.

The door knocker sounded the very next moment. The door was open but as she turned she saw Alistair waiting in her doorway. "Hi there! I am so glad you didn't cancel on me."

"I would no do that! The day is bonnie, no? It should be fine for a good ride. If yer ready, we can go?" He gestured to his lorry idling in the drive. Clarinda grabbed her gloves, and locked the door and walked to the vehicle.

Alistair got the door for her. She was impressed by his chivalrous manners. "Thank you."

"Ye are most welcome." He got in the drivers seat, put the lorry in gear and pulled out of the drive. "So who was on the phone? I don't typically pry, but ya' said it was strange. I hope it was no bad news?"

"Strange, but I don't know who it was. I guess it was just a crank caller. Funny they didn't speak, but I could hear someone on the line and they didn't say they had the wrong number. Just odd."

Alistair nodded and then began to discuss his plans for their ride. He described the two steeds, their quirks and attributes. He talked about the trails they planned to take. It all sounded wonderful to Clarinda. When they arrived at the MacDonnell's farm it seemed no one was home. Clarinda mentioned this fact to Alistair. She wanted to make sure they weren't trespassing and it was alright with their owners that their horses were about to be ridden. Alistair assured her even though the MacDonnell's were not around, he had already made these arrangements and they were perfectly happy to have their horses exercised even if they were not present. Alistair walked into the stables and introduced Clarinda to Pewter and Toby. These horses were clearly named for their appearances. Clarinda was to ride Pewter, a lovely dappled gray mare who was on in years. She was solid, not too tall, with wonderful soft eyes and looked to be a safe and compliant mount. 'Toby' was named after Tobermory, the whisky from the Isle of Mull. He was a bright sorrel gelding with a mischievous look. Alistair explained he was young and needed to be ridden to gain experience and discipline. They groomed the horses, saddled and bridled them up, and were on their way. They started out on the dirt road by the farm, but soon Alistair took them onto paths in open fields.

Clarinda was having the time of her life! This was like the dream she had only a few months ago. Pewter was a willing mare and was a good sport and would willingly gallop or canter as long as Toby was in the lead. Alistair was not only riding Toby, but also treating the excursion as a training session. The horse had shied at rocks and trees, but Alistair held him to the course so the colt would learn and become more docile. Clarinda couldn't believe an hour went by when Alistair came upon a lone tree in the middle of the heathery field and suggested they take a break. Clarinda was thoroughly enjoying herself, but she was glad for the respite. Her legs were not in top riding condition and as she dismounted she felt muscles she forgot she owned complain. Her legs were like rubber. Alistair untied a saddlebag and a blanket which he spread out and invited Clarinda to sit. She couldn't be happier to oblige his request. He knelt down next to her and unpacked the saddlebag. He had stored some English Stilton cheese, cheddar from Orkney, and lastly some local goat cheese. Next he produced a small loaf of bread and come crackers. Finally came a bottle of wine and two plastic wine glasses.

"I know this ~~is~~ fare is more French in nature, but it travels well."

Clarinda was impressed by Alistair's thoughtfulness to bring some lunch and remarked her appreciation.

"When I said I would take care of the rest, did ya' no believe me?"

She smiled at him and prepared some bread and cheese morsels for ~~both of~~ them. The horses grazed nearby as they sat under the tree, drank some wine, ate some bread and cheese, and let the day pass by lazily.

"Thank you Alistair, for asking me to join you. I am having a really great time."

"The pleasure is mine, I assure ya'. I dinnae like to ride alone. First it is no safe, but also if I bring a lunch like this, I am too pissed to ride home if I drink the whole bottle meself. I am glad ya' could come so I could show ya' some of the lovely countryside in our wee town."

"I hope those are not the only reasons. I would like to think that present company might be considered."

Alistair blushed. She was right. He enjoyed spending time like this with her. This excursion was equally as fun for him. She was an excellent rider, as he had earlier surmised by looking at the strength of her legs. She was calm with the horses. He had learned one can tell a lot about a person based on the way horses and other animals respond to them. Mean and cruel people brought about fear. Nervous and flighty actions caused them to be skittish. It took a firm, but calm hand to gain the respect of an animal with such a temperament. His clients always proved to be a good barometer of personal character. He liked this woman, fine, but he couldn't give into his heart or his desires. He knew his was a life destined to live in solitude. It has served him well so far, and he was not about to change his ways. It could be too risky. Better to not fall in love than to suffer a broken heart. He had seen what love could do. His sister gave her heart to a man and he died. She was devastated and never loved again. It was clear to him Janet's love for a man ceased when Richard died. Alistair didn't want to be morbid, but he knew if he gave his heart to someone and they left him, it would be more than he could bear. However when he looked into Clarinda's gentle blue eyes, he felt something for this woman. He just had to make sure it didn't turn to love. She raised her eyebrows at him in a quizzical manner and he realized he hadn't answered her question.

"Aye, the present company is also welcomed. Ye are a fine rider and good with the horses." Alistair wanted to tell her that he liked to be with her, but he felt that could be too revealing. He had said too much at her house the week before. He wanted to establish a more neutral ground with this woman.

Clarinda wasn't going to let his coy behavior get the better of her. She was going to get to know her mysterious companion. What made him tick?

"Alistair, have you always lived in Inverwick? It seems this town is rather small for a man who seems to possess a worldly education. I have given you a glimpse of my sordid life, how about you tell me a little about yours?"

Once Clarinda asked the simple question she regretted it. Alistair's face went very dark. She had ruined the afternoon by prying.

"Sorry I asked. I didn't want to offend you. I guess I have hit upon a sore subject. Forget I said anything."

Alistair shook his head. "It is no that. I just have a hard time reliving me past. Some of it was good, but some if it was horrible. I try to live me life in the present and not dwell on sad histories. They can be filled with ghosts that are better off not disturbing."

He left it at that and Clarinda acknowledged she was not going to get much more from him. She picked up the wine and refilled their glasses. She took a sip and let the silence heal the moment.

Alistair began to speak again. "I will tell ya' some. I was the pride and joy of me parents. Me Da was delighted when me Ma birthed him a son. Me sister Janet was happy to have a living doll to fuss over. As ya' can see, she has no stopped doin' that!

"Our lives were happy and I thrived under me parents' and sisters watchful eyes. Me Da took me fishin' and I learned the ways of the forest and how to ride horses and all the typical things one learns in a rural Scottish town. Janet grew up and went to university in Edinburgh. She worked her way through school. When it came my turn, I went to Aberdeen and followed her example. I worked on fishing boats to get some money to pay for books and boardin'. It was hard work, but the money was good. After university, I got a job in finance."

Clarinda would have never guessed and her raised eyebrows made Alistair go back and explain.

"I guess we all had a good head for numbers. Janet worked in retail stores, but I found the banking business fascinatin'. I studied hard in school and I got a job working for the Royal Bank of Scotland in Aberdeen. I know ya' would never guess to look at me now, a lowly smithy, but I guess ya' could say I had a life changing experience a few years ago." Alistair paused to sample some bread and cheese. Clarinda didn't want him to stop with his life's history, so she remained quiet hoping he would continue. After a few moments he resumed but as he spoke, he didn't look at Clarinda. He kept is eyes down or looked to the horizon. Clarinda sensed what he was about to tell her was deeply revealing and it was easier for him to recount if it seemed he was speaking aloud, but not directed at anyone.

"I was doing quite well at the bank and I lived in a small flat with a few lads I had met at university. We would work during the day and live it up at night. Me friends were very popular with the lasses, so we always had a lady on our arm. Not that any of them were serious, it was more we were enjoyin' our youth and the freedom to live in the city. During the weekends we would play polo or go hunting. I guess I have always liked horses and me mate Duncan, had stables and several horses for playing or huntin'.

I was quite good at polo. I like the fast pace of the game, and it requires not only good horsemanship, but also good coordination. Our team was one of the best and we won several awards. In fact, there is a plaque at the polo club with me name on it for the most goals in a season — I won that in me thirties so I still had the skills of younger men."

"So what happened?" Clarinda hadn't even realized she had spoken aloud. She wished she hadn't but luckily Alistair resumed.

"It was a rainy afternoon. We were playin' a team from Sterling and we were ahead by two goals. The ground was clarty and slick and the weather dreich. The combination of water and mud in our eyes made it hard to see. I had the ball, and me pony and I were racin' to the goal when she slipped. It all happened so fast. She fell on top of me. The other riders were right behind me. Some of the horses were able to jump and clear us, but others couldn't help but run right over us. Me pony had broken her leg and was trying to get up, but couldn't. Her struggles were making it worse since I was still pinned under her. I knew I had broken me leg, and me ribs were on fire and I could barely breathe. I couldn't feel me arm which was crushed under me horse. I had broken it too, as well as my collar bone. I was lucky I didn't break me neck."

Clarinda couldn't believe her ears. She instinctively covered her open mouth with her hands. Her eyes felt as if they were about to pop out of her head. She was horrified by the pain and anguish this man must have suffered. "Oh my Lord, it is awful! But you don't walk with a limp so I guess you were able to recover from this?"

"Well the accident was bad, yes. But it was the beginning of my ordeals." Alistair got up from the blanket and was slowly pacing. Clearly, it was painful to relive this tribulation, so this nervous movement made it easier.

"When they took me to hospital, they discovered I had punctured a lung which is why I couldn't seem to catch me breath. They were able to reset the bones, but I had broken my femur, so I had to spend the next four weeks in bed. My lungs are what really gave me trouble. I had to lie flat from the ribs and collar bone injuries and the punctured lung didn't heal quickly, so I developed pneumonia. I became weaker by the day and I could no longer do anythin' for me self. I took a leave of absence from me job since I hadn't been able to go in over a month. I had become a consultant within the bank for several businesses and it required extensive travel in the UK. Since I couldn't leave me bed, there was no way I could travel and serve me clients' needs. Me mates would come and visit, but they were not able to care for me. I am so blessed to have a sister like Janet. She was living in Skye and came home to care for me. I was released from the hospital three months after the accident. I could barely move. Me leg was still in a cast, as was me arm. Me ribs and collar bone were very sore and it was agonizin' for me to even move from a chair to the bed. I lost over two stone and was a shell of me former self.

"I began to reevaluate my life. I didn't know if I wanted to continue living. I didn't see the purpose of what I was doing. It would have been so easy to give up, quit and end it all."

"You can't mean that?" Clarinda was shocked to hear a man who was the picture of health want to give that all up. "There is always something to live for."

"Aye, there is, I ken that now, but when yer entire body is in pain, and to suffer the humiliation of yer sister as yer wet-nurse, it seems very hopeless. But ya' know Janet. She was no goin' to let me quit. She got me to believe I had somethin' to live for and got me on a regimen to get me strength back. She fed me well, and took me to physical therapy. The arm healed well, but I needed further surgery on me leg. It was almost a year later when I was able to return to me job at the bank. The heid bummer was happy to see me and offered me back me position. I tried to travel but it was exhaustin'. My heart wasn't in the work either. I realized life was very precious and I didn't think I wanted to live it in an office with four gray walls. I had no one; I had always liked the bachelor lifestyle, so I decided I could go and start me life o'er again. I wanted to be outside and I needed to do somethin' that would give me back strength—mostly physical, but I suppose needed some emotional mendin' too.

"When I was ill Janet had come to care for me and we lived in me parents' house. They had died several years ago, and it had stood empty except for when Janet or I would come and see to its upkeep. It was a good place to rest and readjust to a slower pace of life. I was accustomed to Aberdeen's busy city life, but I was unable to keep up the pace. Here in Inverwick I was able to heal in at me own time, and it seemed easier."

Alistair went on with his story and explained how he felt about coming back to his small home town. When he was able to move about the town, he had to introduce himself to everyone all over again. It was as if he had become a stranger in his own town. The time he spent out of Inverwick was a necessity, but he was glad to be back and was soon welcomed into the fabric of the Shire.

He explained he didn't become the town smithy by choice, it sort of came upon him. Gordon Turner had taken Alistair as his apprentice when Alistair was wondering if he could help the old man wield the hammer. The work made him feel good—to finally feel he could help someone else and he acknowledged he was not as helpless as he felt. It was a good trade and he made fairly good money and the town would need a new farrier after Mr. Turner planned to retire. The occupation was what Alistair needed to convalesce. The hammer would continue to strengthen his arm, and holding horses' hooves between his knees would strengthen his legs. He would be outside and his clients weren't going to say much, so he decided a simple life would be his for the rest of his days. At the end of his story he fell silent and then shrugged his shoulders as if to indicate 'that's life'.

"Alistair, I am sorry to hear of your accident. I cannot imagine the pain you went through." Clarinda regretted her choice of words. He didn't need sympathy; he needed someone in his life that would not see him as an injured man, but as just a man. She tried a new recourse.

"You would never guess to look at you today. You are one of the fittest men I have ever met." She figured best to leave it there. Too many compliments may appear as a false flattery.

"Thank ya'," he simply replied. "I have worked hard, but I cannae seem to think I will ever be able to feel whole again. I am not sure what it is I am missin', but I think I will never feel strong enough again."

"Maybe it is not brute strength you need, but instead something to make you feel strong inside. Perhaps what you are seeking is someone to love?" Clarinda could not believe her own ears. Was she a character in a romance novel? What was this gibberish she was spewing? Oh Lord, save her from her own tongue. "Actually what I meant was…"

Alistair cut her off. "I ken what ya' meant, and yes I have considered a woman in my life could be fine, but I am no the sort of man at me age to take on a new challenge. I have me work, me sister and I dinnae need more complications."

Clarinda listened to this blatant lie of an excuse and decided to get into the thick of it. If this man was candid enough to tell her his most excruciating life experience, the least she could do was argue some reasoning into him.

"I don't believe that is true. When I first came to town, you were involved with that young girl, Lauren wasn't it? As I recall your sister thought the two of you were going to become engaged. So you must have felt enough about her to consider proposing."

"That is true, I was seein' the Lees lass, but Lauren was no the right woman for me."

"Ah ha! So Lauren may not have been the *right* woman for you, but you admit there might be a woman who is?"

"No, ya' are tryin' to change me words. I meant I liked her well enough, yes, but I am a loner and she was expectin' a weddin'. I figured it was best to break it off before she became too attached to the idea."

"You still didn't answer my question. If you met the *right* woman, would you be willing to commit yourself to her?"

"Clarinda, don't get me wrong. I hope I have no lead ya' to think otherwise, but the kiss in yer kitchen was just that. A kiss. Could it have gone further—yes. But sex is nae love. I think we need to be pickin' up now. It is starting to get dark and it looks like it might rain."

Well I guess that is that, Clarinda thought to herself. Apparently she had hit a nerve, but good for her! They gathered up the effects of the picnic and mounted their steeds to head back. They rode with only a few spoken words between them, but in an attempt to beat the weather they needed to keep a brisk pace.

They barely beat the rain. Just as they neared the farm the clouds broke and it started to pour. They galloped the horses into the stables and laughed at their luck they didn't get any wetter. Clarinda was glad their outing would not end on a strained note. She removed the tack from Pewter, brushed her and gave her some grain for a job well done. She was still petting the mare's neck when Alistair came over to see she had tended to the horse properly.

Clarinda wanted to thank him for the wonderful day and repair what might need mending in their relationship.

"Listen, I didn't mean to pry. You told me some very private feelings and I didn't mean for you to feel defensive. Thank you for sharing your history with me. I am glad you consider me a close friend to be able to do such a brave thing."

God she was a wonderful woman, he thought. *She knows how to say the right thing to make everything better*. He decided he didn't need to say what he thought, he would show her. He took her in his arms and brushed her wet bangs from her face. He held her tight and gazed into her eyes. They were captivating—clear blue pools revealing her soul. She was honest, straightforward and good. She was everything he had desired in a woman. Her lips were parted in anticipation and he leaned to kiss her. Her lips were soft, warm and smoky sweet. She tasted salty from perspiration, and she smelled so good. His tongue was met with hers and they both delved for deeper exploration. He was kissing her with a force which could not be stopped. She was responding and moving her hands through his hair and down over his back. His muscles felt like a hilly topography and she clung to him as they engaged in this embrace of passion.

He moved his hands to explore her breasts. She gasped as he ran a thumb over her bra-encased nipple. He began to move his hand under her sweater and to reveal her firm and perfect mounds. Her hand moved down the front of his jeans. She could sense his hardness as she caressed him. He groaned low and deep like a wounded animal. They continued to explore each other and Clarinda thought her legs would not hold her any longer. It had been a long time since she had been with a man. And here she was in the arms of a man who held such passion, she knew he would be a fantastic lover. She needed to have him, and he her; even if it was in this lowly barn.

Alistair had to gain control of himself. He was not about to take advantage of this woman in this drafty barn. She deserved better. He needed to stop himself now before he couldn't stop. He pulled away from her, but she continued to stay with him. He looked away and the embrace ended. "Clarinda," he gasped, "this is no proper. I do want ya', but I cannae do this here."

Clarinda realized where she was and nodded her head. "OK, but I have an empty guest house. How about there?"

Alistair didn't want to disappoint her, but could not see a way to take the gentlemanly highroad. It was not as if he didn't want her, but he also did not want to disappoint her. It had been a long time and he was unsure if his performance would be worthy of this woman's passion.

"Let me take ya' home. Then we will see where this goes." They ran to the lorry and raced to Clarinda's.

They were surprised to be greeted at the door by Janet holding a tray of tea and goodies. She was trying out new biscuit recipes for the houseguests due in a few weeks. Although they were a tasty treat, Alistair and Clarinda eyed each other with a longing for a treat of a totally different nature. When it comes to a battle of patience, Janet is the victor. She waited until Alistair was finished and then asked the fitting questions which would signal to him he was needed elsewhere. She was naive to the glowering looks she was getting from either side of the table, but there was nothing they could do or say that would not embarrass Janet.

At long last, Alistair decided to leave. Clarinda saw him to the door and they shared a quick kiss. Alistair touched her face and then turned and left. Clarinda waved after him and then turned to go inside and gave Janet some details of her splendorous afternoon. Janet smiled, not only to hear how much Clarinda had enjoyed herself, but happy to hear her brother did as well.

The afternoon gave way to dusk, and time for Janet to be in her own home. "Well I need to be goin' now. See ya' in the morn." Clarinda smiled. After waiting patiently for Alistair to leave, it was only minutes later when Janet bid her farewell.

Clarinda was alone in the house and listened to the rain fall on the glass. She started a fire and poured a glass of wine. No sooner had she settled on the settee, when a knock came at the door. She opened it to see a raw site—Alistair. Soaking wet.

Chapter 17
Asking for Directions

"I will not tell you a thing! It is you who chose to throw it all away, so don't think now that you have a change of heart I will help you to hurt my friend again. I will not tell you where Clarinda has gone!"

Fran was going to be loyal to her friend and keep her whereabouts secret to everyone—even people she knew Clarinda had once cared about. When Fran visited her friend, it was apparent she was making a new life for herself and Scotland was her home. Fran thought if she was lucky, she might even find love again. Fran recalled how the brawny Alistair had seemed to take an interest. Yes, Fran was going to protect the tender new growth of her friend's happiness and not let anything damaging bring about an unexpected assault.

"She's in the UK, isn't she?" the voice on the line whispered as if he knew the secret and didn't want anyone to hear. To Fran it sounded like an asp, and equally as vile. She gasped at this truth—how did he find out? She hoped he had not heard her involuntary reaction.

"What don't you understand about the word 'no'? I am not going to tell you a thing. I have better things to do than deflect your questions. I will not tell you a thing. Good-bye!" Fran replaced the phone receiver in its holder with finality. She would not take any more calls from that number again.

She was a bit flustered from the conversation. The call had left her unnerved and her seethe made her heart was beat faster than normal.

This was soon followed by the moral debate. She wondered if she should call Clarinda to warn her. She wrestled with this notion overnight and the next morning when she had calmer emotions, she determined it was best not to raise Clarinda's alarm. After all, Scotland was a long way away, and Inverwick was a dot on the countryside. Unless someone knew exactly where to look, they were not going to uncover Clarinda Tetrick.

chapter 18
a night like no other

"How long have you been standing there? You are going to catch pneumonia!" As soon as the phrase left her lips she wished again she would keep from speaking hurtful words. "I'm sorry, it is an expression. I hope you don't think…"

"I ken I am drookit, but I hope you will still let me in?" Alistair smiled at her underneath his hair which now soaked to the skull resembled a mass of seaweed atop his head.

"Come in and shut the door, but stand on the rug. I don't want you dripping all over the floor. Emily will have a fit. Wait here. Let me grab you a towel."

Alistair didn't hear everything since Clarinda took off and was racing about the house for Lord knows what while he stood in the foyer. The cold had gotten the better of him, his skin was of gooseflesh and he slightly shivered. He crossed his arms to preserve any calorie of warmth and waited for Clarinda to return, but as soon as he heard her near, he uncrossed them. A Scotsman would not admit the weather was inhospitable.

"Here you go." She held a towel out for him. "You best take off that shirt. I will toss it in the dryer and you can come in here and warm up by the fire." She didn't know if he was going to think her forward for the 'take off your shirt' comment, or if he would think of her as a 'Den Mother' and all business. After all, this man stood in the rain for almost and hour to see her again. She understood his plan. He had driven his lorry back to his home and left it in the drive so it would appear to his passing sister, he was indeed at home. Then he trudged in the rain the mile or more back to The Heather & Thyme Guest House and waited until his sister left. Clarinda had to wonder why secrecy was so important to him. He had stated reasons before, but to become ill because of them seemed fanatical.

"I have just poured a glass of wine, but I think you need a dram to shake off the cold?" Alistair was using the towel to dry his hair but pushed it back to voice his agreement.

She prepared his whisky and returned to the settee and waited for him to join her. He sat next to her and his chest was glistening from the moisture. She felt like a letch and couldn't take her eyes off his sculptured torso, the tuft of hair that sprung from his sternum, and the smoothness of his skin. He was one of the most perfect men she had ever seen. His hair was disheveled from his drying efforts and fell about his face and into his large, dark eyes. He thoughtfully removed his boots and sopped socks, and to Clarinda even his feet seemed elegant. She didn't even realize she had sighed until her own ears heard the reaction. She tried to make it seem a sigh of fatigue, but she feared it was not convincing.

"I guess the events at the barn were compelling enough for you to brave this cold and wet night to return, or am I wrong?" Clarinda felt there was no use trying to skirt the issue that stood in the room as large as an elephant.

"No, ye be right about that, lass. I needed to come back and see ya' again. Me bloody sister would nae leave!" They uttered an embarrassed laugh about this happenstance. "First, I feel we need to be clear about where we stand."

Clarinda couldn't believe this man. Was his only exposure to romantic dialogue from sappy soaps? What heterosexual male who looked like this man, and was as passionate as he was, wanted to 'talk'? Clarinda wanted to call Ripley's because this was just unbelievable.

She must have looked at him with a quizzical eye, because she was seeing the same expression directed at her. "Alistair, I am not sure where we are headed, so does it make a difference?" She was speaking from a place in her mind that only wanted to enjoy the bodily pleasures of lying with him. Her defense mechanisms would prevent her from giving him her heart.

"No, I guess not, but as I have said before, I dinnae want this 'affair'—for a lack of a better word—to become the gossip o' the town. Ye are new to Inverwick, and tryin' to start a business and I dinnae want to do anythin' to spoil what ye have kindled. Ya' need to realize the culture of Scotland is no the same as New York's. It is no easy to have a relationship in this town where everyone is aware of yer doin's. Also, there is yer personal reputation to consider. I dinnae want to effect how people view ya'. I want them to see ya' as the smart, sweet and considerate woman ya' are."

For sure, he said all the right words and Clarinda decided her reputation was worth forsaking for this brief moment of pleasure. To stop his words, she placed her lips on his and he responded in kind. His strong arms wrapped around her and he kissed her with an emptying need. He was forceful, but not hard. His was taking her all in via the union of their mouths and tongues. He tasted of salt and peat, and she of butter and tartness.

Clarinda ran her hands over his sculpted chest. He was so strong and magnificent in his splendor. She breathed in his scent and it was warm, yet wild. She felt she was grasping a wild animal in her arms and one which was willing to be tamed by her ministrations.

His hands softly caressed her breasts. She gasped as her excitement grew and she would not be able to stop her desire to have this man. They eased themselves onto the coarse rug in front of the fire. He pried her shirt off her shoulders, and she was working the buckle of his pants while continuing to be joined in an unending kiss. Alistair abruptly pulled away and stood up. He worked the fly of his jeans and pulled them down over his hips and stepped out of them. Clarinda was on the floor looking up at him and panting from their energetic kissing. She was undone by the beauty of the man who stood before her. He was strong, not only in muscle but also in spirit, mind, and heart. A deep scar on his thigh was his only flaw. His stomach was ribbed and lead down to an area that showcased a marvel most women will never see. He was standing proud, in more ways than one and if he didn't kneel down to take Clarinda to a fantastic place of pleasure right now, then she was about to reach up and take it for herself.

"Alistair," she gasped. "Come to me!"

He knelt down and buried his face in her neck. He gently kissed her and ran his fingers softly over her face and through her hair. Clarinda felt she was being examined by a blind man. His touch was soft, sensual and he was exploring all her sensitive areas. He unbuttoned her blouse and slowly slipped it off her. He tossed it aside and began to massage her breasts. Clarinda wanted to get that bra off! It was a barrier to greater yearning, but Alistair was taking his time and creating an urge she could barely endure. He reached down and undid her jeans and began to kiss her belly as he slowly slid the denim over her hips. Her stomach and thighs quivered from the attention.

Alistair marveled at the beauty of this woman. Most her age did not possess this youth. She was comfortable in her body and was not afraid to yield to her sensuality. Her warmth, the length of her legs, and the fullness of her breasts had captivated him and all the blood in his body had surged to his groin. His mind told him to be a gentle and satisfying lover to his woman; but his nature was to conquer. At the moment he was able to restrain himself and rather than take her quickly he wanted to escalate her desire beyond boundaries. He felt time spent now would certainly be redeemed later.

Clarinda could not believe the rapture she was experiencing. This man was not the most skilled of her lovers, but his raw magnetism and desire to please her was overwhelming. He was not trying to impress her, only to give her an experience unlike any other.

He had removed her bra and panties, and sat on his haunches to admire her. Clarinda continued to moan from his touch. She reached up and placed her hand around his neck and pulled him to her. She kissed him firmly and drew him down on top of her. She could feel his harness jabbing into her stomach. Lord was she ready!

Alistair kissed her and slid his hand down to the downy apex of her legs. He gently spread them and touched her most sensitive area. Clarinda arched her back and trust her hips in response. She was in ecstasy and not sure she could hold back any restraint and moaned a low growl which came from deep within. She was completely awash in her desire and her body served only as a conduit for more. Alistair kissed her once more and then looked at her. Clarinda's eyes were closed, but she opened them when she felt his ragged breath on her face.

"Clarinda, ya' are lovely. I need ya', and I hope ya' feel the same."

"Yes, yes!" She could barely wait any longer.

"Just checkin'." He smiled at her eagerness and placed his hands aside her shoulders to bear his weight and moved his hips to meet hers. He placed his knees between hers and edged her legs aside to accommodate his hips. He slowly moved over her and began to enter her. She gasped as he began a slow and deliberate penetration. She was so warm, moist, and tight it was almost more than he could bear to continue in this delicate manner. Once he was fully inside her he pulled out and entered her again with a firm thrust. She cried out. He repeated the motions at the same time he stimulated the module of her sex, and she arched her back and thrusted to meet his rhythm. They moved as one. She writhed with abandon under him and he drove himself to take every last part of her. When Clarinda did not think she could take any more her body began to spasm and she uttered a cry as savage as the ages. He joined her chorus with is own voracious yell that emanated from a bottomless cavern. He pumped his seed into her until he felt his very essence would be eliminated. They collapsed together, panting, he on top of her and sealed together by the sweat of their bodies.

Clarinda was depleted. Their love-making had completely fulfilled her and she was feeling a warm sensation in her heart and in her belly. She had not felt this good in such as long time. Alistair slid off of her and propped himself on one elbow. The exertions had left wisps of her hair glued to her face. He gently brushed them away and she kissed the palm of his hand. She was amazed by his tenderness and caring. How could this man be so sensitive to others, yet remain so alone? It was a conundrum and she hoped she could solve it.

Alistair didn't strive to be uncouth, but he was not comfortable with awkward moments. Typically at situations such as this he would get up, go to another room and wait for the lass to leave. He was a master at the 'one-night stand' and liked it that way. But now he was older and wiser and realized there was something about Clarinda which made him want to alter his preferred method of gaining sexual release. She 'got' him. She understood him and let him be himself—even with his aged emotional and physical scars. He wanted to remain close to her—to watch and look over her. He was feeling the usual drowsiness, but fought it off to stay with her. "Clarinda," he whispered.

"Shhh," she pressed a finger to his lips. "Don't say anything. Let us treasure this moment in silence." She smiled and closed and opened her eyes dreamily. It was unlike her not to want to say something, but at this very moment her mind was racing reliving the splendor of their accouplement. She was content and wanted to savor the feeling without shattering it by undue conversation.

Beginning to feel cool from the brisk temperature in her house countered by skin covered with sweat, she grabbed the throw on the couch and tossed it over them. She leaned over and kissed Alistair. The smile on his face belied his satisfaction, and Clarinda could see sleep was going to get the better of him.

What is the proper course of action? she wondered. *Do I invite him to my room, or let him fall asleep here?* Of course if she invited him to her room he would leave immediately. If she left him here, he would sneak away when he awoke like a call girl. She thought it best to tough it out on the hard rug.

"Clarinda?" he asked. She turned to face him. "Can we seek a more comfortable lie? This rug is suitable for love-makin' but nae for resting me elbow."

The moment of truth. She would ask him to spend the night with her. A deep breath precluded her invitation to join her in her bed. Before the words had fully left her lips he was standing and gesturing for her to take his hand. He pulled her to her feet and secured the blanket around her and they ambled toward her quarters. When she opened the door, Alistair turned, "I'll be right back." She lit a small candle, pulled back the crisp comforters and sheets and slid inside the envelope of coziness. As soon as she had assumed her favorite position, Alistair returned. He dumped the armful of clothes on the floor and joined her between the sheets. Turning her so they were both looking out the window to the west, he held her close and kissed her neck and blew out the candle. "Thank ya'."

The statement was so simple and revealing it brought tears to Clarinda's eyes. She didn't know how to answer so she just kissed his hand resting on her shoulder. She sighed and closed her eyes. Her dreams were of the Scottish highlands again; this time she was soaring like a bird, high over them.

Alistair remained awake for a brief while, watching the magnificent woman in his arms fall into slumber. He tried to recall when he was this happy and decided the mental exercise was not worth the effort. He closed his eyes, breathed in the fresh scent of her hair and let sleep come sweetly.

chapter 19
the morning after

Clarinda awoke with a start. After a few moments of recollection, she recalled the prior night's events. The warm body next to her continued to breathe evenly, Alistair remained asleep. Turning ever so gently, she rolled over to spy this astonishing man. When she turned to face him, she found his eyes already open. She smiled at him, and he back at her. She didn't want to ruin the magic of the moment by speaking. She closed her eyes and opened them again, and he was still there. It was not a dream, but actual reality. She was a very happy and content woman.

"How long have you been awake?" she purred.

"Long enough. I like to watch ya' sleep. Ya' seem verra peaceful."

She nodded and tucked her head into his chest. He smelled warm and musky. Breathing in his scent she moved closer to him. He took her into his arms and kissed her head and moved his fingers through her hair. Before long they were kissing, and reviewing the contours of each others bodies once again. Alistair was amazed how well she fit him, her soft curves matched his hard planes in all the right places. Clarinda threw a leg over his, and he groaned deep in his throat. Using his hands to survey her body, his mouth surveyed her breasts. Exploring her sweet cleft with his fingers, he ~~and~~ found her ready for another joining. Lord this woman was made to love! She was giving and receptive and exciting. It was all Alistair could do to restrain himself. She could feel his strong need pressing against her. She leaned forward to kiss him and as she leaned back, she slid over him and took him inside her. A guttural moan revealed his pleasure. As she rocked over him, he continued to fondle her high breasts and stroke her hair and back. She was lost; she closed her eyes and embraced the rapture. They moved as one and Alistair felt her clamp around him has she reached the summit of her pleasure. She moaned and collapsed over him. He held her close and rolled her over onto her back. "Now ya' will be mine," and drove himself into her animal-like abandon. Yelling to announce his release, he collapsed onto the softness of her breasts, his chest covered with a sweaty sheen. They lay still until their panting subsided.

"It's a real pleasure to start the day this way," he murmured.

"Mmmm," she agreed.

The moment was broken by the sound his growling stomach. "I guess me stomach is tellin' me I am hungry for more than just ya'."

Clarinda pulled the sheets up to her chest and slid out of bed. Alistair loved watching her round hurdies jiggle as she walked to the closet. With her hair tousled and her eyes still sleepy she was a vision to behold. He wished he could be her partner for life, but she was something he could not have. He was too old to be changing his life, and she would want bairns and he was not able to handle that kind of responsibly. He didn't want to be tied down. He was too busy doing what, he had to think, but he was busy just living his life the way he wanted.

"Let me go and fix you something." She dropped the sheet

and began to pull on some clothes. She wiggled into some jeans and pulled a sweater over her head. Even dressed as she was, she was still alluring.

Reality finally faced Alistair. He leapt out of bed and rushed to pull on his clothes. He felt if he consummated the night with a morning breakfast, he would be lost forever. "Clarinda, I am sorry, but I am late and I need to make up the time. Please understand I need to be goin' straight away. I will ring ya' up later. Thanks so much for the evenin'."

Before the words left his lips he realized he had made a grave mistake. The look on her face went from bliss to disappointment.

"OK," she stated very calmly, "I understand. Have a great day. Do you want some coffee?"

"No, but thank ye kindly." He had just created the very chasm he wished to avoid. How could he explain to her—it was not her fault, it was his. He hurriedly pulled on his shirt, and Clarinda kept her back to him.

She was trying to hide her disappointment. She had been used again. It didn't matter the country, it was the same around the world; men were caring lovers when they chose to be, and when they were done satisfying their own needs they were quick to be off. Alistair was no different. She thought he was, but she was wrong. She kept her back to him so he wouldn't see her face. Struggling to keep her emotions in check, and she was afraid if she faced him the flood gates would open and he would see her only as a sniveling little girl.

"Clarinda," he came up behind her and grasped her shoulders. "Thank ya' so much, it was a lovely evening." In fact, it was one of the best he could recall in many years, but he couldn't let her know she had such power over him. "I hope ya' don't think my need to rush off has anything to do with ya'—it doesn't." Truth was it was because of her, she was capturing his heart and he couldn't let that happen. "I need to be on me way, I hope ya' understand."

She nodded but still did not turn to face him. It was just too much to bear. "Goodbye. Have a good day."

Carefully padding through the house, he let himself out and began to walk back to his wee house. The murky morning air was crisp, and he could see his breath. It wasn't raining at the time, but clouds gathered and threatened to provide nasty weather later in the day. His heart felt about as nice as the weather—dark and cold. He regretted his shabby treatment toward Clarinda. She brought him so much joy, she didn't deserve her kindness to be met with his indifference. He would make it up to her, if she let him. He had gotten so spooked; he was afraid of his feelings and he was not sure how to react. Clearly he had not performed as a gentleman. Taking a deep breath of the cold morning air he picked up his pace.

It was only a few weeks until Christmas. Where did the time go?

chapter 20
another chore

"Hullo! Hullo! Is anyone here?" There was a shrill voice coming through the house. Clarinda wasn't expecting anyone, but then again her house was now open for guests so she supposed she should be ready at any time to accept visitors.

"Hullo my dear!" Clarinda came around the corner and nearly ran into the stout figure of Mrs. Fitzrandolph. "I am sorry to trouble you but I wanted to come by and make my reservations for your Hogmanay supper. I understand from Janet it will be quite a feed and I don't want to miss it."

Clarinda wanted to hug the old dearie, she was so tickled.

"Thank you, Mrs. Fitzrandolph! You have the honor of being my first guest to reserve a dinner with me! Would you like a room too, and avoid driving home so late?"

"Oh no, just the supper is fine. I don't drink so there is no risk there. Thank you anyway." They quickly finished their arrangements, and Mrs. Fitzrandolph got in her old Mercedes and drove off.

Her visit had raised Clarinda's spirits. The last few weeks had gone by quickly, as they always tend to do as Christmas approaches. But not hearing from Alistair weighed on her mind, and because of it she had not really embraced the Christmas spirit. She had purchased some wool and had fashioned a simple scarf for him but she didn't expect to get a gift in return. Quite honestly the only reason for the gift was to keep the peace with Janet, although she would have given him the world if he would have accepted it.

As the day waned ~~on~~, Clarinda's morale continued to soar — the phone would not stop ringing and her Hogmanay dinner was almost half booked. Apparently, Mrs. Fitzrandolph was like a one-woman advertisement. As she did her business about the town she shared her plans for Hogmanay. Not wanting to be left out of the celebration, several townspeople called to reserve their own table at the guest house. Clarinda was not surprised; everyone in town knew of Janet's culinary skills. Of course many of the rooms were vacant. Scots are a thrifty lot and didn't see the value of staying at the guest house when their own cozy beds were only a short safe drive away. She decided to call Janet with the good news.

Janet was pleased to hear about the amount of interest the townsfolk showed when it came to celebrating the holiday at the guest house, but she sensed Clarinda was not her bubbly self, even though she was delivering good news.

"Clarinda, my love, is there something nae right? Ya' don't sound like yerself. Do ye want to tell me?"

Oh sure, Clarinda thought. *As if I am not already miserable, I could open my mouth and really suffer. As if I would tell his SISTER what a loose woman I am, and I have become no more than another one of her brother's carnal conquests.*

"Oh no, everything is fine," she lied. "I guess I must be tired. I am very busy with preparing the house, and the guests coming, and of course, the Christmas rush."

Janet wasn't buying it. Clarinda didn't have to procure much for the holidays, and guests were not due to arrive for another week yet, so something was up. She had an inkling, but it was clear she was going to have to pry it out of the young woman. "Really, it seems both ya' and Alistair are suffering from the same plight. He is listless as well. I have no seen the laddie so blue. Have ya' spoken to him of late?"

Oh dear Lord, please do not make me talk about that man. She was not sure if she was more angry at him, or at herself. Her emotions were still unsettled about this matter and she didn't want Janet to be involved in these delicate circumstances. It could only lead to everyone feeling worse. "No I haven't." The answer was not only true; it was to the point.

Aha, so there is something up between them, Janet deducted. They both were acting despondent so there was probably a kink in the courtship. Janet was sure her brother was the cause. Once a woman got close to him, he would run for the hills. Janet had always hoped the right lady would come along and he would fall madly in love and be happy. However, she knew he resisted unconditional devotion. She blamed herself. Alistair's view on love and commitment was cynical as a result of what happened to her after Richard died. What Alistair didn't understand was Janet would go through the pain all over again to feel love once again in her heart. The auld adage was true: better to love for a short time, than to never feel love at all. She needed her brother to understand this concept, but his head could be harder than his heart. "Well, then I will have to make sure he pays ya' a visit. I am sure there is something he can help with."

Clarinda rolled her eyes. She loved Janet like her own sister, but it seemed she was now interfering in her life. It was worthless to argue, the more she protested it would only fuel Janet's intrusiveness.

"Very good. Thanks for thinking of me." The conversation ended with Janet's habitual 'Right-o' and Clarinda hung up the phone. She secretly hoped Alistair would stop by so she could gaze upon him once again, but she knew she also wanted to lambaste him across the head for acting like such a cad. She was equally to blame; she just was not a good judge of men.

"Alistair?" Janet called to her brother. He happened to be tending to her ducks and she was not going to let this fortuitous happenstance be for naught. "I need ya' to do something. Come back in when ya' are finished."

When she explained she wanted her brother to go over the guest house to see if he could assist Clarinda in any manner, he looked at his feet. When she finished describing her orders he presented his protests; he had several clients with horse teams he needed to tack with sleigh bells. This was going to take up too much time and he would not be able to assist Clarinda with random chores. Besides, he was sure George was over there every day so he would just be in the way and would be more of a hindrance. Janet was not sure if he would go, but she applied as much guilt as she could muster.

Indeed, he wanted to see Clarinda again, and he had meant to call her, but as the days waned, so did his nerve. Due to his apprehension, he decided to keep away from her, and he was sure she was thankful for his considerate approach to their awkward situation. It was a small town, so of course they would undoubtedly run into each other, but at least he could try to limit these occurrences. He was sure they would have to swap Christmas greetings, but he would also manage to make this more of a casual exchange so as to not draw attention to their relationship; a simple card would probably suffice.

chapter 21
bolstered by friends

"Thank you very much for the invitation. I would love to come. I need to make sure my guests are taken care of first, but I think I can stop over later."

Hanging up the phone, Clarinda was glad to have something to do on Christmas Eve. She had experienced Mrs. Fitzrandolph's gastronomic disasters firsthand, but she understood this gathering will be a 'pot-luck' function and there will be other foodstuffs made by persons who actually possessed taste buds.

Luckily she would be distracted by happy well-wishers. Typically she went to visit her Uncle Rupert and Aunt Jilly in Vermont. This was her first Christmas in Scotland and she felt very melancholy. She planned to call them to offer them greetings, but it was not the same as celebrating the season New England style.

The tree she had selected was wonderfully fragrant and filled the bay window of her parlor. Once lit it would serve as a welcoming beacon to passersby and guests. Garlands and gold gilded burgundy bows adorned the banisters and drapery rods, and a wreath with shiny bulbs and birds hung on the door. Clarinda had purchased small white lights and some meager ornaments for the tree; she missed the sentimental hand-made ones of her youth. Just as she was beginning to overheat from the efforts and frustration of putting the blasted tree in its holder when her prayers were answered.

"May I be able to give ya' some aid?" Clarinda nearly knocked George over when she turned to hug him.

"George! You have come at precisely the right time!" Two sets of hands made light work of the tree erection, and soon the round balsam filled the window. Laughter spilled from them as they struggled to untangle the lights. Bracing him on the ladder, Clarinda guided George as he insisted he string the lights on the top of the tree.

"Have ye an angel?"

Clarinda sadly shook her head and regretted she didn't, but a well placed bulb would have to be sufficient. Once the lights and globes were placed on the tree, they plugged it in and clapped to their merriment of their handiwork.

"Come on," Clarinda suggested, "let's have some tea to celebrate our success of a decorated tree without bodily harm."

George agreed, but suggested some eggnog with whisky was more to his liking. Clarinda whipped up some of the rich concoction and ladled it into their small cups and added whiskey to George's, and rum to hers.

"This is some of the finest eggnog I have had the pleasure to sample. Ya' need to serve this at Hogmanay."

Clarinda nodded her agreement and penned out the directions and gave them to her friend. "In case you have the urge at home, it is very simple. Drink it in good health."

> *Holiday Eggnog*
> *From the Kitchen of Clarinda Tetrick*
>
> *6 Eggs*
> *2 c. sugar*
> *Vanilla*
> *2 pints Heavy cream*
> *2 pints Half & Half*
>
> *In a large mixing bowl, beat egg yokes and sugar until thight and like yellow. Add vanilla to desired taste, cream and Half & Half. Beat egg whites until peaks form. Gently fold into liquid mixture. Sprinkle with nutmeg and serve with Whisky or Rum.*

"Clarinda, this has been a bonnie visit and I had a verra good time decoratin' yer wee tree, but I need to tend to me other chores. I need to be sayin' me goodbyes. Oh, I wanted to tell ya' to put me down for the Hogmanay. I hope ya' still have a place for me?"

"Of course, I would come to your house and drag you here in case you thought you might want to stay home! You MUST be here! I have saved you a wonderful seat. Janet is making something special for you," she winked. She was sure George's visage was beginning to color, and smiled. At least there was someone in town who was enjoying the romance of the season.

She waved as she watched George drive off, and Clarinda did feel a bit happier about the season. Decorating the tree had given her a small dose of holiday cheer. She supposed if she spent the remaining days of the season surrounded by friends and distracted by the needs of the guest house, she would be able to handle the season's emotional toil. The ringing phone broke her out of her reverie. The voice on the other end boosted her spirits even further.

"I suppose it is a picture-perfect holiday there. After all everyone is wearing plaid so I suppose this is the one time of the year they don't appear to clash." Upon hearing Fran's voice Clarinda couldn't help but laugh until her stomach ached and she could barely catch her breath.

"I can't imagine the kilt is keeping their parts warm enough — better to have those chestnuts roasting near an open fire, no?" In between Fran's one-liners and Scottish observations, they shared their most recent news. Clarinda didn't mention Alistair and prayed Fran would not broach the subject, but no such good luck.

"So tell me how that handsome, wild Scotsman has been. You better tell me you have been cultivating a more meaningful relationship with him." Fran's inquiry was met with silence on the other end of the line. "Clarinda? Are you alright? Tell me."

Clarinda so desperately wanted to reveal her feelings to someone, and Fran's easy manner made her an ideal confidante. The story began with the horseback ride, and the rain, and then his clandestine return to the guest house. Fran begged for the details about the night they shared, but Clarinda balked explaining a 'lady doesn't tell'. There were moments of both laughter and tears and once she had finished, Clarinda remained quiet waiting for her friend's advice and rebuttal.

"This is simple. You are over reacting. He clearly is afraid of making a commitment, so you have to move slowly. I am sure he does care for you, but like a horse, you don't want to break his spirit in trying to tame him. I am sure he has missed you as much as you have missed him. For God's sake, girl, don't be so sensitive. You mentioned you were going to a Christmas Eve party. Try to see if you can make amends there. People will be around so he has to be civil."

Clarinda agreed that perhaps she might have been holding onto a misdirected emotion. She reasoned if she could speak with Alistair and ascertain his feelings she might be able to regain his friendship and affections. Her friend's chat had been cathartic, improving her mood and giving her a goal and plan of action for when she next encountered Alistair. They said their goodbyes and bestowed best wishes for Christmas. Clarinda valued her friend; even though Fran was thousands of miles away she was able to sooth her troubled heart—a true friend indeed.

The scarf Clarinda had intended for Alistair was finished. Even though she had earlier decided she would not have the chance to give it to him, she now felt it would come in handy. This gift and one other for her hostess were needed for Christmas Eve. A small house warmer and a few other gifts and she would be set. She was going to have a good time, even if it killed her.

chapter 22
little things mean a lot

"Clarinda will be there!"

At the sound of this announcement, Alistair's shoulders slumped. He dreaded seeing her. Actually, that was a complete lie—he had not stopped thinking about her, but he could not believe she would want to see him. He had behaved so badly and since she had not called him, he feared the worst. A woman's wrath was one thing, but the 'silent treatment' was a far greater torture.

What did she think of him? he wondered. He was soon to find out and he prepared himself, both mentally and physically for a battle.

"Ya' better bring her a gift. I am sure she has one for ya'." How would his backbone be able to sustain the weight of this added burden? He was sure he was now demonstrating the posture of an 'O'.

"Stand up straight. What is wrong with ye?" His sister was eyeing him carefully and he felt she was secretly enjoying her torment. "Ya' do have a wee gift for her, don't ya'?"

His blank stare answered Janet's question. Actually he had

been thinking of something but had not purchased anything thinking his gesture would be for naught. This could be quickly remedied—he could have a present in hand on no time.

"Yes, I do. Don't ya' fash, I am no a complete clot-heid." Perhaps his sister was convinced by his feeble recovery, but that now he had a plan, he needed to get into action.

I think I will wear the hunting colors, he mused. And now he needed to get into town and procure the gift. Once he was finished at his sister's he hurried off.

There, thought Janet, *I hope I can get those love birds back on track.* She had noticed both Alistair and Clarinda had not spoken to each other for several weeks. She also surmised from some carefully placed questions to Clarinda, he had not stopped by as she had urged. This called for some more drastic measures, and getting them together at a crowded party in a small-roomed house seemed the proper tactic. Meddling came to her easily, but there was a fine line between romance assistance and creating a blight to wipeout a budding relationship. If she wanted to get to get these two moving in the right direction, her aid needed to be administered carefully. Pleased she could get him focused on gift-giving to someone other than herself was at least getting him to consider a reconciliation.

"Do ya' have the necklet with the wee thistle in the center?" Alistair was clear about what he wanted to give Clarinda. He had spied a lovely silver necklet at the jewelers in Inverness and as he surveyed the proprietor's inventory, he did not see the piece he had placed in his mind's eye.

"It is about so wee, and hangs in the middle." Hoping his further descriptions would jar the shopkeeper's recollection.

"Oh, aye! Ye were here about a month ago, no? I remember now."

The store keeper had recognized him, but that was not calming Alistair's worries. "So, do ya' have the one I was looking at?" urging the wiry little man with the wild red hair to search his stock.

"I think I do. I believe I hae one left. Let me check in this drawer here." After only a second of searching the man presented the open box to Alistair. It contained a lovely thistle design held by two delicate silver strands. The center of the design showcased a single amethyst which had a self-illuminating luster.

"Tis lovely," the jeweler volunteered. He could see his customer was entranced, and wanted to close the sale. "Tis for a lady-friend, no doubt? I am sure she will be verra delighted. This is me last one. They are hand-crafted and I only was able to get three this year. See hear, they are numbered. This one is seventy-two out of only one-hundred and five. Seems like an odd number, but I guess the artist grew weary of makin' 'em. Verra special piece."

Alistair had been sold enough. He had his designs on this item since he first saw it and knew it to be perfect for Clarinda. He didn't need to be convinced further. "I'll take it, and will ya' please gift wrap it for me?"

With a nod and a "verra good" the little man was quick to perform the task. He was back in no time and handed Alistair a small bag containing the precious article wrapped in deep-colored tartan paper topped off with a burgundy bow; very rich looking. He smiled to himself as he stepped out of the store and ran smack into…

"Oh my, I am sorry ." Clarinda's jaw dropped. She was more focused on keeping a hold on her packages rather than determining what to say. "I wasn't looking." *Of course not you ninny, you plowed right into him*, her inner voice chided.

"Hullo," was all Alistair could muster. *Lord, can't ya' say something with a few more syllables?* he self flagellated.

Time had stood still and neither moved nor spoke but remained frozen from fear of breaking the spell. *Better to be thought a fool, than to open yer mouth and remove all doubt*, was running through Alistair's mind.

"Getting some last minute gifts?" Clarinda attempted to break the awkward silence.

Alistair looked at the bags in his hands and nodded. *Say something*, he goaded himself. "Aye?" *Oh great, can't ya' say more than that?*

"Yes," she replied. "The stores are very busy." *As if she was the only one with X-ray vision who could surmise this obvious fact. Duh.*

Alistair nodded again. *For God's sake, say something. Tell her how ya' meant to call,* his conscience goaded.

"Well, I must be off." Clarinda wanted to say it was good to see him and couldn't they get together for a quick pint at a pub, but she couldn't tolerate his silent treatment. It was clear to her he was uncomfortable talking to her and wanted to make a hasty retreat. Clarinda was merely trying to facilitate that end and still keep her self-esteem intact.

"Oh. I was hopin' ya' might hae time for a pint. I ken a pub in the next close with cold Strongbow." He didn't move his head, but he peeked at her under his dark eye lashes. Clarinda was taken by his boyish approach and couldn't refuse the invitation.

"Alright. I have some time. Sure." She was trying to determine whether Alistair was trying to be gracious and make amends, or if it was just willing to see her in Inverness where the prying eyes of Inverwick were not present. She guessed the latter; after all there were pubs located in Inverwick too. It had to be he was only comfortable to be with her in a town where no one would see him associating with her. Despite her sentiment of feeling like a second-class citizen, Clarinda still walked with him to the pub. Even if he was ashamed to be seen with her in Inverwick, she could at least gaze upon his countenance for the duration of their beverage consumption. The stroll was wordless, but once inside Blackfriar's he guided her with his hand at her back, wrangled the packages into the other, and served her a pint of cold, crisp, golden cider.

"Sláinte mhath," he offered and clinked their glasses.

The tartness of the cider tingled Clarinda's tongue. "Hum. This is nice."

"Aye, it is. I like to drink it at this time o' the year. It is good mulled as well, but it will get ya' pissed quick if ya' no pay attention."

At least he was saying more than he had on the street, but conversely Clarinda felt a loss of words and drank her pint silently. She noticed the small bag from the jewelers where they had collided. Clearly he had moved on and was buying trinkets for another woman. She needed to heed the message and get over her infatuation with this man.

She gazed into her glass; it was almost half gone and neither had uttered another word—this was excruciating! Someone had to say something; Clarinda took the chance. Anything was better than this.

"Alistair, thank you for the pint, but I know this must be as uncomfortable for me as it is for you. I think it is best if I go. I know you are tying to be a gentleman, but it is clear this is a gesture of mercy. If you seek my forgiveness, you have it."

Clarinda rose and began to collect her bags but he grabbed her arm. "Wait. Please don't rush aff so. Cannae ye no sit for a few more minutes?"

"Sure, I can but what will that accomplish? More stares into our cider? It is clear we don't have anything to talk about, and I am sure you have a busy day, so why don't we get on with it?" Clarinda was hoping her tone was tempered so she didn't come off sounding like a shrew.

"No, I do have something to say. Please stay." His eyes looked as if they were pleading with her, but his voice was steady and commanding. Clarinda reoccupied her seat, and second guessed her decision at the same time. She really didn't want to be humiliated in a pub in the heart of Inverness.

He slid his chair closer to hers so his knees were on either side of hers and he clasped his large hands together. He looked down as if to pray and then looked up to fix his gaze on her tranquil blue eyes. "Clarinda," he began slowly, "thank ya' for yer forgiveness, but I dinnae deserve it. I meant to call."

Clarinda couldn't believe her ears! The old 'I-meant-to-call' excuse! Really! This was stupid; she didn't need this and attempted to rise. His hands pressed on her legs and firmly urged her to resume her seat.

"Wait," he continued. "I know that is lame, but it is the truth. Clarinda, there is another truth I want to tell ya'. I have no stopped thinking about ya', the night we shared, and the next morning, since I left yer house. I behaved badly, I admit."

There was a whirlwind of retorts she could use in her verbal arsenal, but when she sifted through them the best she could deliver was: "So why?"

"I dinnae ken. But I can tell ya' this: I would do anythin' to be able to relive that morn. I would stay and make *ye* breakfast, I tell ya' that! I shouldna have run off like a scared boy. I was feelin' trapped. Ya' shared with me a glorious night and I was feelin' things I dinnae ken how to handle, so I ran. Please let me try to make it up to ya'. I have missed ya' verra much. As I said, I meant to call or stop by, but me pride and stubbornness were in the way."

His delivery and words seemed genuine, but Clarinda was not going to fall for it. She had been with enough men to know they use this little apology to get back into good graces, but it is really another technique to make them feel better and break it off later. She would accept it for now, but she knew it may not last. He spoke no further but did not lose eye contact. Clarinda assumed he was looking for her to acknowledge his apology and perhaps express a similar statement on her behalf. She wanted to tell him that she too had missed him, and wanted to be with him, and was sorry she didn't call—wait a minute!

She was not the man; she was not supposed to phone. Granted, these were modern times, but she had hoped this man who moved so gallantly might have some small measure of chivalrous tendencies. That he might understand the rules of engagement after a night of lovemaking meant HE was supposed to call HER;

and within the next week—not a month or more later. Her hard heart was melting as she stared back into his dark round eyes, and she decided to be pleasant and accept his apologies, not only for their sakes, but for Janet's, and the sake of the guest house and its impending début. They could wrestle this out later, once the Heather & Thyme was more stable.

"Alistair, I accept your apologies. I am not sure I understand your reasons, but you seem to truly wish to attempt a reconciliation. I have to admit, I have missed you too. I really enjoyed the glorious day and the night we shared, and I admit; I was disappointed when it was so short lived. I hope we could start over and try again?"

He nodded vigorously and his hair fell into his eyes. He was certainly well skilled at making his appearance speak for him. He casually brushed his locks away and leaned in closer to Clarinda; their lips parallel. He moved very slowly so as to not startle her, and tenderly gave her a kiss. Seeing this one was met with success, he kissed her again. This time he was more wanting and his tongue sought to explore hers. With this, the old desires in Clarinda came flooding back. She responded to him and returned his ardor with equal vigor.

This was the ice breaker they needed. Once they separated the words flooded in. They spoke of their recent news, Janet and other friends they had in common. Another pint of cider was shared and many hours of the afternoon flew passed. As the skies darkened, they realized they needed to make haste back to Inverwick; they both had many more duties they needed to complete by Christmas. They held hands as they exited the pub, kissed each other good bye and walked to their respective parked vehicles. She walked about ten steps and turned to look at Alistair. He didn't turn, but kept walking. She turned and continued on her way. Another five steps and Alistair turned to look at Clarinda. She was almost to the block where she needed to turn; she did not look back. Alistair turned his collar up, looked at the wee tartan box, smiled, and walked to his lorry to drive home.

chapter 23
going somewhere?

David Kline's executive secretary knocked before entering, but without needing an acknowledgement proceeded directly into her boss's office.

"Yes, Melinda?" David heavily relied on her and she kept his life in order. Her loyalty was commendable and her work ethic diligent. She was able to juggle both office tasks and his many relationships seamlessly.

"I have your travel documents. Do not forget your passport." She reviewed with him the e-tickets she had placed for him, the arranged hotel and guest house reservations, and assorted train schedules. "I don't mean to pry but I only placed these for one person; I assume that is correct."

"Correct," David confirmed stoically. "I will be traveling alone."

"As for Christmas Eve, I did not make reservations per your instructions, so I wanted to remind you that you do not have a confirmed room to stay."

"That is fine. Thanks for making these arrangements, and have a Merry Christmas."

"No problem, Mr. Kline. Thank you, and enjoy your holidays as well. I have heard Scotland is a lovely country."

Chapter 24
Presentation of a Present

"Yes Uncle Rupert, I am well, and I have been keeping warm." Clarinda called her Aunt Jilly and Uncle Rupert to wish them a Merry Christmas. Heeding the time change, she called them on Christmas Eve to span both the Eve and the Day. In lieu of telling them her most recent news, she first had to field her uncle's barrage of health related questions. "No, I have not gotten damp, and, yes, I have been taking my vitamins."

She shared with them her holiday plans: the promising bookings for Hogmanay and her plans for Christmas Eve. Her uncle was relieved. "I am so glad you will not be alone. The holidays can be a very dismal time." Clarinda knew her uncle's words were true, but this year she hoped she would not feel the pangs of loneliness. After all, she and Alistair had reconciled and she hoped they might spend some time together tonight.

They ended their conversation; she hung up the phone and prepared herself for the party. She elected a long dark green velvet skirt, and a silk shirt of pale lavender. The combination highlighted the golden flecks in her blue eyes. She admired herself in the mirror, and saw a happy glow in her cheeks. Was it from the joy of the holiday season or from the giddy feeling at the promise of seeing Alistair this evening? At any rate, she was experiencing the good cheer of the season.

"Missus Tetrick, Missus Tetrick?"

Clarinda rushed down the stairs to heed the call of her guests. "Yes, what is it?" She matched the stress of her guests' alarm. "What is up?"

"I wanted to let ya' know it is snowin'! Isn't that brilliant? It may be a white Christmas after all!"

"Yes perhaps. Isn't it lovely?" Clarinda let her gaze drift into the night and was mesmerized by the random pattern and flight of the individual snowflakes. They clung to her eyelashes and feathered onto her cheeks. It was a glorious night and the snowfall put her into a festive mood.

Once she and the guests had calmed from the merriment of the precipitation, she inquired if they further required her services. They ensured her they were settled for the evening, but in case they should need anything, she introduced them to Kyle, the night manager, and to seek his assistance in her stead. She gathered her pumpkin-pecan pie, her gifts, and donned her wool cape and ventured over to Mrs. Fitzrandolph's to revel in some holiday cheer.

Arriving at Mrs. Fitzrandolph's she was greeted by the jolly hostess, who took her pie, the gifts and cape, and handed her a hot mulled wine. The taste was divine and warmed her down to her toes. The house was filled with decorations and partygoers, some she knew and others she didn't. She made the rounds and chatted with the guests and sampled some of the goodies. Spying Janet in a far corner, she made her way to share some quality non-work related conversation. "Have ye seen Alistair?" Janet queried once Clarinda got within earshot.

"No," answered Clarinda. "I just got here a few moments ago. So I guess he is here?"

Janet smiled as she watched Clarinda careen her neck to get a better look at her surroundings. It was clear to Janet that her

THE CELEBRATION OF HOGMANAY

friend wanted to chat with other guests, specifically her brother.

"I think he may be in the kitchen samplin' the whisky," Janet offered.

"Really? Do you mind if go to offer him my season's greetings?"

"Och, no, me dear friend," Janet punctuated her instruction with a wink. "Go and see of ye can pull the man away from the other sotted laddies."

Clarinda could hear the loud boom of men's laughter as she neared the kitchen, but before she could enter the male sanctuary, she was confronted by a large male chest, which smelled as if it was doused in alcohol, blocking her path. "Oh, so sorry!" she exclaimed. Looking up to see who she may have offended, there was a mirthful smile over Alistair's face.

"I hope ya' were comin' to look for me?" he grinned down at her. It was clear he had sampled some of the various whiskies and was not feeling much pain—but probably would be come the next morning.

"Yes yes, I was. I wanted to wish you a Merry Christmas. I brought you a gift."

"Really? A gift?" He seemed surprised but equally delighted. "What is it?"

Rescuing it from Mrs. Fitzrandolph at the door, she had tucked it under her arm and now produced it with cradled hands in front of Alistair. It was a simple gift, but made from the heart, however Clarinda felt inadequate with her choice. After all, Alistair had made a new start in their relationship, so perhaps she needed to present him with something more valuable.

"Let's go sit over here, so I can open it." He indicated a spot over by the window seat. There was only room for one, so as soon as Alistair had taken a seat, he pulled Clarinda upon his lap. "So let's see what ye have here fer me!" He gave her a gentle kiss on the neck and then focused his attention on the gift. The paper was instantly ripped off, the box pried open, the tissue paper shredded until he got his fingers on the contents. "It certainly is soft. What is it?"

Now Clarinda felt downright childish. "It is a scarf," she explained. Taking it in her hands she tried to place it around his neck to demonstrate its use. He grabbed her hands and took the scarf from her and placed it around her shoulders. Using the garment as a lasso, he pulled her toward him and gave her a vigorous kiss. Apparently the alcohol had made him willing to publicly display affection, and Clarinda wasn't about to complain. He was not completely drunk, only inebriated enough to feel liberated and without inhibitions.

Clarinda needed to feel worthy with her gift-giving choice. "So, do you like it?"

"Aye, I like it fine, and if I can get a kiss with it every time I wear it, I will like it all the more."

Taking the scarf from around her neck, she successfully placed it around Alistair's.

"It is verra soft," he repeated. "I like the colors. They are Campbell colors, ye ken."

Clarinda nodded acknowledging her obvious design choices. "I know." She didn't admit she chose them because they also brought out the mysterious darkness in his eyes.

He seemed to be searching for the right thing to say, and the words appeared to be in an actual confrontation inside his mouth, but he finally spoke what was on his mind. "I love the gift, yer verra thoughtful. I have a gift for ya' too, but I dinnae think to bring it here with me."

"Oh please, don't worry about it. It will make the anticipation so much more fun." She winked at him—he winked back.

"Clarinda my dear?" he asked. "Me leg is tingling and I think I may need another dram. Do ya' think we could stand for a spell?"

Happy to oblige, Clarinda was on her feet before he could finish the request. "Of course. I think I could use another wine myself." They both made their way to the kitchen, greeting and giving holiday wishes to those they passed on the way. Glasses were refilled, jokes were shared among the men folk, and then they made their way back through the other rooms to enjoy the home's decorations.

Out of the corner of her eye, Clarinda saw the petite Ms. Lees. She was busy chatting with other guests. No sooner had Clarinda noticed her, when Lauren glanced in their direction. What would happen now? Would Alistair leave her side to run to hers? Alistair turned to see what held Clarinda's attention and once he realized it was his old flame, he gave her an amicable nod and turned back to his conversation and curled his arm around Clarinda's waist with more concentration. Clarinda offered a small wave, and Lauren waved back. That was it, simple—no snarling and no bickering. It was clear to both women who Alistair had chosen and tonight there was no doubt it was Clarinda. Her heart was elated and she felt the delightful tight feeling in her chest which only comes from that very emotion. The night continued, guests chatted, and Alistair was complemented on his scarf which perfectly matched his kilt and his features. It was a wonderful evening of warmth, community, and togetherness. As the night waned, Clarinda realized she needed to be going to attend to her patrons and the guest house's other needs. She started to make her good-byes to the guests, Janet, and Mrs. Fitzrandolph, and made to fetch her cape.

Alistair stopped her. "The weather is no good for goin' alone. Let me see ye home." He had sobered considerably so she delightedly accepted the escort, and took his arm to leave. All in all, it was a wonderful gathering, and to be leaving with the most handsome man at the party, or in town for that matter, was beyond her imaginings.

Walking out into the snowy night, Clarinda felt as if she had been transported back to Vermont and into the Currier and Ives type of setting she had known during her childhood. Alistair showed her to her car, but to the left hand side. He got in the driver's seat and started the Mini into motion. In no time they were back at the Heather & Thyme. "Thank ya' for taking me home," Clarinda confided.

"'Tis no trouble, me lass. I hope ya' will favor me with a kiss as payment for this deed."

"Of course, but I hope we can do this right and not in the front seat of my car. Please come inside?"

"As ya' wish, me lady, please let me come around and get ye door," he affected.

Kyle greeted them as they made their way into the foyer of the guest house. "Did you have much trouble tonight?" Clarinda asked her night manager.

"Och, no. In fact, it seems ya' have a full house tonight. A Mr. Kline checked in after ye had left for the Missus Fitzrandolph's. He didn't have a reservation, but since ya' had a free room, I went and rented it. He plans to be stayin' until Hogmanay, so I hope ya' approve."

Clarinda felt wobbly and her knees weakened. To Kyle it appeared she was beginning to pale and she vigorously wrung her hands. "Mr. Kline, you say?"

Kyle nodded and with that Clarinda fainted. Luckily Alistair's reflexes were swift or her head would surely have hit the floorboards.

chapter 25
an unwelcome christmas delivery

"Lass! Lass! Clarinda! Can ye hear me?"

Alistair was slightly slapping her cheek, but 'light' in his vocabulary felt like a sharp slap to Clarinda. Opening her eyes to assess her bearings, she found herself lying on the floor of her foyer with Alistair, Kyle and some other guests crowding around her.

Kyle was clearly troubled to see his mistress on the floor and unconscious "Ya' gave me quite a start. Are ya' feeling yerself? Let me fetch ya' a glass of water." He ushered the guests to the parlor to provide some privacy.

Clarinda tried to sit up, and luckily Alistair was tenderly at her aid. She was not confident of her strength and still felt a bit woozy. She looked steadfast into Alistair's eyes and tried to speak. At last she spoke one word: "David?"

Alistair's heart sank. She was looking at him but calling him by another man's name. It was abundantly evident why he couldn't become attached to this woman. By the mere verbalization of this single utterance Alistair felt himself slip in her ranks from the man of the hour to the clown of the season. Clearly Clarinda still had feelings for this man—she just spoke his name in a questioning manner. It was apparent to Alistair she had been biding her time with him until her true love could regain his place by her side—once he came to his senses and realized what he had almost lost. Yes, she was a prize and it was folly for Alistair to consider he could find happiness with her—or any woman. A heart never heals—his sister was living proof of that fact. If he wasn't so concerned with Clarinda's welfare, he would have dropped her right there and made for the hills to cleanse his soul of this cruel woman. She spoke again, but Alistair's ears were closed to more of her mumblings about her true love.

"Please tell me David is NOT here! Oh Lord, when will this stop? I cannot—and WILL NOT—have him here! I need to get up and kick him out into the cold snowy night!"

As she rambled her words became fiercer and Alistair and Kyle were relieved to see her gain her strength and usual determination. Kyle gave her a glass of water and she gulped it down, and it reacted as if he had poured petrol into a car; she was struggling to get up, continuing to mutter commands and expletives.

These expressions were counter to what Alistair had expected. *Wasn't she glad David was here? Why is she so upset?* he pondered. He stayed by her side not because of devotion, but because he did not want to see her lapse again and injure herself. But he knew her well enough to see she did not seem pleased by the mystery appearance of her latest guest and was preparing to do something about this situation. Had he wrongly surmised the circumstances? Was she enraged this Mr. David Kline was here?

He took a brave and daring tactic. "Clarinda, are ya' no glad ye lover has come for ya'?"

"NO! No, I am not! Why does he need to come here and ruin

the new life I have started? Isn't New York a big enough city to exhibit my shame, but he feels he needs to spread it around the world! And on Christmas Eve of all times! Where is he?"

Alistair tried, but couldn't conceal a small grin. Clarinda was still acting a bit loopy and trying to smooth her skirt and restore her appearance, but her determination reminded him of the cowardly lion in the Wizard of Oz. He would not have been surprised if she next challenged him to 'put 'em up, put 'em up'. Could he have been wrong about her attachment to a long, lost great lover?

"Clarinda? Are you looking for me?" A voice floated down from the landing of the staircase.

Footsteps softened by the cushion of thick carpeting made their way down the stairs. First black shod feet, black trousers, and at long last the torso and head of the enigmatic Mr. David Kline. When Clarinda took in his visage, he seemed to not have changed at all. He stood tall, still ensconced in black, and looking every bit the successful New York businessman. As he neared the small group of three, he provided introductions.

"Hello there, I am David Kline," and offered his hand to Alistair. David took in the Scot who was at least a good six inches taller and certainly had more bulk even though David had not slacked from his vigorous workout routine. He also didn't think Scotsmen actually wore kilts, but perhaps Christmas was the one and only time these garments were actually publicly put on display. He then nodded to Clarinda. "My dear, it is lovely to see you again. You are as beautiful as I remember from the last time.

The last time, really! thought Clarinda. *I think I was bawling my eyes out so I am sure I was really looking and feeling my best.* Instead she decided to ferret out his motives and why he decided to show up in Scotland, of all places. "David, what exactly are you doing here?"

Alistair didn't really want to hear the answer to this question, but he wanted to stay as Clarinda's guard should she feel lightheaded. Sensing this was not for his ears, Kyle went to the parlor to attend to the guests, but they easily were able to overcome him and were making their way into the hallway to get a good view of their innkeeper's altercation.

Seeing a good sized audience developing, David thought some privacy might be in order. "Can we go someplace quiet where we can talk?"

"No, you have had plenty of time for talk. This is my house and you are not welcome here. I have changed my mind—I don't want to hear your lame excuse. I want you to leave immediately," and she pointed to the door.

"Clarinda, please, let me explain," David tried to appease her so he could be heard. Alistair had never seen the wrath of a woman as keen as what he was witnessing. He was proud to see Clarinda stand her ground even though he feared her heart wanted to be more reasonable and agreeable to David's justification.

David continued to state his case, "I did not realize what I had when you were with me. I am so, so, sorry and I want to apologize to you. I want to show you by coming here that I am ready to make a change and to ask you to reconsider. Please come back to me; please come back to New York."

There, it was said. David wanted her and Alistair was powerless to do anything. After all, why did he care? He realized he was having an internal debate between his heart and his head. His heart was disappointed he might not see Clarinda again; they might never ride across Rannock Moor again, nor enjoy a long walk along the Great Glen Way nor... but his head interjected and was telling him he wouldn't miss her anyway. 'Don't let the weakness in ya' take rule, be strong.' She would only bring pain, such as this very moment, and it was not needed in any man's life. Oddly enough he felt Clarinda press up against him and use him for her support.

"David. Let me make this very clear, so please try to pay attention so I do not need to repeat myself." Her voice was eerily soft; she spoke slowly and struggled to control her anger as if at any minute it could erupt into a disastrous power. "I thought you made it perfectly clear to me you are not interested in a committed relationship. I gave you my heart and my soul; I thought that was what you wanted. I would have done anything for you." She struggled to keep her voice even and not quake with the overwhelming emotions. After a deep breath she continued. "I understand I am not a cute 'twenty-something', but I still loved you with all my heart. Yes, you taught me many things, and I would have sacrificed my job at the firm to become a proper wife for you, but in return you decide it is better to make me the fool than to make me your partner."

She was so angered she needed to grasp something, so her hand reached behind her and found Alistair's right thigh. Her hold was strong and the pressure on the old injury made him wince. His heart was matching his leg with pangs of its own, but he would not back away nor lessen his stance. If nothing else he wanted to act as her 'cheering section'. She may be lost to him, but she was doing a hell of a job telling this worthless clout where to go, and he was proud to see a woman be this brave. If he didn't know better, he would have thought her to be Scot!

After taking hold of something sturdy, she took another breath and continued her diatribe. "Do you think it was easy for me to leave my friends, my Aunt and Uncle in Vermont? No, it wasn't, but I did it anyway because I had been ruined in New York—thanks to you. But I moved here to gain a new life. And you know what? It is a good one! I work hard, I have made some friends, and the country here is beautiful. At first it was very hard for me, not only with limited money, but also to cope with loneliness. But I have finally made some roots here. I have some guests," and she indicated to the growing gallery in her foyer, "who may never visit my doorstep again, but I have tried to be careful and not fall for men like you. I don't need to ever again go through the pain of ever loosing a love held so true."

Clarinda's firmness was about to dissolve so she stopped spouting and looked at the floor. Alistair gripped her shoulders but she took no notice.

Taking advantage of this pause in her discourse, David tried to explain his reasoning. "Clarinda, I know I was cruel to you in New York, and again, I am sorry. I wish I didn't have to say it over and over again, but I guess I am not getting through to you, so I will say it again and again until you realize I am truly sorry for my actions."

"David, you can say it until you turn blue, they are empty words. Your actions told me your true desires, and it is clear they do not include me. So after many months, you decide to come over to the UK, and expect me to accept your apologies, abandon my guest house and the investment I have made in this business, and come back to New York with you? Am I getting this right?"

"Yes—I thought you would be happy to see me. Tell me its not true? I wrote to you and told you the same thing I am trying to tell you now. Fran told me you weren't seeing anyone so I hoped you still had feelings for me."

"Fran? Fran? You spoke to Fran? Did you ever consider the fact my friend is very loyal and she might have told you things to protect me? It is not your business if I have a new man in my life."

David directed his next retort to Alistair. If there was going to be a row, why not make everyone miserable. "So I assume you are Clarinda's new bedfellow?" To this accusation, there was a hush from the gallery of guests horning in on the conversation from the parlor.

Not knowing how to handle this accusation, Alistair remained silent, but was shocked at the brazenness of this cad. He might not deserve Clarinda for himself, but this pompous jerk certainly didn't deserve this fine woman either.

"Leave Alistair out of this!" Clarinda was vehement. "He is the brother of my head chef, and is kind enough to drive me home from a neighbor's party."

Alistair was not about to let a woman, even one as determined and fair as Clarinda, handle his defense. He attempted to take a step forward to which Clarinda pushed him back as an attempt to keep the two men out of striking distance and not allow the quarrel to come to blows.

"Look, Mr. Kline," Alistair began slowly but with a firm voice. "I don't ken ya' from Adam, but I ken ya' are makin' Clarinda upset by your arrival. Dinnae you think if ya' leave now, it will prevent her from further upset."

His ear untrained to the Scot's brogue, it took David a few moments to discern what had just been said. "Look yourself—Alistair, right? I think you need to stay out of this. After all, Clarinda made it clear to both of us that you are just a relative of the hired help. I was her fiancé! Why don't you give us some privacy so we can handle this ourselves?"

"I am no about to leave Clarinda's side. Based on ye actions, it is clear to me ya' are no more than a feartie, spoiled child. Ya' had the love and devotion of this fine lass, and ya' cast it away without a thought. Now ya' want back what ya' threw away. Well, she is no a toy or a pet you can just reclaim on a whim. I have seen her thrive in our wee town, and she has made some dear mates here who love and cherish her. She has changed our lives here for the better, and I pray she doesn't go back to you, because we need her here."

Wanting to see the sincerity in Alistair's eyes, Clarinda looked back and looked up at him. *Was he really talking about her?* She had hoped he might care for her, but he had made it clear he didn't want to be confined to a relationship, perhaps now he was having a change of heart? The scowl of confusion troubled Alistair and he spoke directly to her. "Aye, lass, ye have brought hope, and a magical light to Inverwick. Dinnae ya' no see it? Ya' can't go. We need ya' here."

"We, or do you also mean 'you'?" Clarinda wanted to know if he was speaking in generalizations, or he did care for her as she did for him.

"Aye lass. Me too."

David was about to release the contents of his stomach onto the plaid carpeting if this ridiculous conversation didn't cease this instant. He came to reclaim his lover, but he could have possibly driven her into the arms of this huge, plaid, Highlander. "Clarinda, look at me. Please. I'm here, in Scotland to beg for you to forgive me. I will do whatever it takes. If you want to get married, so be it. What is it that you want and I will make it so?" David felt pathetic having to succumb to such plaintive pleading. He realized his dignity was in shreds, but he was not going to give her up to an uncivilized dolt who couldn't even speak the English language correctly.

Clarinda took a deep breath and began to explain her feelings. There was no point in creating a scene in front of her guests, so she hoped her words would be accepted without the need for a harsh delivery.

"You know what David, your proposal for marriage is a little late, and I have to tell you, my philosophy on the matter has changed as well. There was a time I wanted to be your wife, and it was a desperate longing. But the act of marriage was not going to solidify the relationship. You need to give of yourself, and it is not displayed with the offering of a ring. It comes from an unselfish love. To hold a heart in your hand and understand it is under your care. You are not capable of this kind of devotion. You do not give into what your heart tells you to do, but rather your actions come from what makes you feel good, and to avoid any commitment for fear of loss. To find love is to accept there might be pain, and as horrible and scary as it might be, the chance for utmost happiness is the reward.

"Once you realize this basic concept, you might be able to truly see the light and love in other people. You haven't learned this yet, and you came here to try to reclaim the closest thing you had to it, but it is not the same. You still don't want to take the risk. For you it is better to 'settle' than it is to risk it all, and find your true soul mate.

"What you have done is a brave thing—unwanted yes—but very brave. Why don't you apply this same courage by freeing your heart and accepting the love of someone? I am sure you will find her, but it won't come from reason, it comes from here," and she took her hand and placed it solemnly over her heart. She was not in tears, but close to it, and she took another breath to keep the tears at bay.

No one spoke, the conversation was over. There was a sniffle and Clarinda looked over to see one the elderly ladies stifle a small sob into her hankie. Apparently it had moved someone to tears, but she didn't deliver this monologue for the benefit of her guests. She hoped the man standing behind her had harkened these words.

David saw the imploring look in her watery eyes and realized he was not about to accomplish his goal with this impromptu visit to Alba. Clarinda hadn't yelled, she'd spoken from the heart. For the first time in his life David realized falling in love wasn't always all about what *he* wanted. He knew he had lost, and it was his turn to deliver a speech—one of concession.

"I am sorry Clarinda. You are right. We had a good thing, but the timing was not right for either one of us. I suppose I best be going. I have caused enough distress for one night. I don't suppose there is another inn in town where I can get a room?"

"Please stay. I can't bear to think I threw you out into the cold on Christmas Eve." Actually she had thought about doing that very thing a short half-hour ago, but it was clear roles had changed in the same span of time. Clarinda was now the teacher, and David was the pupil. David began to understand what she was trying to convey. He hadn't appreciated what she had offered him before, but he was starting to comprehend the tremendous loss he had created by his selfish actions. He might not leave Scotland with Clarinda as his again, but he vowed he would not make the same mistake. Yes, it was better to love, than to never feel the wonder of the emotion at all. Valuable ticket to the UK yielded and equally valuable lesson learned.

"Thank you for your compassion and hospitality. I guess I better go and retire. I think your guests have had enough excitement for the evening." He turned and solemnly made his way back up the stairs to his previously assigned room.

As if on cue, Kyle jumped into action. "Alright everyone, why dinnae you all retire, or I will be happy to serve an evenin' beverage in the bar? Nothin' more to see now, let's all move along."

Clarinda smiled. Kyle was behaving like a copper at a traffic accident. The rubber-neckers—her guests—wanted to see more blood and gore from the wreckage of the relationship, but he was determined to not let his boss's open argument escalate into more public entertainment. The guests moseyed off to their rooms or to the wee bar for one more libation. Clarinda was not about to leave the scene of the crime. She turned and faced Alistair. "Thank you for being here. I am not very strong when it comes to this sort of thing, and I was glad to have some moral support to get me through this wretched ordeal."

Not strong? Not strong? Did Alistair hear her words correctly? "Me lass, I have no seen or heard a woman with more strength and heart as yeself. I am glad yer are plannin' to stay in Inverwick. I ken me sister would about die if ye were to go."

"Really? Janet would be sad, huh? Well I guess so."

"Clarinda." Alistair took her chin in his palm and directed her face to meet his gaze. "The speech you gave was no just for David's benefit, was it now?"

This was a tricky moment. Clarinda was feeling some relief from deflecting the unwanted affections of David, but indeed she had spoken those words for Alistair as well. He also seemed to not fully understand the wonder of love, but rather he seemed to fear and resist the emotion.

"Alistair, I spoke those words to David to try to demonstrate to him how I felt then, and how I feel now. I didn't intend to provide a doctrine for all to live by."

Alistair nodded his head, but he still felt he was also an

intended recipient of her discourse, despite her confirmation ~~of~~ that he ~~it~~ was not.

"Are you feelin' alright? Are ya' still shoogly? Why don't ya' come into the parlor and I can get you a wee dram to calm yer nerves." He gently guided her into the parlor and made her place her feet up on the divan. "Just stay there a wee bit, and I will be back directly."

Alistair returned quickly with two shot glasses of amber liquid. He was right, once Clarinda took a sip, she felt the whisky begin to settle her nerves and still her shaking hands.

"Sorry about the scene we caused. I am sure my guests will never visit my doorstep again. What a disaster. I am sorry for ruining your Christmas Eve."

"Och, no lassie, ya' dinnae ruin me Christmas Eve, and I think it was quite somethin' for yer guests, so dinnae fash about that either." His voice was soft and he stroked her hair. She could restrain herself no longer and the flood-gates opened. She held her head in her hands and sobbed. She needed to get the pent up emotion out. Of course, she was embarrassed to have Alistair witness this childish behavior, but she couldn't help it.

"Go on, and greet, it will do ya' good." He was gentle and soft, and continued to stroke her hair. In a few moments, Clarinda was able to regain her composure. Alistair provided her with his handkerchief and she wiped her wet eyes and nose.

"S-s-s-sorry about that." Her words hitching as a result of a good cry. "I don't typically break down in front of strangers."

"Lass, I ken when a person needs to have a deep greet to cleanse the sourness they feel in their gut. I ken women need to do this more than lads, but it is no different. And since when am I a stranger?"

She began to laugh. He was right, she felt closer to him now than she ever had. He had been her support when she needed it, and was equally kind and gentle when she needed to release her emotions. "I guess I am wrong about that—thank you so much for being my friend."

"And I am no just yer friend either, am I? I think that since I hae seen yer fine hurdies, I am more than just a friend?" He was teasing her.

"You are right about that too. You are more than a friend as well. But this makes me think; how do I refer to you? Are you a 'good friend', or just a 'lover'? Hum, what do you think?" She could taunt him just as well.

"I dinnae ken, I guess I will have to think about this, but for now you ken I will be there if ya' need me."

"Thank you. Thank you very much. I certainly did appreciate having you here with me tonight. However, it is now very late, and I need to be up early in the morning to see to my guests. Your sister is serving a special Christmas Breakfast for everyone. After all, Santa Claus won't come unless you are fast asleep." Clarinda didn't want him to leave, but she had to be reasonable and began to get to her feet.

Luckily Alistair was still at her side, her feet were not quite under her and she stumbled and fell against his chest. His arms reached around her and pulled her up to him and he placed his lips on hers and gave her a deep and longing kiss.

"I think Santa has given me what I want already," he grinned and kissed her again. Clarinda was more than obliging and returned his ardor. Their tongues were intertwined with each other and they were breathing for each other.

"Ah lass, ye are definitely what I be wanting' for Christmas." He dipped one shoulder down, outstretched his arm and in one smooth motion gathered Clarinda off her feet and into his arms. She reached her arms around him and buried her face into his neck. He smelt warm, clean and masculine. She caressed his back with one hand and peppered his neck with soft kisses. She felt a soft moan in his chest and knew he was enjoying her attentions. Luckily, the door to Clarinda's apartment was ajar, and he deftly used his foot to open it fully, gently delivered his delicate cargo onto the bed.

He then reached and took his shirt off, and flung it to the floor and climbed on top of Clarinda. His hands grazed over her breasts and she gasped in excitement. He cupped them and began to unbutton her blouse and kiss her neck as he worked his way down her silken body. She touched his back and worked her hands down to his hips. Typically this is the time and place she would begin to unbuckle a man's belt and trousers, but since Alistair was still wearing his kilt this presented some intriguing opportunities. She began to run her hand up along his thigh until she reached the crease of his hips. Then gently she began to stroke him near his most sensitive area. Alistair sucked in a breath of air, but continued to focus his attention on suckling her breasts. They both were beginning to become lost in the rapture and urged each other to reach the next plateau.

Alistair sat up on his haunches and held Clarinda's arms over her head with one of his large and strong hands. Delicately, he took his time to unfasten the remaining closed buttons on her blouse and eased her out of her camisole. With equal care, he began to unzip her long, full skirt. Occasionally kissing her on her tummy, and her breasts, he wanted to take her in, to be intoxicated by her essence. She reached for him, but he held her at bay. He wanted to revel in the beauty of this woman bathed in the soft blue light of the winter's night. "Clarinda, ye are the most beautiful creature that graces these eyes." He lowered himself down to her and softly kissed her waiting lips.

"Alistair, let me please you now."

He couldn't believe his ears, he was already feeling more delight than he ever had before, and now she wanted to please him. This was not typical of other lasses, yes girls, he had bedded before. In the hands of this woman, he didn't know what to expect.

She indicted for him to roll over onto his back and she straddled him. She slowly caressed his thighs while administering kisses, licks and gentle bites to his torso and nipples. He began to pant and wanted to use his hands to guide her, but she would push them aside, replicating his previous method of torture. She slowly slid his kilt up his leg and reached under to fondle his manhood. In response, Alistair arched his back and uttered a low, deep groan of desire. His head rolled back; his eyes and jaw were clenched shut in deep concentration. Clarinda could not believe this untamed, rough and mysterious man was in her bed—again! This time she would make it an experience for him like no other in hopes the morning after their love-making would not end as before. She teased him with her tongue, licking him here and there, and finally took him into her mouth. This was more than Alistair could withstand and his hips began to buck and rock to match her strokes. She would stop to let him regain some composure and then slowly begin the process again. His longing was so intense; Alistair was not sure if this was the epitome of pleasure or a gentle form of sheer torture. He knew he would not have the control to be able to contain himself any longer. Grabbing Clarinda, he rolled her over onto her back and placed his knee between her legs. Reaching down to her hidden clef, he found her slick and ready to accept him. He thrust into her with wild abandon. Clarinda shrieked, arched her back and clung to him. Her nails scrapped his back, the sting adding to his ecstasy. They moved together as one, his thrusts deeper and stronger with each succession. Clarinda had never felt such searing desire. This man was taking her like no other; he was holding nothing back. She felt his wild carnal need rush over her as he exploded into her. Still panting from the excursion, they clung to each other as drowning victims do when afloat at sea on a raft.

    She kissed and softly rubbed his shoulders, down his arms and to his hands. He took hers in his and kissed the back of her capable, yet delicate fingers, and then kissed her mouth. "These have brought me pleasure like no other I hae ever felt b'fore. Ye are most enchanting, Clarinda Tetrick." He knew he should offer her some kind words on par to what he was feeling, but those emotions were beginning to make him anxious and ensnared.

Clarinda could see him turn and look away from her, as if longing for the freedom of the moor outside the window. She didn't want to make him feel like a penned animal, and tried to redirect his attention. Her hand ran down his torso again, and she could feel his hardness under his still donned kilt. "What do you say we have another go?"

Before she could get the words out he began to powerfully kiss her. "This time, I think I need to be the cat, and ye can be me wee mouse." He grabbed her arms to hold them over her head and began to explore her body with his hands and tongue. She was on fire wherever he touched her. She could no longer endure the longing he was fueling inside her. She cried out for him to take her and when he came to her, it was as powerful and forceful as before. She wept tears of emotion when their coupling had ceased.

"Clarinda, me love, I have caused you harm? Oh Lord, I didn't mean to." Alistair brushed her hair from her sweaty brow. "I am so sorry, it is just you made me lose " Clarinda brought her finger to his lips to silence further words.

"No, you didn't. These are tears of joy. I have never felt such joy, and I guess I didn't know how to react. Shhh for now, let me just watch you."

Blissful sleep came upon them as they gazed at and embraced each other. The morning would come soon enough and the truth with it, but in the small hours of Christmas Day, they were delighted for the gift they had shared.

chapter 26
the strange gifts
christmas can bring

    Alarm clocks have a ringing clamor that can only be described as bad-mannered. They are relentless, and Clarinda felt the clock on her night table was trying to play hide and seek while she groped to find it. In real time it was only seconds, it seemed like hours until she had grasped the infernal time piece and submitted it into silence and registered the hour.
    "Oh Lord, it is six o'clock! Damn! I need to be ready for guests in only a half and hour." She bolted upright in bed and was surprised to find herself naked until she remembered what had taken place the night before. She smiled at the large, smooth back of a Highlander facing her, rhythmically rising and falling with the shallow breaths of slumber. Clarinda bound out of bed, grabbed some clothes and dashed into the bathroom. She didn't have time for her standard morning ablutions; she hastened to become merely presentable.
    "Lord, I hope Janet is here—I am so late!" she whispered. The jolt of her leaving the bed must have awoken Alistair. When Clarinda

returned to the bedroom, the sight of him stretching his long lean body in front of the curtained window was enough to make her forget about her guests and take the Scot back to her bed.

"I'm sorry. Did I wake you? I didn't mean to but I realized I am running horribly late. I need to help Janet with Christmas breakfast and begin to prepare Christmas Dinner."

"Aye, lass, I heard ya' get up, but I typically have risen by this hour anyway."

"By the looks of you, you already have risen at this hour," Clarinda teased after spying a jutting pinnacle of his anatomy.

Alistair blushed. "Well you seemed to want me to rise to the occasion last night!"

"Yes and if I had more time, I would take advantage of your 'rising' right now!" She ran up to give him a quick kiss, and then dart toward the door, but he held her arm and swung her back to face him.

He kissed her deeply, and then whispered, "Happy Christmas."

"Merry Christmas, to you too. I wish I could stay and give you another 'present', but your sister is probably wondering what is keeping me. I am sure she would be some surprised to see you here this morning. But you can duck out the side door if you want to go undetected and avoid her scrutiny." She recalled his hasty departure the last 'morning after', and wanted to provide him with escape options if this was going to be his standard modus operandi.

"Aye, I am certain she will be, but I bet the details of last night's row will be more entertaining to her than to see me beggin' up to the table for some breakfast." Alistair watched her face for some sort of reaction. He knew he behaved badly the last time, and he was not going to mess things up again. Last night was too perfect, and he wanted to preserve its magic for as long as it could be sustained.

"OK then, I will see you out there. Take your time." She kissed him again and slipped out the door. The smell from the kitchen wafted in, and Alistair smiled. His sister would be surprised, but so would Clarinda. He trounced into the bath for a shower.

Clarinda dashed into the kitchen. "Where ya' been lass? I was thinkin' I was gonna be the only one pulling this feast together. Oh, and Happy Christmas!" Janet was teasing and gave her a peck on the cheek, but Clarinda felt small regardless.

"Sorry Janet, I guess I overslept. Merry Christmas to you too." It was a fragment of the truth, she didn't get much sleep last night, and when she finally did get some rest, it wasn't enough.

"Ah, ya' had a good time at Dottie's?" referring to Mrs. Fitzrandolph, "I saw ya' walking around with me brother at yer side. You two make a nice pair—both tall."

Oh Lord, this is not what I need right now, Clarinda consoled herself. This day was going to be a long one, and Clarinda knew Janet would not let up until she knew every detail. She just wished she could first get breakfast served before she had to reenact the *Jerry Springer Show* held in the foyer the prior evening.

"I understand yer auld love came here to Inverwick. So, how is that goin'?"

"Who told you?" Clarinda was exasperated. Was there no sense of decorum this holy morning? "I suppose Emily? Oh well, I might as well tell you, but can we get the food organized? I want to keep my mind focused on one thing at a time."

Janet smiled. She enjoyed this mild torment. Yes, she had received the full story from Emily who in turn got it related to her by Kyle. No need for a lot of mobile phones in Inverwick when the old grapevine system worked so efficiently. She was delighted for her friend, it seemed perhaps she had found a man after all, and Janet was pleased it was her brother. Could it blossom into something more romantic? Walks home and horseback riding was platonic enough, but what they both needed was some honest-to-goodness passion in their lives.

"Fine, yes. Ya' ken I do this every morn, so I have most of the pudding, sausage, and bacon done. The scones are almost ready to come out of the oven. Why don't we see what kind of eggs the early risers would prefer and we can get this Christmas Breakfast underway?"

Clarinda walked out into the dining room where some of the guests were starting their breakfast of toast, marmalade with tea or coffee. Her waitress, Kate, was attending to everyone nicely. When some of the guests spied her, they waved and looked sympathetic which made Clarinda all the more sheepish. She walked over to one of the tables and wished her guests a very Merry Christmas. This helped to break the ice, and soon after greeting everyone in the room, the spirit of the place was of joy and good cheer. Kate began to deliver piping hot plates of food, and Clarinda could see her guests were enjoying their holiday and might possibly dismiss the previous night's shenanigans.

Clarinda walked back into the kitchen and Kate and Janet and the other cooks were performing their well rehearsed orchestrated dance, and Clarinda realized she was not needed for the remainder of this meal and started to organize herself for Christmas Dinner. She had reviewed the planned menu.

Menu:
~ Goat Cheese Comfit
~ Mushroom Turnovers
~ Pumpkin Curry Soup
~ Roast Turkey, dressing and gravy
~ Green Beans
~ Creamed pearl onions
~ Garlic Mashed Potatoes
~ Neeps
~ Tossed Salad
~ Candied Yams
~ Plum Pudding and Hard Sauce
~ Cheeses, coffee, tea

This meal was going to be served 'family style' as they say in the States which would help add to the community of the guests; passing dishes to each other would allow them to get to know each other a bit better. Some of her guests were staying with her while visiting nearby relatives, so not all of her patrons would be dining, but she planned on having more than enough, just in case there were some late additions. She was so engrossed with the menu and determining the necessary portions she didn't notice the back door of the kitchen swing open.

"Happy Christmas! Smells great — can I hae some?" Clarinda was not sure who was more surprised — herself or Janet — to see the tall figure standing in the kitchen, still donning his kilted attire from the previous night. He looked disheveled from his shower and it was clear he had just come from Clarinda's apartment. "You two birds look surprised, hae ya' no seen a hungry man b'fore?"

"Er, no, well aye, I have, but I dinnae think I would see ya' here so early," Janet stammered.

"I am no hear early, I'm late — I hae no left since last night," he walked over and tenderly kissed Clarinda upon her blushing cheek.

"Really?" Janet gave both of them the 'raised eyebrow look' of one who knew better. "Well, I guess it was quite and eventful evening here at the guest house last night? I suppose I could spare you some breakfast." Janet prepared a plate of hot goodies for her brother and instructed him to sit at the kitchen table. She walked over to Clarinda and whispered, "You have quite some story to tell me later!"

Everyone continued in silence, even Kate did not make any notice of Alistair at the table but she did announce the arrival of 'the man from New York City' when she brought his order into the kitchen. "Very peculiar, this egg-white thing."

Clarinda saw to it his plate was as he preferred and sent Kate to deliver it. Leaving him a few moments to sample his meal, Clarinda gathered herself up to discuss his travel arrangements.

With luck, he planned to leave Inverwick today. However, the train schedules would not be typical due to the holiday, so perhaps this was wishful thinking on her part. She was not going to be such a shrew to cast him out of her guest house on Christmas, but she hoped he might have made other arrangements, optimally outside of Inverwick. Once she gathered up her courage and made sure she was presentable to the dinning room, she walked through the swinging door and found David already had a visitor sitting at his table. There was not mistaking the broad shoulders of Alistair Campbell who was sitting facing David. Their voices were normal and it did not look as though a brawl was to break out so she turned tail and walked back to the safety of the kitchen. She had been so focused rehearsing her 'departure speech' she didn't even notice Alistair slip out of the kitchen. "What could they be talking about?" she asked aloud to no one in particular, but Janet's keen ears heard the query.

"Who, my dear?"

"Alistair is out there talking with David." Her voice was soft, as if she was distracted by a daydream. "What on God's green earth do you think they are talking about? I hope it doesn't come to blows—that is the last thing I need."

"Why, ye silly, of course."

"Huh?"

"Ye. They're talkin' about ye. I don't think ya' ken much about me brother, but he is very competitive, and he will no back down when faced with a challenge. It is clear he is no about to give up and walk away when ya' have another man who could interfere."

"Janet, I am sorry to have to say this, but I am going to speak the truth. I think your brother would welcome some interference. I care about him very much, but I do not think I am any different than his earlier lady friends. Of course, he is gorgeous, and who wouldn't want to have him by their side. But he made it very clear to Lauren, he was not about to marry or settle down; and I don't think I'm going to change his mind. I would be happy to be his companion for a short while, but I think he is too set in his ways to be committed, or even fall in love."

"Clarinda my dear, you're right about the past. But he has nae met someone like you before. Trust me on this. I think you ken how he feels about love; this is because he has seen the pain I went through when Richard passed. But what he dinnae ken about love is that it is better to feel the pain of it leavin' than never to feel the joy of it growin' in yer heart. I think ya' ken this to be true, no?"

Clarinda nodded. She understood completely.

"Sae ye see, me brother is afraid to have his heart broken, sae when he feels he might be vulnerable he takes the easy way out and breaks it off. I think what ya' need to do is to show him the joy of love, not the pain that might come of it. I hae told him this, but he is no goin' to listen to auld Janet for his love-life advise. In some ways he has lived through a lot, and in others he has only begun to understand life."

The two women worked in silence until Alistair came back into the kitchen. "David would like to say good-bye to ya', Clarinda." He gently clasped her shoulder as he passed on his way back to her apartment. "I will be going, I have some things I need to be doin' today before dinner."

"Will ya' joinin' me and Clarinda, dear?"

"Count on it! I wouldna miss it for anythin'. Make sure ya' have a large turkey; I will be hungry again when dinner comes to be served." Clarinda smiled when she thought of a different version of his insatiable hunger. Watching the swaying kilt pass into her apartment she hoped it would not be the last time she would enjoy the thrilling sight.

"He's waitin!" Janet was trying to break Clarinda's reverie. Good Lord, this love-sickness was trying her last nerve.

"Who?" Clarinda questioned.

"Ya' daft? David! He's waitin' to say farewell. You better get him out of here while you still can. The weather may change to snow and you will be stuck with him here another night! Now go!"

Clarinda walked to the front desk in the foyer and David had his coat on and bag ready. "Thank you again Clarinda for your kindness to let me stay here. I hope I was not too disturbing to your guests last night. I guess you and I are known for making scenes." He was struggling to keep the conversation light in this awkward moment. "I have learned something here that I never understood before and I have you to thank for it."

"What is that?"

"Someone's love is much like a glass object. Even though the glass may be very thick and look durable, it can still shatter and break if not treated with care. I didn't realize this at all, I thought if I was happy doing what I wanted, the other person would be happy as well. It is entirely the other way around. If I can bring joy to someone else, I will feel the better for it. Thank you for helping me to understand."

"You are welcome." She paused. "Where are you planning to go? It is Christmas Day, and I can't have you leaving without arrangements for someplace else."

"I do have plans. I can still get a train from Inverness this afternoon, and I have called and made reservations at the Swallow Craigmonie and they are expecting me. They are even serving a Christmas Dinner; but I will sorely miss dining here. Thanks again Clarinda. You look terrific, and that large man you have will treat you well; at least much better than I did. Bye now."

Turning, he gathered his bag, and walked out into the drive where a local cabbie was waiting to take him to the depot. The moment was melancholy—she was glad to see him go, but she knew she would probably not see him again. This was most likely his one and only trip to Scotland; and likewise, Clarinda wondered if she would ever visit New York City again. So much had changed in just the span of a day—even on Christmas Day.

chapter 27
the emotions of the season

"Yum, what good eggnog ye make! The guests will love this concoction. I must make sure we hae rum and whisky for them to spike it if they choose."

Janet was noisily slurping down the creamy drink and Clarinda hoped there would be some left for their guests. Appraising the foods before her, Clarinda was quite pleased with their lovely presentation and scrumptious aroma. Some of her guests, drawn by the wafting odors had already gathered in the bar to enjoy an aperitif. The group would be small, but intimate. If she couldn't share the holiday with Uncle Rupert and Aunt Jilly, than at least she was glad to have some company about her. Janet and Alistair would serve as her adopted family, and for many reasons she was so thankful.

Late in the afternoon, soon after George Wallace made his entrance, Alistair arrived and to Clarinda, he was even more handsome than ever. He had forgone the kilted attire; he donned an Aran sweater over dark gray trousers. He was freshly shaven, his hair was still damp but groomed—wild and refined at the same time. To Clarinda, she was always amazed

THE CELEBRATION OF HOGMANAY

how his appearance forever mirrored his character. Janet attempted to put him to work immediately, mostly to make sure the wood pile by the door was sufficient for the next few days so Clarinda would not have to mind it. Before he went to perform his assigned chores, he pulled Clarinda aside.

"Clarinda," he whispered in her ear and kissed her neck. "I hae no stopped thinkin' about ye all day. I want to wish you a very happy Christmas. Last night you gave me such gifts, but I dinnae hae yers with me." He handed her a small box. Clarinda blushed; not only from the gift but she began to recall the previous evening. She was sure the 'gift' he gave her the previous night was going to have much more meaning than whatever the small box would yield.

"Oh, Alistair. Thank you. You really didn't have too. Very thoughtful."

Alistair nodded his head to encourage her to open the store-wrapped gift. When she looked upon the shiny thistle necklet, her eyes lit up. "This is lovely! Perhaps this makes me a Scot? Certainly not by birth, but I perhaps by choice. I love it!"

"Aye, a Scot by choice. That is a bonnie idea. Welcome to the clan." He motioned for her to turn so he could assist her with the fastener. Her hand went to her neck as she continued to admire the details with her hands. The silver shone in the candlelight of the parlor, and the amethyst lit up her entire face. She had been wrong, this was a simple gift but one of great meaning. She was wearing the flower of Scotland around her neck, given to her by a Scotsman. She was accepted into the fold, and by Alistair Campbell, no less. And all she had given him was a stupid scarf!

Wanting to thank him the best way she knew, she reached up and gave him a deep kiss upon his soft and reddened lips. They were lost in the embrace when Janet gave them a gruff 'A-hem' and they broke from their dreamy hold on each other.

One hand on her hip and a wooden spoon in the other, she used the latter much like an orchestra conductor would his baton. "All right, you need to get back into the kitchen," she instructed Clarinda. "And you," indicating her brother, "outside to see to the wood and coal." Using this as an escape ploy from Janet and her kitchen, George joined this newly assigned task force.

In no time at all the finishing touches had been made, and the fire roared in the hearth. Clarinda declared the feast to be served with the two simple words: "Let's eat!"

The meal was served family style and all the goodies were placed about the table, and each guest took their place about the largest table.

"A toast!" Alistair raised his glass. "To each and all, I bid ye a happy Christmas, and to Clarinda, thank ye for havin' us at yer table."

"Here, here!" was repeated by all. Clarinda beamed in the candlelight. Rich with nostalgic imagery of her childhood in Vermont, she couldn't quite remember a Christmas this wonderful. The snow had started up again; the house smelled of pine and balsam boughs, a genuine turkey dinner; and the tree sparkled in the window. Her guests were joyful, and she was blessed to have found this wonderful town to live in and doubly blessed by the friendships she had forged.

"Thank you," she blushed. "Please take your seats and let's enjoy."

The meal was exceptional—she was delighted to watch her guests enjoy themselves. Alistair rarely took his eyes off of her; each time she looked to see him, he was looking at her and she would smile and blush. Another night of 'gift-giving' was indeed in order, she decided. These gazes and coy looks were not only being shared by Clarinda and Alistair. It seemed when Janet and George were not watching the 'lovebirds', as Janet put it—they were sending each other glances of equal zeal. Romance was in the air, as was the feeling of good will toward men.

After the guests had enjoyed the Christmas Plum Pudding and Hard Sauce and further libations, they made their merry way out into the night for some caroling, or up to their room for some canoodling.

As the tryptophan began to take effect Clarinda was glad for the extra hands in the kitchen to help with the clean up. The many hands made the work light, and soon she, Janet, George, and Alistair retired to the parlor to enjoy a dram of Bunnahabhain.

"Lovely meal, lass," George complimented. "I ken I enjoyed every wee bit, especially the plum pudding. I think yer guests did too. Well done."

Alistair sat beside Clarinda on the divan and whispered into her ear, "Aye, very well done, but I hope I can have more deserts?" She looked at him and could see by his smirk and gleam in his eyes; he was not referring to the pudding. The clues were enough to prompt Janet and George to take their leave. George was eager to see Janet home, and Clarinda wondered if a kiss would be shared under the mistletoe Janet had hanging over her stoop. If George has his way, there would be and it warmed Clarinda's heart to see the two of them find happiness in each other's company.

As for herself, she was exhausted and knew the minute her head hit the pillow she would succumb to her weariness, but she knew Alistair had other plans. Luckily, Janet could handle the standard breakfast fare the next morning so perhaps she could sleep in. Once they closed the door from bidding their good-byes to their friends, Alistair firmly grabbed Clarinda's hand and lead her to the apartment. The rest of the house was fairly quiet. A few guests continued to converse in the bar, but Kyle was seeing to their needs. No more distractions for the rest of the night, God willing!

He shut the door behind them as they entered the room and directed Clarinda to sit on the bed. She reached for him, but he held her hands and rested them in her lap. "No my sweet lass, I hae somethin' I need to say to ya'." He kneeled on the floor in front of her. "I hae to explain me behavior toward ya', so yer no confused by me later actions." To Clarinda, this sounded serious, but she couldn't have him torture his knees on her hard floor and motioned for him to sit beside her, but he refused. "No, I want to make sure I can see yer eyes."

He held her hands and gave them a gentle kiss and sighed. Clarinda remained quiet. This was his moment, not hers; she would listen patiently. At long last he began, "the first time I saw ya', I kent this is no ordinary lady. Ye are very capable, and strong, not only in yer frame, but also in yer heart. I hae no met someone as brave, and as lovely."

"Thank you," she softly countered, but he put his finger to her lips.

"Shh, please I am no done with what I hae to say." Again, a long pause before he continued.

"As ya' ken, I was seein' the Lees lass, Lauren, when ya' first come to Inverwick. Aye, she is a sweet thing and I ken she truly loved me, and wanted to make me a good wife. I hae no doubt she would hae tried her best, but I would no be able to make her happy. We would be actin', she as the dutiful spouse and I as the honorable husband. But I kent we would grow apart. She would want more from me than I would be able to give her, I dinnae love her. I dinnae want to bring bairns into the world without a lovin' ma and da, but she would want them, so it would create another wedge between us. So you see, I had to break it off. Lauren was no the first who tried to get me down the aisle. I had plenty of willin' lasses in Aberdeen, but there has no been love in me heart to give."

This was a curious confession for Clarinda to grasp, and the questioning look on her face belied her thoughts.

"Wait, I will get to that," Alistair responded as if reading her mind. "As you ken, me sister, Janet, once was married. He, like you, was an American and a nice enough lad. Me sister was as happy as anyone has a right to be. She loved this man with all her heart; even left our fair land to go to America just to be with him. And of course, ya' ken what happened to them?" Not waiting for a response, he answered his own question. "Yes, he was killed in war in the Persian Gulf. He was no even a soldier; he was a trainin' to be a physician, ya' ken. Clarinda nodded, Janet had given her some of the history, but Alistair was filling in the details.

"Well after she got word that her man was no comin' back, me sister became morose with sadness. She dinnae eat, sleep, and she moved back to Scotland, but sequestered herself on Skye, of all places. Of course, Portree is lovely in the summer; it is no place to live in the winter, especially alone. She would come to Aberdeen to visit once in a while, and I could see the drastic change in her."

"As a young woman, me sister was one of the loveliest in the Shire. She could cook, naturally, but she also sang. She would sing as she performed her chores. She had the voice of an angel. She was a happy woman, and it radiated in her face. After Richard was killed, that spark of joy was extinguished. She sang no more, she became thin as a rail, and she no longer was the happy lass I kent."

"She seems to be somewhat happy now," Clarinda interjected. "It seems George fancies her, and you know I couldn't live without her; and she, too, seems to be glad to work here."

"Oh aye, she does like cookin' and being a part of your guest house. This is the best thing for her, to feel useful again. But that is no the point of this tale." He sighed again and shifted his weight in his knees but continued to hold Clarinda's hands very tightly.

"I saw what me sister went through all because of the love of a man. I was a young lad just about to enter university, and I vowed then and there I would no let a woman take me heart. If I dinnae fall in love, I could no be hurt by someone. This has been me philosophy and it has served me well thus far."

Clarinda couldn't believe her ears. "Oh Alistair, that is no way to go through life. Love is one of the most wonderful things people can share. It is what gives us hope, compassion, and generosity to others. It is one of the most glorious features of human beings."

Alistair nodded, but he was not yet finished with his discourse. "Aye, me sister and me mates hae told me the same thing, but I dinnae believe it. Again, I had seen the ravages of the emotion, and I fully believe it is better to shield yourself from a possible unsought of agony."

"But that is exactly the point," Clarinda argued. "You won't know the joy of love unless you allow it into your heart. You might get hurt, but you won't know unless you make an attempt. You will never find true happiness in this life without love. Don't shut yourself away. You don't know what you are missing." She was pleading with him, not so much for herself, but to help this enigmatic man find what he so desperately needed to experience for himself.

"Aye, yer sayin' the same things they hae told me. But, I dinnae think I will change. This is what I want to tell you: I think ye are fine and I hae enjoyed our time together, and I hope we can continue to be friends and lovers. But I also want to make it clear I cannae be yer man, as you might expect. One of the things I admire so much about you is your independence. I ken you will be all right, even if we end badly. I hae seen your strength, and you are able to withstand the torment of a broken heart, but I cannae. I am sorry." He bowed his head and rested it on her hands. She was not sure, but it seemed by his breathing he was trying to keep his emotions in check.

Wrenching a hand free from his strong grip, she stroked his hair. "Alistair, I am so sorry for you. You don't know what a wonderful place the world is when you see it through the eyes of someone you love. It is magical and pure."

He muffled his reply. "Dinnae feel for me. I am not the one who got her heart broke by the bloke from New York, and I dinnae have to suffer from the anguish."

His next words were sharp, "You might think love is so wonderful, but it is no. See, ye ken firsthand the cruelty of love, don't ya'!"

Clarinda nodded, somewhat taken aback by his rapid change of emotion. "Yes, I did suffer from a broken heart, but I experienced a deep love for David. He was not right for me either, but I would do it all over again to feel the tenderness and warmth of loving someone. I think you are missing the point. It is not about what you feel, but how you make someone else feel. Love is to give of yourself, not to take from someone. Never mind, I think my words are wasted on you!" She abruptly stood up and Alistair simultaneously leapt to his feet, but he still had a hold on her hand and swiftly whirled her around until she was facing him.

"Give to someone, aye. Well let me give ya' something!" He kissed her hard and forcefully on the lips. "Ya' think it is easy for me to watch ya' each day, and fashin' ya' might injure yeself, or wonderin' if there might be some deranged guest in ya' house who could harm ye. I ken ye are strong, but I also ken the harm others can do. I fash about seein' ya' get hurt, and livin' here all alone."

He was ranting, but Clarinda let him continue to vent his emotions. No doubt about it — the man was confused alright! He vowed he didn't love her in one breath, and in the other he is raving about his concern for her welfare. She was not sure, but this might be what happens when the wall he had so well mortared around his heart was beginning to quake.

He grabbed her and held her close. "I ken I'm haverin', but I cannae bear to see you in any distress. Not only would it kill me sister, but I dinnae think I would be able to." He kissed her again. His emotions were running wild, and taking Clarinda along with him. Stunned by his frankness, however, she wasn't going to disagree with him in this agitated state. She felt for the hurting he was feeling, but at least he was feeling something! Willing to not only help him grapple with his emotions, she would behave as an absorbent sounding-board. Wherever he was going with this, she would follow.

"Clarinda, Clarinda." He began to kiss her while murmuring her name. His hands vigorously explored her body and she was willing to have him take her as she wished. Before long they were in her bed, and he in her. Their lovemaking was strong and physical. Whatever he needed to exorcise, she was the conduit. They collapsed from fatigue and were enveloped by slumber.

chapter 28
a change of heart

Clarinda woke up with a start. Once she recalled the events of the previous night, she reached out expecting to find Alistair lying near her, but only found an empty void in her bed. Disappointed yet again by his lack of 'staying power' she grabbed her pillow and rolled over to take a few moments to collect her thoughts and outline her day. A constant thudding sound was disturbing her thoughts, and she couldn't assess the source of the annoying cadence. At last, when she could stand it no more she shed her bedcovers and peered out the window which faced her backyard. There was a sight most women in Inverwick would spend several pounds to witness. Despite the cold and the previous night's snow, Alistair was shirtless and swinging an axe. By the looks of the growing woodpile and the sheen on his back, he had been at this activity for some time. *Well at least he is servicing some of my needs in an odd way*, Clarinda thought to herself. She got up, washed, dressed and made her way down to the kitchen. Even though Hogmanay was still six days away, it was only six days away.

Clarinda ambled into the kitchen and muttered a 'Good morning' to Janet who was finishing her breakfast chores. She grabbed a cup and poured herself some coffee. She wasn't feeling 'hung over', but she wasn't feeling quite right either. Hoping the coffee would yield some medicinal relief, she drank it black.

"Is it?" Janet countered. "I hae no seen Alistair take to a woodpile like that before unless he is fashin' about somethin'."

"We had an argument, I think. I am not sure what's going on. I guess I better let him cool off, and release the axe from his hands before we try to reconcile."

Wanting to change the subject, she asked Janet for the next call of action.

"So where can I help you. Hogmanay is only six days away and I think we are still cleaning up from Christmas."

Janet suggested some chores to Clarinda, and she took to them, happy to be able to focus her attention on something other than Alistair and his comments. The man was an enigma!

By mid-morning the assigned tasks completed, the guest reservations reviewed, and the rooms inspected, Clarinda felt much better prepared about the upcoming holiday. Double checking the champagne stores, she didn't want to run out and ordered another case. Everything else seemed in order.

At long last Alistair barged into the kitchen to take a break from the wood pile massacre. It seemed to Clarinda the physical exercise had been a good method to release his tensions. He was back to his calm self, but seemed very guarded, even around his sister.

"Can I see ya' outside please?" he quietly requested of Clarinda. Donning a coat to keep from getting chilled, he stepped out onto the front porch and waited for her to join him. She was feeling lucky he didn't go into the backyard again; where the axe was still present. Not that she feared him, but he had been acting very strangely since last night.

As she walked out onto the porch she found him staring over

the moor, and he didn't hear her approach. She placed her hand on his arm and he slowly turned to face her, with redness in his eyes. What ever was troubling him, she could see it was serious.

"Clarinda, I want to say first of all that I am sorry for last night. It is not in my nature to loose control as I did, and I am sorry if I harmed ya'."

Shaking her head, she reaffirmed to him, "No, you didn't hurt me, although they may sting, the words you spoke were true. I am fine, let's forget what we said to each other and move on."

"No lass, I dinnae mean me words, but I am thankful for your forgiveness of me callus remarks. No, what I mean is I hope I didn't physically harm ya'. I dinnae ken what came over me to take you in such a savage fashion. I'm verra sorry."

Struggling to keep her smile from deflating him, she bit the sides of her cheek and measured her response carefully. "Oh, Alistair, my love, no, you did not harm me. I wanted to be with you, and you did not engage in anything improper. I find your raw animal magnetism is very exciting." She smiled slightly and Alistair could see she didn't harbor any ill will. He was amazed at what he still didn't know about women!

"Is that all you wanted to talk about?" she asked. Her toes were beginning to freeze and the warmth of the house was tempting.

"No. I have something else I need to say." Ideas of returning inside were dashed, but Clarinda was still rapt to hear what he needed to convey.

"I was thinkin' about what ya' said last night, in particular how ya' would do it all over again with David just to feel love. That is a powerful idea. To knowingly sacrifice yer lifestyle, and run the risk of heartache to have the love of another is very courageous. Ye also said it is no about what ya' feel, but the love ya' give to another is what is important. These ideas have shaken me and I hae to strongly consider their meaning. I don't know why, but while I was working at the wood, I felt I couldn't control me emotions. I don't know why, and it was a bit upsetting. I think I need to take some time and sort through some things. I am sure ya' will think me a bastard for saying so, but I think we need to stop seeing each other."

This declaration took Clarinda back. Not speaking she just stared at him, her blue eyes enlarged with disbelief. He could see she was trying to sort his words into their meaning, and her reaction was breaking his heart. He didn't purposely want to wound the spirit of this woman who had been so kind, so exciting, and brought so much pleasure into his life. Yes, he realized he was the worst sort of man; a merciless cad.

She sighed to gain her composure, and simply said, "OK," and turned and walked back into the house. She hastily made her way into her apartment. She didn't want to face Janet, she would find out soon enough from her worthless brother what had just transpired. She needed to be alone to have her emotional meltdown in private.

In a few minutes, Alistair returned to the kitchen where his sister was making biscuits. "What was that about?" Janet inquired. When she saw the look on her brother's face, she had her answer. "Och, ya' didn't? What are ye thinkin'? The lass has been the best thing for ya', and ya' cast her away like all the others. When are ya' goin' to grow up, be a man, and let a woman love ya'?" She was exasperated and returned to her mixing bowl with vigor. "Ya' best go. I dinnae think she wants to see ya' when she comes out."

Alistair shrugged and turned, and walked toward the front door of the guest house. As he passed the door to Clarinda's apartment, he could hear faint sobs coming from within. He didn't think he could feel any worse, but he did. The pit of his stomach was close to touching his shoes and he guessed his stature was no taller than twenty-four inches. He slunk out of the guest house, got into his lorry and drove away. He didn't know where he would go, but he wasn't going to go home just yet.

Clarinda heard the truck start up and peeked out of the curtains to see the lorry turn onto the road and head out of town. Once again, she played the fool! She knew she could never be with a man such as him, and she was stupid to think she could. *Buck up,* she chided, there were more important things to consider—especially her guests and Hogmanay. It had been fun while it lasted, but now had bigger issues to resolve. Namely, she needed to ensure her chef didn't leave her in the lurch from the ruin of this relationship.

Janet had been waiting for Clarinda to resurface and tried to bestow some simple comforts. "Here, lass. Come sit here and hae some biscuits and tea. It will help to calm ya'." Clarinda was surprised by her friend's kindness, truly expecting Janet to side with Alistair and want nothing to do with her or her guest house. She surmised incorrectly. Janet tried to offer words of reassurance to placate her upset friend. "It is no yer fault. The man is a clot heid and daft. He cannae see what is right before him. Give him time and I ken he'll come around."

Clarinda was not hearing any of this. She wanted to put the ugliness of the situation behind her. She might be able to wait for Alistair to change his mind, but she couldn't put off the needs of her guest house. To keep busy was the best way for her to keep her mind off the awful feeling she had burning inside.

"Janet, you are very kind, and I appreciate your gentle and encouraging words, but the main concern I have right now is you. Will you stay and continue to be my head chef? I can't bear to loose you right before Hogmanay."

Janet's face softened when she heard Clarinda's plea. "Och, me friend! Of course I will stay. Me brother's a pure mad dafty, but that has no concern of our arrangement. I'm ye chef, and I willna leave ya'. We are in this thing together, and I ken we can make a go of it. I am no quittin' on ya'!"

Janet could barely breathe as a result of Clarinda's forceful hug. "Thank you! Thank you! I'd hoped you would stay."

"Ya' don't know a stubborn Scot yet, we do nae quit. Now come and help me with these tatties for Cullen Skink."

Before long they were working, and despite the unsettling events earlier in the day, Clarinda found herself whistling. She was amazed when Janet began to sing a little song to herself. It was true as Alistair had told; his sister's voice was lovely. Odd, Clarinda reflected how some things come to be. Her heart might be experiencing a dull ache, but Janet's was beginning to flourish. As she had said aloud so many times before, she contemplated her words to herself. *Yes, it is better to give love to others; it is so much more rewarding.* With that resolve as a booster, her mood improved throughout the day. By the week's end she had almost forgotten about the horrible scene on her front porch, but she still thought about Alistair every waking moment.

Heather & Thyme Boursin Cheese Spread
From the Kitchen of Clarinda Tetrick

8 oz Cream Cheese
4 oz. Softened Butter
½ tsp. Oregano
¼ tsp. Basil
¼ tsp. Thyme
¼ tsp. Dill
¼ tsp. Marjoram
¼ tsp. Garlic Powder
¼ tsp. Pepper
½ tsp. Worcestershire Sauce

Blend all ingredients. Refrigerate for 2 hours or overnight to develop flavor. Let soften at room temperature. Ideal when served with smoked salmon on crackers.

Chapter 29
A New Year, A New Beginning

"Yes, Mr. Clark, I have your room ready. Let me show you the way and Kyle will bring your bags up shortly. This way please."

Clarinda had spent a good portion of the day climbing up and down the stairs showing her guests to their quarters. Some were already ushering in the New Year in the bar. Janet had been slaving in the kitchen organizing the Hogmanay feast for the last three days. The house was charged with excitement, and she was delighted to finally have the place completely booked with pound-paying guests. She had worked so many months preparing for this event, and thus far everything was going without a hitch. She prayed her good fortune would not run out.

A jubilant shout emanated from the kitchen. "Happy New Year!" She walked in to find George planting a kiss on Janet's cheek and hoisting a bottle of champagne in the air. "Happy New Year," he cried to Clarinda and repeated the embrace. "I came by to see if ye two birds could use a hand."

No sooner were the words out of his mouth when Janet had assigned him all manner of chores. Mostly she wanted him to see to the wood and coal supplies for the fires and wood stoves. The weather continued to be cold, but New Year's Eve was clear and sparkling, and the fires would keep the guest house inhabitants warm and cheery. Once he was clear of the tasks, he went to begin his celebration in the bar. It was soon to be dinner time, but he wanted to get some well-wishing in beforehand. Dragging Clarinda and Janet to join him was a struggle, but he knew they needed a break before they began to set out the feast. Seeing some local mates, he grabbed a dram and proposed a toast. "Lang may ya'r lum reek!"

"Here, here!" came the hearty reply.

"What was that you said, George?" Clarinda asked. "Long may your rum leak? What does that mean?"

"Och no, lass. Lang may yer lum reek. It means 'long may yer chimney smell,' or may ya' always have coal on yer fire; and may ya' have enough money to keep yer house warm. It is auld adage we say at the New Year to wish for prosperity. And since I just finished with coal duty, I felt it was very appropriate, no?"

She supposed it did, and downed her shot of Edredour and then made her way back to the kitchen to give Kate some last minute coaching before the serving began. This was going to be a fun night no matter what! Her guests were having a good time, and that was what truly mattered in the grand scheme of things. She served the Boursin cheese and organized the glasses for a champagne toast; one of many to come in the night ahead. Once her guests had gathered for the toast they then sat to enjoy their other courses. Her guests raved about the goat cheese salad, the chateaubriand was by far the most popular entree and Clarinda had never seen a crowd enjoy warm sticky toffee pudding more. Once they were satiated with food, she instructed her guests to return to the bar to resume their holiday reveling so she, Kate, and Janet could secretly clear the tables.

Kyle had his hands full helping the bar staff, and Clarinda was grateful her intuition guided her to order the extra case of champagne. The night was turning out to be a huge success, and she knew she could not have pulled this off without Janet—she was the major reason her guest house was full. The word-of-mouth praise that would come from this night would foster months of bookings. She decided she would give the lady a bonus for all her hard work and steadfast loyalty—she was certainly worth it! Clarinda's dream of owning and operating a successful guest house had finally become a reality. The triumph of this night was proof.

The eleven o'clock hour came and went, but her guests showed no sign of waning. Even more townspeople had arrived after the end of the meal. Her small bar was packed and guests spilled out into the foyer and parlor. Liquor sales are very profitable, so Clarinda didn't mind the extra patrons, but hoped the fire brigade would not stop by to check occupancy standards. Janet and Kate had cleaned up most of the kitchen and decided to join the party. They didn't want to miss New Year's either. George handed Janet a glass of champagne and held her close. He didn't want to miss the opportunity to give her a proper New Year's kiss when the minute struck.

Kate's beau was one of the local Scots who had come over to enjoy the festivities and she joined him with a hug and a playful squeal. Clarinda was left high and dry without a suitable person to embrace at New Year's and didn't want to take her chances with some of the more randy and ragged looking men becoming rowdy and intoxicated in her bar. She decided the safe thing to do was to call Fran. Granted it wouldn't be midnight in New York for almost four hours, but she wanted to greet the New Year with someone she loved.

"Long may your lump reek?" Fran was similarly perplexed by the expression, but it got Clarinda to enjoy a wholehearted laugh. "So no one to get a smooch from, huh?"

"Boy do you know how to kick a girl when she is down," Clarinda bantered. "No, I don't have a hottie to swap spit, so you are as good as it gets for me tonight."

"What happened to the kilted god? Tell me you haven't bedded him yet?"

"That is really none of your business, but I will tell you it was marvelous as long as it lasted." Clarinda wistfully fingered the thistle necklet around her neck.

"So you did bed down with the highland king?" Fran was giddy and wanted details which would be too painful for Clarinda to divulge.

"Yes, I did, but it was short lived and he has decided he is 'no the man for me'," she imitated his brogue. "Oh well, at least I gave it the 'ol' college try', as they say. Why can't I find a man to be with, who wants to be with me? Hmm? Answer me that?"

"Because you are too much woman for one man. They can't handle the tiger. No really, I don't know. You have so much to offer, it is a shame they can't see these things for themselves until it is too late."

"Ah-ha! So you did know about David, and his plans to come here. I thought so! Why didn't you give me a clue. Do you know I passed out in my foyer in front of all my guests when I saw him? And you call yourself a friend?" It was teasing and all in good fun, but she hoped she had gotten the point across.

"I didn't think he would go through with the trip," Fran used as her defense. "But I NEVER told him where you were, and he asked plenty of times. I have to hand it to him; he took the time and effort to track you down. I guess his plan didn't go as scripted since you are still in Scotland. You know you could still come back and I know he would still want you. Of course, I, too, would love to have you on this side of the pond."

Clarinda had never considered this option, and why would she? She had decided she didn't love David as much as she had thought, and she had chosen to be with Alistair instead. But now that prospect had run aground, would she want to go back to David? *No*, she answered to herself. She was going to stick it out in Scotland. Her business was going to be a success and she was sure there might be at least one or two other men in this entire country that might be interesting. David was over and out, so now on with the show.

"Naw, Fran my friend. I think I will stick it out in Inverwick for a while longer. Tonight's party is a wild success, so I think I will stay. Who knows, I might meet a Laird and become a Baroness or something. You never know."

"Ten! Nine! Eight!" Clarinda could hear the countdown to the New Year shouted out in unison from the bar. Janet rushed over and was pulling her away from the phone to join the jubilant crowd.

She hastily hung up with Fran, "Gotta go! Happy New Year!"

She didn't get to hear Fran's farewell as she was yanked into the bar area. "Four! Three! Two! One! HAPPY NEW YEAR!"

Everyone in the bar tossed confetti (Clarinda wondered where that came from) and began to kiss anyone within arms length. George was delivering a kiss to Janet the likes of which she would not forget. Hoping to avoid an unwanted smack on the lips from a local patron, Clarinda raised her glass to her lips to taste the bubbly dry champagne.

"Happy New Year," she toasted to herself. A strong hand held her arm and prevented her lips from touching the glass. In one smooth motion she was turned and a strong mouth was placed over lips. Initially she tried to resist, not wanting to catch some sort of human "hoof-and-mouth" strain from a random swarthy Scot; but once she recognized the technique of her surprise-attack kisser, her struggles ceased. *What is he doing here?* ran through her mind.

He held her shoulders tight and when the kiss was over, he pushed her away from him, but never lost his grip and held her firmly. He looked directly into her eyes and said something that very rarely comes from the mouth of any man: "I was wrong."

This statement almost drove Clarinda into a swoon, but the embarrassments of succumbing onto the floor of her bar gave her the needed strength and resolve to remain standing. "Did I hear you correctly? You are what?"

"Ya' heard me. I said I was wrong." The din of the festive crowd made conversation impossible so Alistair took her and led her to the front porch. Realizing party-goers had already claimed the porch for their merriment, he doubled-backed and led her into her apartment. Once inside, he shut the door and locked it. She did not fear for her safety, she trusted Alistair would never harm her, but his determination was startling. "Clarinda, I came here tonight to tell you I was wrong, and I have been all these years. The last few days hae been some of the darkest in me life—even worse than when I was hurt. I think I finally ken what ya' have been strivin' to tell me. I love ya'! Yes, I love ya'! And I cannae spend another day without ye by me side."

Clarinda couldn't believe her ears and his words were gushing forth so fast she could barely comprehend their meaning. *Did she hear him correctly? The man who would never consider love, was now falling for her?* Clarinda didn't know whether to scream or rejoice.

"The burnin' question I have for ya' is this: will ya' take me back?" He let the question settle in and said no more. It was her turn to reveal her desires.

She paused. Took a deep breath and began to reply. She strived to keep her voice even. "Alistair. I am shocked and surprised by your dramatic change of heart. It seemed to me you made it very clear you were not about to change your lifelong beliefs and accept a loving companion to share your bed and your heart. What has happened in the last six days?"

"I have been miserable. I dinnae ken if this is love or no, but I do ken I have been so glum I have made meself sick. I always feel alive with ya' and if that is love, than that is what I want. Will ya' take me back, and be with me?"

"Let me think about it. You know you really hurt my feelings; go ask your sister. I really don't want to go through that again. If you are not serious, please if you feel for me at all, tell me now."

"I won't make ya' feel any pain ever again. With you as me wife, I would never let any harm come to ya'."

"Hold on cowboy! Wife? Wait a minute! Are you proposing marriage?"

"Aye, I guess I am—but I dinnae think I am a cowboy. I dinnae realize I said the words but I hae been thinkin' about it. Yes, I am asking ya' to be me bride."

"For a man who didn't want to be saddled with even a girlfriend, I guess I am not convinced of your sincerity. I believe you think your words are true right now, but once the romance of the night has worn off, you will most likely feel differently."

"No Clarinda, I am no pissed. I hae thought about this very seriously. I hae lived as a shallow shell of a man all me life, and I didn't think it was love that was missin'. But after I left you on Christmas, I realized I hae been given a great gift—you. Ye opened me heart and me eyes to the glory of devoted companionship. This has changed me life and I want it to stay that way. Please, accept me proposal. Please become me wife." He was on one knee and held her hands in hers pleading with his eyes for an affirmative answer.

"Alistair, let's take one step at a time. I will accept your proposal." He face beamed with delight. "But, on one condition."

"What is it me love, please tell me and I will do it."

"OK, good. Here it is. Let's say we are lovers and companions for now. If we are still enjoying each others companionship, than you can ask for my hand in six months time. I don't want to agree to something neither one of us is prepared to fulfill. I love you very much Alistair, I have since the day I first laid eyes on you. I want to be your wife, but I only want to engage in matrimony when I know my heart's affection will be returned."

"It will be returned two-fold. I agree to your condition, and I will prove to you I am good on me word. But first," he wrapped his arms around her and gave her a deep, but soft and loving kiss. She could sense a change in him. He was no longer afraid to love, but was open and willing to let it sweep over him. He was going to finally find happiness in his life, and Clarinda looked optimistically to bring it to him.

"To show me words are laudable, please come with me now." He took her hand and led her back into the bar where the party had thinned, but those left were showing few signs of tiring. Janet and George were still present, and getting on quite well with each other. Clarinda noticed George's hand on Janet's knee, and hoped their bond would reach new heights after this evening.

Once they had a place where they could fully address the assemblage, Alistair blew a shrill whistle to get their attention. The conversation slowly ceased. "I hae somethin' to say to ya', me neighbors and me friends. I want to present to you Miss Clarinda Tetrick, the mistress of this fine guest house where ye are present. I hae asked this fine lady to be me wife." Immediately cheers and accolades rose from the group.

"But did she say 'yas'?" someone heckled.

"Aye, she did, but only if I ask her again in June. I will invite ya' to be witnesses!"

He was giddy and she was caught up in his joy. This man might well be the most mysterious man she had ever met, but Clarinda presumed this could be the perfect ingredient to an exhilarating and never dull union. He took her in her arms and gave her a passionate kiss in front of all of her guests. Pride be damned, he soon led her back to her apartment where his proposal was consummated. Clarinda couldn't sleep, but remained awake staring at Alistair. He was sleeping peacefully in her bed, where she hoped he would forever lie.

epilogue

The sun rose once again in the east and with it New Year's Day began. It was like any other day except for one major transformation. Alistair awoke, and once he assessed his surroundings he felt warm and safe. He turned over to look at the slumbering woman by his side. He loved to watch Clarinda sleep. She looked peaceful, and as soft and ethereal as an angel. He wanted to gently touch her soft cheek, and stroke her soft hair, but he didn't want to wake her so his restraint prevailed. She slowly opened her eyes, looked at him and smiled. "I love you," she whispered.

"Happy New Year," he whispered to her. "I love you, too."

She closed her eyes again, relishing the phrase she had longed to hear. She slowly opened her eyes again. "This year will be the best one in my life, and it will be because of you."

"Same for me. I cannae wait until June when you will become me bride. How many bairns to ya' want?"

"Bairns? Babies?"

"Aye. Don't ya' want bairns?"

"Yes, of course. I just didn't know if you did."

"Aye! I do. I hope you would want to bear me some sons and daughters."

"Oh Alistair! Of course I want to have your babies! We should have at least two. A boy and a girl."

"The laddie will look like me and the lass will be your miniature. We can start our wee family when you become me bride."

Clarinda looked at him very seriously and then a devilish smile spread over her face. "Alistair, I want to wait until June to be wed so we can get to know each other better and enjoy time alone before we start a family. But when it comes to 'preparation', I think practice makes perfect."

"Aye, it does lass. I think we should begin rehearsal right now?"

They dove under the covers in a tumult of kisses and titters. The rays of first morning sun of the year shed its light over the moors, danced on the Inverwick River, and warmed the two intertwined lovers nestled together in the Heather and Thyme Guest House. The blessings of Hogmanay were fulfilled.

appendix

Basil
Instructions:

Cloth: 14 count white Aida Cloth
Grid Size: 95 x 78 stitches
Design Area: 6.79" x 5.57"
Floss: DMC – Use 2 strands for all full stitches and 1 strand for all back-stitches.

Legend:
- ◆ 598 Turquoise - Lt
- ○ 747 Sky Blue – Vt Lt
- ◣ 905 Parrot Green - Dk
- ▲ 937 Avocado Green - Med
- ✛ 964 Sea green - Lt
- ■ 3051 Green Gray - Dk
- ● 3347 Yellow Green – Med

Back-stitches:
- 598 Turquoise (Lt) – This is shown as a dotted line around the ribbon. This is to be stitched as standard back-stitch – no gaps.
- 905 Parrot Green (Dk) – These are depicted as 'tracks' at the end of the stems, but they are to be stitched as solid straight lines.
- 3051 Green Gray (Dk) – This color outlines the leaves and stems and is depicted as a solid line. These are to be stitched as shown.
- 904 Parrot Green (Lt) – These are shown as dashed lines in the center of the leaves (veins). These are to be stitched as straight lines.

Photocopy the pattern and enlarge at least 200% for better legibility. Begin at the center and work darker colors first. Once all full cross-stitches have been completed, then the backstitched can be added on top of the full x-stitches. Block to frame, or stuff to create door pillow. Add tassels or fringe as desired.

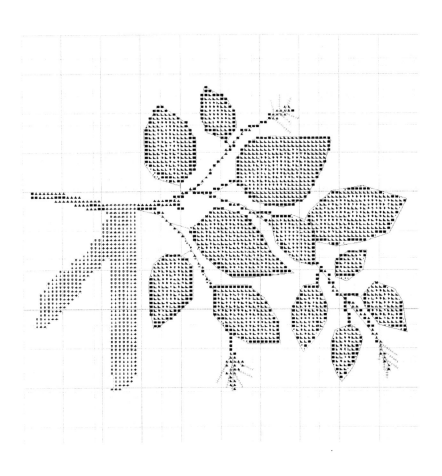

Savory

Instructions:
Cloth: 14 count off-white Aida Cloth
Grid Size: 56W x 3.36" (50 x 47 stitches)
Floss: DMC – Use 2 strands for all full stitches and 1 strand for all back-stitches.

Legend:
- ♥ 209 Lavender - Dk
- ▶▶ 340 Blue Violet - Med
- ◆ 452 Shell Gray - Med
- ◼ 3362 Pine Green - Dk
- L 3835 Grape - Med
- ● 522 Fern Green
- ▼ 524 Fern Green – Vy Lt

Back-stitches:
- 3835 Grape – dashed lines around the ribbon and the word 'Savory'. These are to be stitched as straight lines
- 164 Forest Green (Lt) – These are found throughout the savory branches and are stitched as shown.

Photocopy the pattern and enlarge at least 200% for better legibility. Begin at the center and work darker colors first. Once all full cross-stitches have been completed, then the backstitches can be added on top of the full x-stitches. Block to frame, or stuff to create door pillow. Add tassels or fringe as desired.

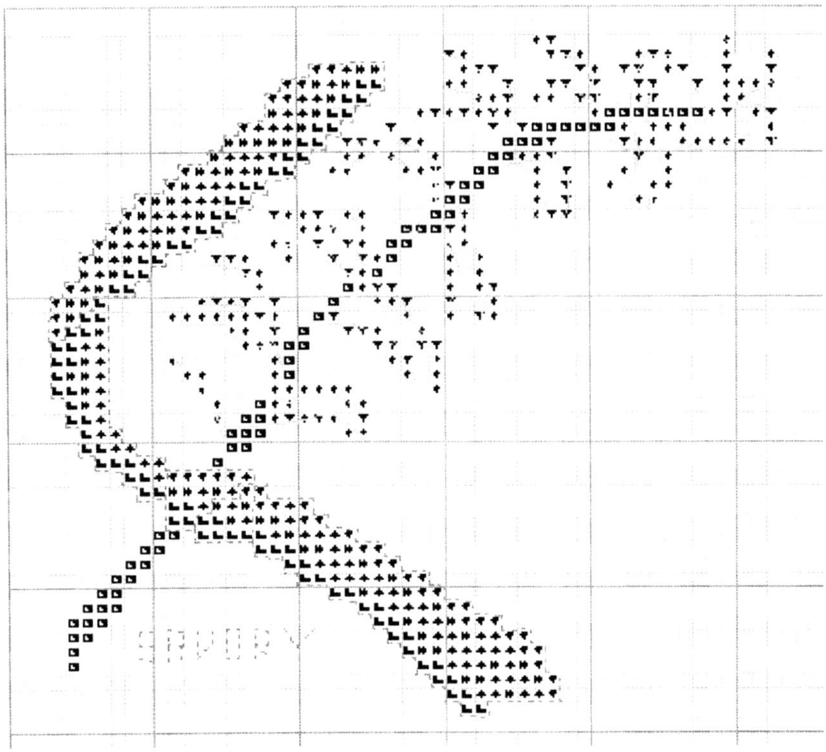

Thistle – Flower of Scotland

Instructions:

Cloth: 14 count white Aida Cloth
Grid Size: 56W x 56 H
Design Area: 3.86" x 4.00"
Floss: DMC – Use 2 strands for all full stitches and 1 strand for all back-stitches.

Legend:

Symbol	DMC	Color
X	648	Beaver Grey -- Lt
⊗	762	Pearl Grey – Vy Lt
●	799	Delft Blue – Med
▪	3023	Brown Gray – Lt
ͼ	3042	Antique Violet – Lt
☐	3790	Beige Gray – Dk
♥	3803	Mauve – Med
▸	3835	Grape – Med
■	3815	Celadon Green – Dk
◆	502	Blue Green
ͻ	912	Emerald Green – Lt
◥	3837	Lavender – Dk

Back-stitches:
799   Delft Blue – dashed lines around the ribbon.
3790   Beige Grey – Squiggle lines at the base of the flower blooms. These are to be stitched as straight lines.
3803   Mauve – These are dashed lines, found only on the small bloom. These are to be stitched as straight lines.
3835   Grape – These are dotted-lines found around the edge of the large bloom. These are to be stitched as straight lines.
3815   Celadon Green – These are shown as 'tracks'. These are found among the leaves. These are to be stitched as straight lines.
3837   Lavender – These are straight lines found on both of the blooms.

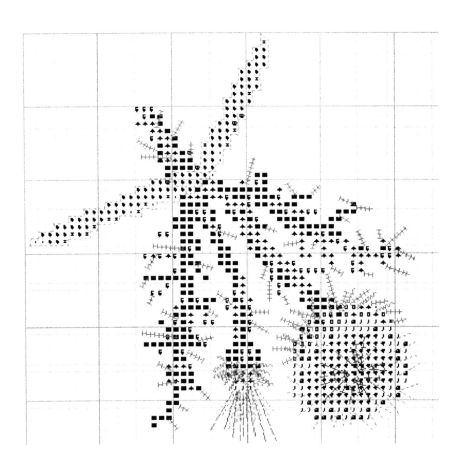

Printed in the United States
53291LVS00004B/208-285